Daphne H Ellis is a retired teacher. She has a degree in divinity and worked with Cardinal Hume's committee for Catholic Jewish Relations to implement the changes in the RC-Church post Vatican Two. After retiring she helped at a preschool for two- to four-year-olds and joined a creative writing group. She lived for some years in Vienna, enjoying the musical life of the city and endeavouring to learn German. Daphne now lives in Kent.

Let this not be the measure of me.

Daphne H Ellis

THE MEASURE

A Struggle with Guilt

AUSTIN MACAULEY PUBLISHERS™
LONDON * CAMBRIDGE * NEW YORK * SHARJAH

Copyright © Daphne H Ellis 2022

The right of Daphne H Ellis to be identified as author of this work has been asserted by the author in accordance with sections 77 and 78 of the Copyright, Designs and Patents Act 1988.

All rights reserved. No part of this publication may be reproduced, stored in a retrieval system, or transmitted in any form or by any means, electronic, mechanical, photocopying, recording, or otherwise, without the prior permission of the publishers.

Any person who commits any unauthorised act in relation to this publication may be liable to criminal prosecution and civil claims for damages.

This is a work of fiction. Names, characters, businesses, places, events, locales, and incidents are either the products of the author's imagination or used in a fictitious manner. Any resemblance to actual persons, living or dead, or actual events is purely coincidental.

A CIP catalogue record for this title is available from the British Library.

ISBN 9781398426474 (Paperback)
ISBN 9781398426481 (Hardback)
ISBN 9781398426504 (ePub e-book)
ISBN 9781398426498 (Audiobook)

www.austinmacauley.com

First Published 2022
Austin Macauley Publishers Ltd®
1 Canada Square
Canary Wharf
London
E14 5AA

I am very grateful to Sian Thomas, my tutor at Creative Writing, for her criticism and encouragement throughout. This story began as a piece of classwork with the title 'Broken Object' to be completed in one week. It grew and sustained me throughout the months of solitary lockdown due to the Covid-19 pandemic. Sian's suggestions for a more effective piece of writing were always accompanied by appreciation where it was deserved.

My thanks too to Judith Carpenter and Colin Nice, who, as the writing neared completion, gave me the benefit of their suggestions for improvement.

Thank you also to Ken and Sue Baker for their help in setting out the manuscript correctly, and to Jackie Mount for helping me with checking the first proof.

Table of Contents

Chapter One: At the Benedictine Monastery, January 1960	12
Chapter Two: Escape from Warsaw, April 1943	18
Chapter Three: Back at the Benedictine Monastery, 1960	35
Chapter Four: From Dieppe to England, April/May 1943	38
Chapter Five: Settling Down and Making Friends	55
Chapter Six: Changes and a Happy Reunion	68
Chapter Seven: Visitors, Visits and Surprising Revelations	86
Chapter Eight: The Truth Revealed, 1960	112
Chapter Nine: Charles Tries to Deal with His Guilt	122
Chapter Ten: A Happy Christmas Holiday, 1960	135
Chapter Eleven: New Horizons	140
Chapter Twelve: A Bleak Day	155
Chapter Thirteen: The Struggle Ends	191

Early one winter morning, a teenage boy is found lying outside the gates of a monastery. The monks take him in and eventually, in terrible distress, he tells them that he has killed his father. This story follows the life of the boy's father and the discovery the boy makes about his father's past and his struggle with guilt.

Chapter One
At the Benedictine Monastery, January 1960

The young novice monk faced the novice master, kissing his robe, a sign he wished to speak to him urgently. Father Andrew led the young novice to a cupboard, one of a few 'talking places' in this monastery.

"Father, there is a broken object outside the gates. I think it might be a human being."

"I don't understand what you are trying to tell me."

"Well, it's a bundle of clothes on the ground. It moves a little. I think it might be someone who is ill."

"Very well, my son, go back to your duties, and I will deal with it."

Father Andrew went out, walking steadily in the early morning gloom, through the turn, which marked the access to enclosure, the area inside the house to which the public were not admitted, and out into the front drive. The tangled trees rustled and groaned either side of the path, their dark greenness marked out against the grey shroud of the time just after dawn. It was a cold winter morning in the bleak days after New Year 1960. Sure enough, as Father Andrew reached the gate, he could see an object lying on the ground. He opened the gate, bent down and touched the untidy heap.

It was indeed a human being. He knelt down. A young man lay there, with no immediate signs of physical injury but conscious, though mute and vacant. Father Andrew drew the boy's left arm around his own shoulder, slowly pulling him to a sitting position whilst supporting him as best he could with his own right arm. He saw that he was just a young lad.

"Can you stand, young man? Can you manage to walk a few steps with me into the house?"

Slowly, their progression marked by many stops, they made their way into the back of the house and to the small infirmary. Father Andrew and the young monk in attendance lifted the stranger onto the nearest bed and covered him with a blanket. An elderly monk sitting nearby, his arm in a sling, watched but did not speak.

"A hot drink, please," Father Andrew quietly said, and the young monk disappeared into the kitchen to make a cup of tea for the stranger. When he returned with the tea, Father Andrew told him that he would have a hot soup and bread sent down. He instructed the young monk that the boy was to stay in bed and be kept warm.

The boy had made his way to the monastery, which lay on the outskirts of a small village near Quidenham, in a very rural area of Norfolk. It was a large old house, which might at one time have been described as 'grand'. Looking at it from the front, it was quite easy to see that over time additions had been made to the house, but it was still imposing, with some acres of grounds surrounding it. It housed a community, at this time, of about thirty monks ranging in age from a few novices of eighteen years, to the eldest who was eighty-eight. A church was attached to the house, to which the scattered local community came to hear Mass on Sundays and Feast Days.

The abbot was Father Vincent, and it was to Father Vincent that Father Andrew now went, in order to relay to him the events of this early morning.

After lauds had been completed, the first of the community prayers of the day, Father Vincent made his way down the cloisters to the infirmary.

He leaned over the young man.

"What is your name, my friend?"

The boy made no reply, giving only a fleeting glance at Father Vincent.

"Well, you've come to the right place if you want to remain silent," said Father Vincent with a gentle smile.

He noted that the boy seemed uninjured and clean. His breath was free from any hint of alcohol. Not the usual casualty that sought their help. His blonde hair was most noticeable. Perhaps he was still a schoolboy. Then Father Vincent realised that he had seen this boy before.

"Do not be afraid. We will look after you, and I will come each day to see how you are progressing. When you are ready, I hope you will tell me how you come to be in this broken state. For the moment, you need only try slowly to feel better. By the way, I am Father Vincent."

Father Vincent did indeed visit the boy. Each day, he spoke a little to him, just ordinary topics, maybe how the garden was progressing as they moved towards spring.

He got no reply, and the boy made no eye contact. Father Vincent realised that he had in the community's care a deeply troubled young soul. It would take time to bring about a healing.

One day, in the first week, Father Vincent gently asked the boy if there was anyone he should contact on the boy's behalf, perhaps a family member who would be worried about his welfare. To his surprise, this enquiry elicited an immediate response from the young man. He shook his head violently. Well, Father Vincent thought that was at least a response. He left instruction that the boy was to be helped into a chair and to be given some reading matter. When the afternoons were sunny and dry, he was to be encouraged out into the garden. Father Vincent did not tell the boy that the monastery had already had a visit from the local police regarding him.

They had enquired about a young lad, actually almost an adult now as the Sergeant was quick to acknowledge, who had left home suddenly and whose parents were anxious about him. In response to Father Vincent's enquiry, the Sergeant said that no crime had been committed but that there had been a somewhat violent altercation between the father and his son. The Sergeant's description of the lad certainly fitted the young man now sheltering in the monastery, and both Father Vincent and the Sergeant decided to leave things as they were for the moment. As Father Vincent reflected on these things, he realised that he knew the boy. He came to Mass on a Sunday from time to time, sometimes with a woman who was probably his mother. The spiky, untidy blonde hair shone out like a beacon in the dusky church and couldn't be missed.

As the boy lay in the infirmary, he wanted at first only to feel warm again. But gradually, his mind returned to the terrible events he had just lived through. He could not believe what his father had told him. Surely, it could not be true? And how had he reacted to what his father had told him? He remembered throwing the thing at him and running. He thought his father had fallen. But he had kept running. Each time these memories came to him, he buried his head in the bedclothes and tried not to think anymore. Gradually, however, he began to recover physically and would sit in the chair beside his bed and read, anything, but no thinking. He certainly did not want to think. He was the only one in the infirmary, and eventually, he thought he felt strong enough to venture out into the garden.

One morning, Father Vincent, pleased to see the boy's chair empty in the infirmary, sought him out in the garden. There he was, wandering through the vegetable plots. Father Vincent noted the athletic-looking stature and the blonde hair falling in an unruly mass about the boy's face. He bade him good morning and indicated they should sit on the gardener's bench next to the big greenhouse. They sat in silence for a while. Then the boy, his face suddenly contorted and full of pain, pushed out the words he had kept tight inside himself for over a week.

"I've killed my father."

The voice was strangled and almost inhuman. Father Vincent sat quite still, allowing the boy to sob uncontrollably. Better that all the emotion flow out than be once again stemmed to wreak its havoc, he thought.

"When you can compose yourself a little, would you like to tell me about it?"

The sobbing and moaning gradually subsided.

"I hit him. So hard." The boy put his head into his hands and began to rock back and forth on the bench. "I had the thing in my hand. I threw it at him." The boy was gasping and finding it difficult to speak. "It hit him. Really hard. I saw him fall as I ran. I ran. I ran. I didn't stop to see what I'd done. Oh, Papa, forgive me, forgive me."

The horror of these events engulfed the boy again, and for a short time, Father Vincent let the boy rock and moan. Then, judging it was right to bring him out of his crisis, he laid his hand on the boy's arm.

"My son, you suffer greatly, and it is right that you should." He paused. "But I know that you did not kill your father. He is alive and well. I know this because your mother contacted the police when she couldn't find you and the police came here in their search for you. Your father was certainly hurt but is out of hospital now, and we must concentrate on helping you."

There was silence. Then, the boy in a small unbelieving tone said, "Is it true? Can it be true?"

"It is so, my child. And now you too have made the first steps of recovery. You have been very courageous. Try to breathe slowly and deeply through your nose. Then when you are ready perhaps you will tell me your name."

The boy sat, eyes closed, the paroxysm of sobbing and anguish slowly ebbing. His hands, tightened into fists, relaxed, and gradually his breathing became more regular again.

"I'm Gregory. Gregory Hartman." Then, after a short silence, he said, "I should go to the police. I'm in a lot of trouble. I've done a terrible thing."

"There is no need for that. Your father is recovering. Although you did wrong, there are no charges to answer. Your parents know that you are here in our care, and they think this might be the best place for you for a while. It isn't only you, of course, that needs time and space to recover. Now I must leave you, Gregory. I have work to do."

Father Vincent saw that the boy had quite visibly let go of the tension in his body and was breathing deeply. As he walked back inside, he felt that the boy had overcome a big hurdle. He had begun to talk about his experience. We're making progress, he thought.

Indeed, Gregory, for the first time since he had run away, began to think more clearly, calmly and positively. He looked properly, for the first time, at the garden, still in its winter state. But the January chill began to make itself felt and he returned to his chair, and his books, in the infirmary. But he could not read. He thought, now more calmly, about his father's revelations, and his own angry response. I am not a child, he thought, I must deal with this like a grown-up. Getting angry and throwing things at my father will not help. I think it will be up to me to make the first move towards apology and reconciliation. Yet, at the thought of it, Gregory cringed. He was not ready for this yet.

The next day, there was a Chapter Meeting in antechoir. The community gathered in silence to listen to what their abbot wished to say to them. Father Vincent began.

"There is nothing lost, that may be found, if sought. For whatsoever from one place doth fall, is with the tide unto another brought: For there is nothing lost, that may be found, if sought."

He paused. "Brethren, many of you will know that these are the words of Edmund Spenser, a poet who lived in England in the second half of the sixteenth century. I think they are apposite because we have with us here at this moment, a young man who feels himself to be lost. He has been sheltering here for almost two weeks. He is sixteen years old. He is in a crisis from which he needs time to recover. He is not a criminal, but he is indeed in an inner turmoil.

"I propose that we install him in the Gardener's Lodge and set him to work in the gardens and perhaps also with the livestock. I have already spoken with Brother Simon who is willing to guide the boy in this work. His name, by the way, is Gregory. The work obviously requires him to be inside enclosure. The law of the church permits this in certain cases, and I do not see that it should present any problems. If any of you were to meet the boy as he goes about his work, a nod of recognition would suffice. His presence in the gardens should not be an occasion for breaking silence. Father Andrew will be in charge of Gregory's reading and, I suppose we could say, general education. I will see him once a week and for the time being will oversee his general recovery. I tell you all this because I require your consent to what I have outlined. I have not spoken to Gregory about this proposal and do not know even if he would wish it. I suggest, today being Friday, that if by Monday no one has any objections or difficulties, I acquaint Gregory with our plan and see what he chooses to do. Novices, please let Father Andrew know of any concerns you may have. I shall be in my office to hear from any other brother. Let us pray…"

NOTE: There is no Benedictine Monastery in Quidenham but there is a Carmelite monastic community of nuns there, whose church is used by the local Roman Catholic residents.

Chapter Two
Escape from Warsaw, April 1943

Otto von Hartmann was one of a landowning elite of Posen, a province of Prussia at the time when Otto was born there in 1871. This was a notable time in the history of Germany, for that year Bismarck became chancellor over a newly unified German Empire. Posen had a predominantly Polish ethnicity due to Germany's annexation of Polish territories during the nineteenth century.

Poland's history is very much an illustration of the fact that its great tragedy was geographical, being between Russia and Germany, countries that both made claims to its territory. The aim of the German rulers was that the province of Posen should be thoroughly 'Germanised'. The attitude towards the majority Polish inhabitants was to regard them as an inferior race. There was also considerable hostility towards their religion, Roman Catholicism.

Otto was married to Margit, a girl from Hamburg, whose father was a banker. In character, she was quite a contrast to Otto, gentle and ready always to see the best in people. Their firstborn was Klaus, who, in his earliest years, had the great benefit of his mother's unconditional love. Five years later, a second son was born whom they named Karl. Soon after Karl's birth, Margit died, so Karl never knew his mother, and little Klaus inevitably associated the arrival of a new brother with the loss of his mother.

To one of Otto von Hartmann's outlooks, a second son was of little importance, so Karl grew up in the early years of the twentieth century, knowing that he had no particular place in his father's plans. His father's interest was focused almost entirely on Klaus. Neither boy had much experience of being loved. Klaus was the victim of his father's insistence that his eldest son should attain perfection in everything he did, and Karl felt that he had committed an offence in having been born a second son.

A German nanny, Frau Schmidt, imposed a strict regime of reading and outdoor activities for both boys, as instructed by their father, but was not without affection for her young charges. Karl played with Klaus in the times when they were allowed to be together for recreation, but because of the difference in their ages, their studies at home were followed separately. But the boys got on well, an affection that was nurtured by Frau Schmidt, and they certainly enjoyed the time they were able to spend together. It was quite remarkable that young Karl never held it against Klaus that he was so obviously the favoured one. And gradually, Klaus, with help from Frau Schmidt, was able to understand that his mother's death was in no way the fault of Karl.

The boys were raised in a Posen that was nationalistic and militaristic. It was a lovely city, architecturally, and they loved being taken out. They both liked the thirteenth-century Royal Castle, which inspired in them an interest in medieval knights and chivalry. Frau Schmidt would help them read the stories about them in their books at home. But best of all, for Karl, was to be taken as a treat, to a small restaurant on the outskirts of the city, for luncheon. He liked it, not for the food but for the small collection of wild animals kept by the restaurant owner.

When his brother went away to school, Karl lost his only friend, and loneliness became a constant companion.

Karl, unlike his brother, was not old enough to serve in World War One, and at its end, at the Treaty of Versailles, the settlement made against Germany ceded the area of Posen to Poland. The city became Poznan, a province of Poland. This resulted in many Germans from this area migrating west into Germany, Otto von Hartmann among them.

It may have been this turmoil of resettlement that persuaded Karl in 1919, aged eighteen, to go to Munich for his university education. With such an uncertain and changeable background, it is not surprising that this young man opted for certainty and decided to study law. From here, the two brothers lost touch with one another.

Karl met Hans Frank at the University of Munich. Frank was a year ahead of Hartmann, so they met only at social events and never became very close friends. However, Hans Frank was a young man who in the circle of those studying law was well known. Later, he would become Adolf Hitler's legal advisor.

During his time at Munich, Karl had very little contact with his father. He began to regard himself as being alone in the world.

On graduating, Karl decided to go to Warsaw to live, mainly because he had obtained a post with a German law firm practising there. His reliability, and punctilious attention to the details of his duties, made him respected but not particularly popular. There was a rigidity about him, and a lack of humour, that his colleagues found a little difficult to handle. Tall, lean, dark-haired and good-looking, always very well presented, he was nevertheless not very popular with women either. However, to his workmates' surprise, one day he announced that he was engaged to be married to a young Polish girl called Maria.

Maria Swoboda was the only child of Jan and Irina. Jan was a baker and his wife assisted him in their business in Warsaw by making the cakes they sold along with the bread. Jan was a master-baker, and people came from quite a distance in order to buy his bread. As a small child, Maria began to learn from her parents the skills they practised daily in their bakery. Her father had to rise very early in the morning, six days out of seven, in order to start work on the bread making, and there was little time for either parent to play with their small daughter. On her father's day off, however, the family would have time to be together. This day was the highlight of Maria's week. The day being Sunday, the family always went to Mass at the nearby Roman Catholic Church, and sometimes, as a treat, they would go to the cathedral. Afterwards, the day was Maria's, for she was usually allowed to choose what they would do. She was a dutiful child, with a very easy temperament and presented no problems to her parents. She was not an outstanding student; she had a practical mind and not a great deal of ambition.

At the end of her schooling, Maria worked full-time with her parents in the bakery. She grew into a very attractive young woman, her blonde hair and dark brown eyes catching the attention of many young men. It was when she met Karl Hartmann that she began to be interested in any man other than her father. Karl's attractiveness, for Maria, lay not only in his physical appearance but in his air of assurance and his courtesy towards her father in particular. She knew that he was working at a respected legal practice in Warsaw, and as she got to know him, she believed he would be a good husband for her. In fact, she had to admit to herself that she had begun to love him.

The only drawback, if it could be called as such, was that he was German. Perhaps Maria's parents thought that coming from a Lutheran family was also a drawback.

Karl was very correct in his wooing of Maria. He met her first through going to the shop to buy bread. He was, at once, impressed by her beauty, and gradually, as he seemed to need bread more often, by her gentle warmth and friendliness. Eventually, he asked Mr Swoboda if he might call on Maria. Then it became permission to take a picnic together, and gradually, it was accepted that Karl and Maria would get engaged.

And so, in 1930, they married, a simple affair in Maria's local church but a very happy day, with some of Karl's workmates turning out to support him. Karl was twenty-nine and Maria twenty-three. Karl had informed his father of his impending marriage and had said that he hoped he and Klaus would be able to attend, but Otto von Hartmann did not reply. Perhaps marrying a Polish girl, and a Roman Catholic, was too much for him. However, the now elderly lady who had been his nanny, Frau Schmidt, much to Karl's amazement, was seen sitting in a pew during the service. Karl made sure he caught up with her immediately after the ceremony to insist that she join them for the informal reception.

Karl always remembered this act of kindness of Frau Schmidt and often wished he had been more appreciative of her attempts to help him as he grew up. He realised that she had probably loved him much more than she had ever been able to show. She still lived in Posen, now Poznan, and they agreed to keep in touch.

When they said goodbye, she handed him a small, carefully wrapped parcel. A little wedding gift, she told him. When he unwrapped it, he found inside a small, very beautifully made model of the Royal Castle of Posen, which as a little boy had set Karl's imagination alight. Karl, throwing propriety to the winds, kissed Frau Schmidt on the cheek, thanking her very sincerely. It was strange, he thought, maybe he was able to love Maria now, because, without realising it, he had been loved by this rather shy and reserved woman who had had the care of him.

By 1933, Karl was able to establish his own legal practice in Warsaw, specialising in advising German nationals about land law. At the same time, he bought a small house, not too far from his office. With the advent of Hitler's rise to power in Germany, like most German men, professional or otherwise, he joined the National Socialist Movement, later known as the Nazi Party.

When Germany invaded Poland in 1939 and the General Government of this area of Poland was set up, it was not long before Karl received a summons to a meeting in Berlin. He was received by an underling in the Department of the Gestapo, responsible under Heinrich Himmler for the 'Germanising' of the new provinces. Hartmann was required to work in the district of Warsaw as district administrator assisting the Governor-General Dr Hans Frank, who was in charge of this whole area of Poland known then as The General Government. Hartmann now found himself appointed a Nazi officer responsible for the 'Germanising' of the Warsaw area. There was no opportunity of declining the post.

He soon learned what was required of him. The National Socialist or Nazi racial ideology required that the occupied territories should become German as quickly as possible, by force, with a strict procedure of selection. People, including children, who were considered racially inferior and worthless, were sifted from those considered, for the Reich's purposes, valuable. The General Government areas of occupied Poland became a dumping ground for those classified as worthless and a source of cheap labour for the Reich, which was desperately in need of manpower. Many of those regarded as socially or racially inferior, particularly the mentally handicapped, were simply shot. Some Poles, deemed to be acceptable as lower-class Germans, were saved for service in Germany.

The Jews, who were considered to be racially inferior, whether doctors or farm labourers, had no exceptions made. In Warsaw, a huge ghetto began to be formed from what in the past had simply been the area where the Jewish residents lived. It was here that Karl Hartmann became instrumental in establishing and overseeing the conditions in which the Jews would exist.

The worst and most immediate problem in what became the ghetto was the overcrowding. As more and more Jews were dumped there, typhus spread, fuelled by starvation. The dead, often young children, lay in the streets unburied for days. It was a situation from which the Nazi officers exempted themselves. Jewish 'leaders' had been appointed to deal with the ghetto's day-to-day problems, and the Nazis merely shrugged their shoulders, or even in some cases exacerbated the suffering of the people by mockery and cruelty. Any Nazi officer, from Hans Frank downward, must have been fully aware of the conditions. What any individual, who might have had a conscience about it, could have done is a big question. Of course, officers like Frank and Hartmann did not usually go into the ghetto, but certainly, if Karl Hartmann saw any misuse of inhabitants by German soldiers, he put a stop to it immediately. That marked him out as 'different'.

Much of Karl's time was taken up with poring over the new laws that were issued regarding the Jews and then seeing that they were implemented. Gradually, for instance, he had to insist on allocation of housing that resulted in more than one family inhabiting a space normally occupied by just one family group. This was the policy that resulted in the gross overcrowding and the spread of disease. No official outside of Warsaw considered the number of Jews being sent might be far more than could be accommodated. They arrived and were pushed into any apartment, with little consideration of the numbers already in occupancy. The Jewish 'officials' who had to do this had no possibility of objection but had to bear the brunt of the anger of those already living there, if indeed they had the strength left to complain.

No 'Aryan' resident of Warsaw was allowed to employ a Jew, so gradually the buying-power of the Jewish families was reduced to nothing. Karl Hartmann had to enforce these laws of complete separation of 'Aryan' and Jew.

There was no education available for children in the ghetto. They could often be seen wandering around the streets trying to sell trinkets in order to buy food. Some children would manage to slip out to the marketplace outside the ghetto and steal whatever they could manage to get their hands on. It was a very risky undertaking for them.

The ghetto's isolation was completed when Karl Hartmann had to supervise the building of a high wall around it, to keep its occupants in and to shield the 'Aryan' side of Warsaw from the horrors within. Outside the walls, the inhabitants went about their daily business, going to market, meeting friends for coffee, while a few yards from them human beings existed in unbelievable degradation, until the last spark of life was extinguished. Even then, no one cared, and no one among the Jewish population was in a position to be able to do anything to help one another. Each person tried only to survive for as long as the will to live continued to flicker.

At home of course, Karl had a young, very attractive Polish wife. Now, under the 'Germanising' laws, she might be vulnerable. Her hair colouring could attract attention, so that Karl felt uneasy about her safety, especially when he was away from home. He worried particularly when he knew she was going to go to her parents. Although it was not far from their home, Maria had to walk there. The ghetto and its neighbourhood were alive with German soldiers who had little respect for anyone. Young, blonde Polish girls, walking in the Aryan quarter, often became a target, as it was thought they could be absorbed into the Reich as servants who would pass as Germans.

When Karl and Maria were at home together, Karl avoided saying anything about his duties with regard to the ghetto, and Maria was intent upon keeping the house, as far as possible, an oasis of peace and tranquillity. Maria did not want their home to be tainted by any talk of Karl's work for Hans Frank. Sometimes

Jan and Irina would come for the evening with them, and that helped Karl and Maria to feel that there were some moments of normality about their life in Warsaw.

Karl did his best to keep his law practice going, but it was difficult, and gradually his clients became less and less.

At the end of 1941, on hearing of the entry of the USA into the war, Karl began to feel that Germany might not win this conflict. With America now on the side of the Allies, it seemed to him that it was only a matter of time before the Axis powers were overwhelmed and Germany defeated.

Soon after America became officially involved, Heinrich Himmler visited the ghetto. It very soon became apparent to Karl that when Himmler spoke with Frank about the problems presented by the presence of an overwhelming number of Jews, and he heard the mention of new methods of proposed processing, he himself could be involved in genocide. Himmler ordered the liquidation of the ghetto and the deportation of all those who were able-bodied to labour camps within the General Government, a first step to their being transported to extermination camps. Karl was horrified. He knew that if Germany lost the war, there would be a terrible price to pay.

The deportation of the Jews from the ghetto began almost immediately. Without speaking to Maria about his fears, Karl quietly set about obtaining a fake Polish passport and considering how they could get out. Karl did not think deeply about the morality of what was being planned for the Jews. He shuddered inwardly at the thought of a policy of mass killing and did not want to be a part of it. His legal mind knew what the outcome would be for anyone involved in such a scheme should Germany lose the war, and uppermost in his thoughts was his own, and Maria's, survival. His mind was fully occupied, as the weeks went by, with the problem of how to get them both out of this hell that Warsaw had become. That Karl did not speak with Maria about the things he was planning was characteristic of him. Not only was he terrified inwardly of his intentions being discovered but as a young man he had always had to make decisions on his own, and now his natural instinct was to do the same.

Early in 1943, Maria told him she was pregnant. They were both thrilled and happy, but in Karl's mind, this was a complication that made their escape urgent. Now, for the first time, he discussed his plans with Maria. Her immediate response was one of anxiety for how they could safely escape. But, in truth, Maria was deeply relieved at the prospect of getting away from their terrible involvement in what was going on in Warsaw. She knew that Karl was unhappy and uneasy with what he was being expected to do, and the whole atmosphere of their life had become dark and frightening.

She told her parents that she and Karl were very uneasy with what was happening in Warsaw but said no more, as she thought that it might endanger her parents if she disclosed their plans to them. After all, Karl was a Nazi official and the German authorities might well question her parents when their flight was discovered. Maria loved her parents dearly, but she knew that her first loyalty must be to Karl and that their proposed undertaking was fraught with danger. The less anyone knew about it, the better.

Karl went on planning their escape but did not share with Maria any further details of his thoughts on what they would do. He always told himself that his wife should not have to bear any more anxiety than was necessary. England would be the destination he was thinking. But how, from this war-torn and ravished continent, could they get away? He could rely on no one for help; it was too risky.

They must make their way alone.

Karl harboured the wish that his child should be born in England, since it seemed likely to him that it would be among the victors of this war now that America was helping them. Also, it was an ally of Poland. That would help them. Was it better to aim for a town or country destination? How would they live? How could they make the journey across Europe without being questioned? There were so many routes that were closed to them. He would have to risk travelling through Germany to France and the coast. There would be no problem with language until they got to England. Maria had not a word of English. His own command of it was good, he spoke Polish fluently, but he had no doubt that his German-accented English would immediately be noticed in England. As a German, he was proposing to go into enemy territory.

There, in England, would be the greater danger he thought.

Then, whilst his mind was preoccupied with these plans, an uprising of the Jews still in the ghetto occurred. Everything turned into chaos, and all German Nazi officers had their attention focused only on attempts to quell the armed uprising and dodge the bullets. Karl took the opportunity. He warned Maria that they must go quickly, during daylight, because of the curfew and that there would be no possibility of telling her parents of their intentions. Karl had decided that they would head for Berlin initially.

He wore his full Nazi uniform. Having done this trip before, he knew how to make their way to the capital and thought the uniform would prevent any questions. They left the house just as it was, taking with them only one small suitcase with essentials for them both. As Karl locked the door and pocketed the key, he wondered if he would ever see the house again. His office he did not worry about.

He tried not to hurry as they left the house. He was aware of Maria's hand gripping his arm. He was a Nazi officer on his way to Berlin, on official business. That was his mindset as he strode through the narrow cobbled, and mainly deserted, streets. He was aware of the receding sound of gunfire. When they reached the station, he purchased their tickets to Berlin, via Poznan, a direct journey with no need to change, for which Karl was thankful. The city brought back memories of his childhood that were not entirely happy ones.

Once in their compartment on the train, Maria asked Karl about her parents. She was upset at leaving them without a word and hoped Karl would say that they could very soon let them know that they were at least safe. Karl's curt 'it's not possible, Maria' was said in such a way, a way that Maria recognised brooked no discussion, as to silence her on the subject. In any case, she understood the danger any communication between them and her parents could cause them all. Still, she felt sad and uneasy about it and wished they could have brought her parents with them.

Soon, a rotund little man opened the door to their compartment.

"*Heil Hitler*," he said firmly, making the usual salute.

Was he German or was he a Pole wondered Karl. He returned the salute and reached for their passes. The official gave only a cursory glance at them and departed. Maria wanted to know what Karl's plans were. Karl explained that they would stay a day or two in Berlin, where they should be relatively safe, and it was then his intention to try to get to England.

This came as quite a shock to Maria. Karl had never discussed these intentions with her, and her immediate reaction was one of disbelief and fear. She knew better than to argue with him though. She began to realise that they faced a lot of unknown dangers. She remembered a prayer for travellers and silently offered it up.

When the train stopped at Poznan, Karl gazed out at the landscape of the city. He could see the top of the old Royal Castle's battlements. He had packed the little model Frau Schmidt had given them. He wondered if the animals he used to visit at the restaurant were still there. He realised that not every memory of Poznan was bad after all. He wondered, briefly, where Klaus was and what he was doing.

A few people joined the train here, but nobody came into their compartment.

Soon, a young boy came along selling coffee. They bought a cup each and listened to the young shrill voice shouting out 'Kaffee' as he proceeded down the corridor. Maria was thinking about her unborn child. He, or she, would be born in England if they managed to get there. She had little idea what that would mean for them, but in most respects, she trusted Karl to do what was best in whatever situation they found themselves. She had never questioned his work in the Nazi Party because she thought he had no alternative. When he decided to leave Warsaw, she had been very relieved. She was aware of what had been going on behind those high walls of the ghetto and was glad that he no longer wished to be a part of it. She thought once more of her parents and could not help feeling very sad. Would she ever see them again, she wondered. Would they be safe in Warsaw? All these thoughts occupied her mind on the journey to Berlin, so that the couple said very little to one another.

The next stop was almost on the German/Polish border, Frankfurt on the Oder. The early spring sunshine shone on the river snaking its way through the town. It looked peaceful and beautiful, in spite of the fact of being right on the border of two warring enemies. A lot of people got off the train here.

Before long, they were at the Ostbahnhof on Koppenstrasse in Berlin. A short bus journey took them to Friedrichstrasse where they made their way to a small lodging house, which Karl knew. Tucked away on Friedrichstrasse for a couple of days would give Maria a chance to rest, thought Karl, and himself time to plan the next part of their journey. Maria had never been to Berlin, so after a good night's sleep, Karl gave in to her pleas, and throwing on plain trousers and jacket, he set out on a morning of sightseeing.

When they emerged into the street, Maria remarked on the strange smell that hovered in the air. Later, she realised it was due to the burnt buildings some of which were still smouldering. She wondered why she had not noticed it the day before. Karl had his own thoughts. How incongruous, he was thinking, at such a dangerous moment in their lives that they should be wandering around Berlin like carefree tourists. Maria wanted to see the Brandenburg Gate, but the obvious devastation they encountered as they walked along Friedrichstrasse, the result of enemy bombing, alarmed Maria, and she quickly agreed with Karl that they should return to their lodging.

On the way back, they stopped off at the station where Karl bought train tickets to Paris, with a change at Frankfurt-am-Main. The journey would take them about ten hours. Karl decided he would continue in uniform. They were heading for occupied France and perhaps it would still, at least en route, give them some protection.

The next day, they checked out and made their way to the Hauptbahnhof this time, the Main Station, taking the same little bus service that had brought them from the East Station. Karl noticed once again the devastation wrought by the enemy bombing. Would anything be left of Berlin, he thought, when this war was over? They saw, through the bus windows, ordinary Berliners seemingly going about their daily tasks. Was it imagination, or did they look hungry and anxious? Karl felt sad as he surveyed the state of the city.

They got off the bus at the Hauptbahnhof. They had a couchette on the overnight train and were glad, although early, to be able to install themselves there and take stock. They were just settling down when the door was thrown open and a man's gruff voice demanded 'Passports'. The bulk of the tall man filled the doorway in a manner that seemed menacing. For a moment, Karl thought he was going to question them about the reason for their journey. He was glad his Nazi uniform was hanging on the chair, and from its pocket, he took out his own German pass and Maria's Polish one. The officer glanced at them and handed them back to Karl without a word. He closed the door behind him and his voice could be heard, gradually receding, shouting 'Passports!'

Karl felt relieved to have survived that encounter. He was not sure what they would do when they got to Paris. Could they travel on to Calais straightaway? Was Calais the best choice? During the rest of the journey, they were uninterrupted and able to rest quite comfortably, although Karl could not help half expecting the carriage door to be thrown open again and to hear himself ordered off the train.

The journey took just under ten hours, most of which they managed to sleep through. Later, when Karl thought over this journey again, he had no memory of a change at Frankfurt-am-Main at all. Karl was pleased to see that Maria seemed refreshed when she woke. For a moment, her beauty forced the anxieties out of his mind. Her golden curls, tousled from her sleep, the hazel eyes, the slim and 'curvy' body, even in pregnancy, captured him, as it always had. But only for a moment. He returned to reality as the knot of anxiety in his stomach made its presence felt again. The train drew into Paris.

Quite quickly, as they disembarked, he felt that it would be unwise to linger. Paris felt unsafe. He was acutely aware that here, in occupied France, his Nazi uniform marked him out as 'enemy', at least to the French. Without asking any questions, they walked hurriedly around the station and discovered it was possible to get a train to Dieppe, with a ferry ticket across to Newhaven on the south coast of England. Karl asked himself how this was possible in a country occupied by Germany. A country at war! Just like that! A ferry to England! Enemy territory! He felt doubtful about the possibility of this destination and wondered why he had been offered these tickets. It was surely ridiculous to think that the German occupiers would allow travel to a country with which they were at war, or that England would welcome anyone arriving from occupied France without a lot of questioning. As he thought about these things, he began to feel very uncomfortable in Nazi uniform but purchased two tickets for Newhaven via Dieppe anyway and left the booking hall briskly. Then he felt that even having these tickets in his hand marked him out as an enemy. He stuffed them quickly into his pocket. Karl was fast losing control.

He must, as quickly as possible, get rid of his uniform he thought. He was aware of a sense of panic arising in him. He walked swiftly to the toilets where he changed and stuffed his uniform into the little case. He would dispose of it when he found a safe opportunity to do so. Maria was waiting outside. Karl noticed the anxiety on her pale face. He took her arm, and they made their way into a buffet where they had a light meal. Karl thought that Dieppe to Newhaven might be a safer option than the Calais to Dover one, if they were able to do that, and enjoyed a brief moment of optimism, although he was now aware of a feeling of nausea in his stomach. He didn't really want to eat, but he realised that it was important that Maria should have something sustaining. They were alone in the sparsely furnished eating place. Karl's mind was jumping from one thought to another, heightening his tension, although he did not realise it. From now on, he decided he would use his Polish passport. They would be two Polish refugees from Warsaw seeking asylum in England, the ally and protector of Poland and where the Polish Government in Exile was housed. He was pleased to see that Maria had eaten and looked better for it.

Suddenly, the door was flung open and two Nazi officials strode in. Karl immediately felt a rush of fear. The men ordered coffee and took a table close to the counter. Karl spoke quietly to Maria in the little French he had, and they left, Karl muttering a 'Bonjour' to accompany the nod of the head towards the Germans. It seemed strange to him to find himself thinking of his own people as enemies and being so afraid of them.

As he again took Maria's arm, he felt her trembling. He wanted to keep moving. He wanted to get out of this place. He picked up a free French newspaper and tucked it under his arm. Everyone they passed seemed a potential enemy, be they French or German. Karl did not want to be questioned. The time dragged. He began to feel even more nauseous, and the only thing that occupied his mind was getting out of Paris as quickly as possible.

He decided to check their platform. He thought it was safer if they looked like a couple who knew where they were going. If they wandered aimlessly, he was afraid they might be stopped and would have to explain themselves. With some relief, he saw that their train was in, and with no one as yet at the barrier, they walked straight through and on to the train. They found their seats and sat down next to one another, Maria beside the window.

Karl realised that they were in another dangerous situation now. If anyone came and questioned him here, he was Polish, a refugee in France where the Nazis held power and for whom a Pole would represent an enemy. He sat, quietly contemplating what was best to be said in the event of their being questioned. Was he going to be German or Polish? He felt tense and was aware that he was questioning the wisdom of this whole enterprise. He must have dozed. He was woken by the lurch of the train as it commenced its journey and by Maria tugging at his sleeve. In front of him towered a French Railway official.

"He's asking for our tickets," said Maria in Polish.

Karl reached in his pocket for them. "Passports too?" he asked, also in Polish.

The man did not reply, clipped the tickets and moved on. Karl couldn't help wondering why all these ticket inspectors seemed to look the same and present the same kind of threat. Then he realised that the problem was his. Everyone seemed to present danger, and he was, yes, he was afraid. He looked at Maria and at the outskirts of Paris as the train gathered speed. He took her hand, in a rare gesture of affection, trying to reassure her with a confidence he did not feel. Perhaps, although he did not recognise it, holding Maria's hand was also a way of boosting his own courage. They heard the sound of distant male laughter. Probably troops, he thought.

"I'm just going to take a short walk up the corridor," he told Maria, and noticing her immediate alarm, added, "I will only be a minute." He returned quite quickly. "There is hardly anyone on this train," he told Maria.

Maria was more interested in the view from the window.

"Look at this lovely countryside, Karl. It seems to be farming land. I haven't seen any villages yet." Maria, very aware of Karl's anxiety, was trying to distract him.

Dieppe was the terminus for this train, and when they heard it announced, they disembarked. Karl was uncomfortably aware of the incriminating uniform in the suitcase. The ferry departure was close by, and he walked towards it thankfully, feeling that now they would really be on their way to a new life. Everything around the area looked deserted. The entrance gates guarding the ferry ramp were closed. Thinking over in his head the French he required, he politely stopped a woman carrying a basket of fish and asked her about the ferry. She looked at him as though he were crazy.

"Ferry? It has been closed. No one goes to England these days. Do you not know that there is a war on?"

Karl got the gist of what the woman had said. This was a terrible blow. What should they do now? For a moment, Karl felt confused, and he was aware of that knot in his stomach returning. Here they were in Dieppe, and, as he had thought likely all along, they had no way now it seemed of getting to England. They were trapped.

"Let's walk a little," he said to Maria. "The ferry will not take us; it's closed. We can't stand around. I think we must look for somewhere to stay overnight." He sensed Maria's bewilderment and took her arm.

"Do you think we'll be able to find anywhere here?" she said in a whisper, looking from the sea to the simple cottages that lined the harbour. She looked at Karl and saw the grim look on his face. She knew that he was worried and wasn't surprised that he didn't answer. Maria felt as though every little cottage was an enemy, watching, knowing all about them. Karl had his doubts as to whether they could find anywhere to stay here but said nothing. They felt alien and alone and in danger. They continued walking.

A little further along the harbour sat a man on the quayside, doing something with nets. This time, Karl spoke English and slowly explained that he and his wife were Polish refugees who wanted to get across the channel to anywhere in England. At this moment, he wanted an overnight stay somewhere could he help.

The man took a minute or two to reply, looking carefully at Karl and Maria. Karl was about to move on, thinking the man had not understood. Then the sound of aircraft coming in over the sea made them all look up. In the brief moment before they started running, Karl became aware of the high white cliffs marking the sides of the inlet; clearly visible too were the German artillery and bunkers guarding the harbour on the top of either cliff.

"Hurry, we cannot stay here. They are British planes! Follow me."

The man got up quickly, leaving the nets and set off at a fast pace along the harbour. As the three of them turned the corner into a small alley behind the little cottages that fronted the sea, they heard the strafing of the planes as they swooped down and along the harbour edge. Karl and Maria fell, behind the stranger, into a doorway. The door took them straight into a small living room, dimly lit and with shuttered windows.

The sound of the planes' onward progression was ear shattering and it seemed that the little cottage might shudder and collapse under the impact. The stranger went out towards the back. Karl and Maria stood, trying to accustom themselves to the gloom. The stranger returned, behind him the woman Karl and Maria had met at the ferry.

"Please sit. My wife will make a pot of coffee." He lit a small lamp in the corner of the room.

"Thank you," said Karl in Polish and continued, "it is very kind of you and your wife to offer us this safe haven from the bombing." Then he apologised and repeated himself in English, hoping the man would think his accented English was due to his being Polish. The woman smiled at Karl and Maria and without saying a word went out. The sound of bombs dropping continued and Karl took Maria's hand to try to reassure her, although he felt far from confident himself, not perhaps so much from the bombing as from the situation in which they now found themselves. Karl felt that they were very vulnerable. He was uneasy. Could they trust this man?

Then the stranger took charge of things. "I am Pierre. I am a fisherman here in Dieppe. This town is heavily armed with German fortifications, that's why we get quite frequent bombing." Pierre sat next to Karl on a wooden straight-backed chair. He continued, "Last year, there was a massive Allied assault waged from the sea and many were killed by the German artillery, mostly Canadians." Pierre broke off again, noticing that Maria was also on a less-than-comfortable chair.

"Please come and sit here, closer to the fire," he said, indicating a small armchair, which Maria thought would usually have belonged to his wife. Maria understood his gesture and moved, glad of the instant warmth.

Then Pierre continued, "This is a very well-defended port and so is dangerous. You may have noticed the German artillery up on the cliffs. You and your wife should stay here tonight. I'm afraid we have only one small spare room. Your wife looks exhausted. Would it be a good idea if she went up now to rest, and we can discuss what can be done to help you?"

Karl translated what had been said, omitting the details about the German defences, but Maria wanted to stay with Karl. The little room they were sitting in, though very simply furnished, seemed like a refuge to her.

Karl was thinking rapidly. Pierre's English was very good, although he was obviously a Frenchman. That meant he would not see a Polish couple as enemies. Karl had no option but to trust the man.

"Thank you, but I think my wife feels safe with me."

"You were planning on going to Newhaven. You have business in England?" The door opened and in came the woman with a tray of coffee.

"Yes," said Karl, "I am a lawyer by profession, and I have to make contact with the Polish Government in Exile. We have travelled from Warsaw. Eventually, I shall have to try to get to London, but it seems to me that it will not be easy to get into the country."

Pierre said something to the woman, who left the room. Her footsteps could be heard mounting the stairs.

"I think that entry to England cannot easily be made. The beaches are mostly well protected and in some cases are mined, especially on the South, so Newhaven is not possible. It would be better to aim for the East coast of England. But to do this, you would have to go from Belgium." Pierre paused, frowning as he tried to think out the problem with which he had been confronted. "It is dangerous. I can probably get help for you, to get you to somewhere on the East coast. That would be the shortest journey but not from here, you understand? Perhaps the Hook of Holland would be a better starting point."

Pierre seemed to be thinking to himself but aloud, turning over the options in his mind. "It will take me a few days to arrange. You must stay here. It is better that you don't go out. We should also be prepared for a visit from a German officer. No doubt, they saw you arrive. In the meantime, I think we shall have some supper."

"My name—" Karl was interrupted.

"No names. Better that I know little about you."

The woman's footsteps were heard again descending the stairs, and she soon came in with bread and wine and began to set up the little wooden table for four.

Chapter Three
Back at the Benedictine Monastery, 1960

"May I sit with you, Father?" Gregory stood in front of Father Vincent who was sitting on the bench near the greenhouse where the two of them had sat before and talked.

Father Vincent felt greatly encouraged. It was the first time the boy had voluntarily opened communication between them. He did not answer but patted the place next to him and smiled encouragingly. He handed Gregory a thickly lined waterproof coat he was carrying.

"You can't be out and about in this cold weather without a jacket. You'll catch your death, and I have enough problems to contend with," he said with a smile. "I thought we might make some plans. Perhaps you have some ideas about what you want to do next?"

"Father, I do feel a little better," said Gregory, as he pulled on the warm coat. "I don't want to be a nuisance to you. I am really not quite sure what I should do. I don't feel at all ready to go home; I think I am a little afraid of seeing my father again. But I don't really know what to do. I should be preparing for university and thinking about exams and everything. Of course, I should really be at school. Oh dear!"

"Gregory, I think that at this stage we should simply be practical. You say that you need time. I can offer that to you. It is not good for you to be in the infirmary, and the community here would be happy for you to occupy a small lodge we have in the grounds. It is very simple but has what you would require to live for a short time. We could provide you with a hot meal once a day and make sure that you have provisions in the lodge for breakfast and supper. In return, we would like you to do some jobs in the garden. What do you think?"

The boy's head was lowered, and for a moment, Father Vincent thought he had retreated into silence again.

"I can't believe such kindness. It would help me if I could be here for a little. So long as I don't cause you and the monks any trouble. I would like to work in the garden. My father…" Gregory stopped himself from saying more. The boy was not yet thinking clearly, and it was obvious to Father Vincent that he was not yet ready to go home.

"Let's go and look at the lodge, then, and we can begin to get you settled."

The little lodge had a primitive kind of charm. Just a wooden shack really but with a small outside sitting area where a small table and chair were placed. Inside, a log fire was burning in the grate, an easy chair and little table sat under a window, and bookshelves lined one wall. A single bed occupied the other long wall. Father Vincent opened a door at the back. "Toilet and handwashing, but no bath. I'm afraid. For that, you must come, by arrangement, into the shower block. Brother Simon will arrange all the practical issues for you, and if you need to contact us when he is not around, you just come to the turn and ring the bell, like visitors do, and whichever of the brothers is on duty will come to help you. But I think you know that procedure."

Gregory noticed a small neat pile of clothes on the bed. He placed his hand on them, looked at Father Vincent and was about to speak, when Father Vincent continued.

"Well, Gregory, I believe you came without a suitcase, so you need a change of clothes. Laundry can easily be done but arrange that with Brother Simon. The main detail we need you to observe is to be aware that when the bell rings the midday Angelus you must go to the turn to collect your meal. You can return the dishes there when you have finished. Now, Brother Simon will come to see you a little later. I must go."

"Thank you so much, Father." Gregory looked directly at Father Vincent and smiled.

Father Vincent placed a hand on Gregory's shoulder. "God bless you, Gregory."

The next day, Gregory thought he had woken quite early. As he peeped out through the little window, he could see the early mist rising from the ground. A brief wash and dressed in the clean clothes left for him, he emerged into the gardens, wondering when he would meet up with Brother Simon and get his work details for the day. He found a note on the little table on his balcony, a stone carefully placed on it. It read:

"I will come after Mass to see you here. We need to get the soil turned and fertilised ready for the planting of the vegetables. Br Simon."

Gregory went back inside, found his watch, which told him it was 7:30. He knew that Mass was held each day at eight. He had plenty of time to get himself some breakfast and have a look at the books. After he had eaten, he cast his eye over the shelves and took down a copy of The Rule of St Benedict. He became immersed in it. He was impressed by what seemed to him a very humane vision. He wondered to himself why he had thought that it would be otherwise. His present experience of the monks' dealings with him bore out all that St Benedict seemed to be saying.

Later, Brother Simon came and together they went to one of the walled gardens where the vegetables were to be grown that season. Gregory understood the simple instructions and began work, work with which he was familiar. The soil was caked not only with the series of rainfalls it had received that winter but also with a certain degree of frost. The work was hard, but the time passed quickly. Before long, to his surprise, he heard the midday Angelus begin to ring. He went quickly to his lodge, washed his hands and almost ran to the turn. There, just as Father Vincent had said, was a dinner plate covered with a metal lid, on top of which was a set of cutlery. Gregory carried it back to the lodge, sat down at the little table and began to eat.

After lunch, and having returned the dishes to the turn, Gregory went out again to look at parts of the garden he had seen but not explored. He found a series of small walled gardens, mostly now lying fallow. In one, small trees stood like guardians against the brick wall, and he wondered if they were fruit trees. As he walked into the last of these tiny enclosed gardens, he noticed that it led to a large area given over to chicken pens. He determined to ask Brother Simon if he could help here too. It would be just like being at home.

He began to think about home and his parents. He should try to put things right between himself and his father. He had allowed his shock to turn to anger and had not given him a chance to explain anything. He wished profoundly that he had not hit out. But he knew, now that he was calmer, that unless he went home and spoke with his father, nothing could ever be resolved. Yes, it was right that he should soon find a way of reconciling himself with his father, if that were possible. Yet, the thought of trying to achieve that, filled him with dread.

Chapter Four
From Dieppe to England, April/May 1943

It was still dark. In the early morning chill, Karl and Maria stood waiting in the living room, Pierre holding back part of the blind, watching through the window for someone he was expecting to come in a small vehicle.

"Here he is," he suddenly said. "Very quietly now! Goodbye and good luck!"

Karl and Maria, the latter whispering her thanks, got as quickly as they could into the small black van, Maria sitting next to the driver and Karl crouched in the back space intended for goods. The doors were closed quietly, and they were off. Maria was aware that the driver was quite a young man. "You speak Polish?" he asked. Maria replied, also in Polish, saying that they did.

"You will be going to England by air. The aircraft is carrying members of the Polish government back to England. They gave permission that you could travel with them. It will take you to the east coast."

Maria expressed her thanks to the young man. She asked him if he had been fighting with the Allies in France. He was non-committal in his reply, and Maria thought that perhaps she should not have asked this question.

"We are almost at the small airfield where the plane is waiting. When I stop, please get out quickly, close the doors quietly and go straight on to the plane."

As Maria got out of the passenger seat, the darkness surrounding her and the outline of an aircraft quite close made her feel for a moment that she was taking part in an adventure film, not that she felt at all exhilarated by the prospect of this current adventure. Karl emerged from the back of the van; they whispered their thanks and made their way over the tarmac to the steps up to the plane. They found themselves inside a small aircraft and quickly strapped themselves into simple seats, which ranged around the edge of a small centre space. The other seats were already occupied by men who were speaking quietly in Polish. Karl immediately recognised Wladyslaw Sikorski, the Polish Prime Minister. Karl thought he must have been visiting some of the Poles who had been fighting in France.

The group acknowledged Karl and Maria with nods and a Polish greeting, which both Karl and Maria returned. Then Karl leaned over towards his left and thanked Sikorski for his kindness in helping him. They spoke briefly about the state of Warsaw and then the aircraft began to taxi towards the runway. The sound of the plane's engines echoed in the interior and made conversation difficult. Because they were all sitting with their backs to the windows, no one was able to look outside, so everyone's attention was focused on the empty interior and the tension became palpable.

Karl was aware that they were flying through airspace often dominated by the Luftwaffe. Undoubtedly, it was dangerous. Still, he knew that the flight could not be a long one. However, it seemed quite a time before he had the sense that the aircraft had begun its descent. Maria was also aware of the change in sound of the engine and looked anxiously at Karl. She gripped his arm as the plane made a somewhat bumpy landing. The man sitting next to Karl told him they were at an RAF airfield in the East of England, in Norfolk. He handed Karl an envelope.

"Here is a small amount of English currency to help you with your immediate needs. When you are settled, you can return it to our prime minister in London. Remember, too, that we can always use the skills of a Polish lawyer. Good luck."

Karl thanked him for their kindness, and just as quickly as they had embarked, they now found themselves standing on English soil in the early hours of a day they couldn't name, because they had lost count of the days whilst they had been in Dieppe. It was actually a Sunday. Or more precisely, it was Sunday, May 23, 1943. They were at RAF Station 139 at Thorpe Abbots in Norfolk, about six miles from Diss. It was about eight in the morning, and the sun was already shining.

A little more than a month later, Sikorski was killed in a plane crash as he left Gibraltar.

It would be almost a year before Karl was able to repay the loan.

"Can you walk a little way?" Karl asked Maria. Together they found a way out of the airfield and onto a lane. A little further on the lane joined what seemed to be a proper road. Karl felt heartened when he saw what was obviously a bus stop. Karl suggested they walk on because buses might be few and far between, especially this early in the morning. They didn't talk much. They were both aware that they had no idea where they were or where they were heading. The only thing to do was to walk. The road was bounded by hedges and seemed to run through farmland. They came across little habitation. After about half-an-hour, they heard the unmistakeable sound of a bus. Karl waved it down, noticing that the sign on the front declared its destination to be Diss. They got on and with some relief took a seat.

"Good morning," said a cheery-looking man with a small ticket machine strapped around his waist. "Where are you going?"

"We'd like to go to Diss," replied Karl.

"That'll be one shilling."

Karl paid the man and asked to be told when they reached Diss.

"Oh, it's easy, sir; it's the end of the journey. Only about four stops."

Karl noticed a signpost at a junction, which told him they were on a road numbered A143. Gradually, the countryside became less rural, and before long, they were on the outskirts of what seemed to be a small market town. Indeed, they were in Diss. They said goodbye to the ticket-man and walked into the town. They were looking for a simple inn or tavern where they could stay. Karl knew his first task would be to find work and with it, he hoped, somewhere to live. The streets were narrow. As the little lane curved, Maria saw what looked like an old building, obviously an inn on the opposite corner.

"Shall we try there?" she said.

They went in. It was quiet and empty; after all, it was still quite early. A bell stood on the bar. Karl rang it and almost at once a woman came, ruddy-complexioned and with a broad smile. Karl had already decided that he would be as honest as he could about their situation, since he hoped they might settle here.

"Good morning. My wife and I have just arrived here in England. We are refugees from Warsaw in Poland, and we came this morning to the RAF airport with members of the Polish Government. Do you have lodging for a few nights?"

"Well, bless you, my dear. You must both be very tired. From Warsaw? Poland?" The woman seemed amazed by the mention of these far-distant places.

"Yes, of course, we have a room. There aren't many visitors these days. I'll show you where it is. Follow me. I expect you would like something to eat? This way…"

She led them up a small staircase, her bulk filling the narrow space, to a room at the end of a short corridor. It was small but adequate, with a window looking out over the narrow lane from which they had just come.

"I am sure you can't have had any breakfast. We'll go down, and I will bring you a pot of tea and some toast. If you think this room will be all right, you can come back up and get settled."

Maria was touched by this cheerful lady who seemed so concerned that they should eat. The three of them went back downstairs, Karl leaving the suitcase in the room, knowing it was locked and the key safely in his pocket. Karl and Maria had hardly seated themselves when back came the friendly landlady. She placed a pot of tea, hiding under a tea cosy, on the table with teacups and saucers, a jug of milk and bowl of sugar.

"I'll be back in a minute with some toast. By the way, I'm Flo Dickson. My husband and I run this inn."

When the toast came, Karl and Maria realised that they were hungry and soon finished the simple breakfast. The woman reappeared, began to clear the table and suggested that if they would like some lunch, they should come down at one o'clock. They could meet her husband then, and he would take their details if they were going to stay.

"Yes, thank you, Mrs Dickson; we will come down at one."

Karl thought that this woman seemed kindly and welcoming, and he realised now how tense he had been and how much better he felt now that something seemed certain, at least for a while. The man on the bus had been right. They were indeed at the end of the journey. Maria and Karl went back upstairs and looked around at the room, which would be home for a little while. There was a picture of the king and queen on one wall. Pretty floral curtains, matching the bedspread, were draped in front of a black blind at the window. Two small easy chairs either side of the bed and a small dressing table completed the furnishings. A cupboard in one corner served as a wardrobe. There was a rug either side of the bed; otherwise, the floorboards were bare. On the back of the door was a hook, and Maria took off her coat and hung it up there.

Then she opened the door onto the corridor again, looking up and down. "I'm looking for where there might be a bathroom." She disappeared but then quite quickly came back in. "It's next door," she said. "I'm going to get a bath."

In the room, Karl sat on the edge of the bed, his head in his hands. He felt only a great wave of relief and utter exhaustion. He was in the same position when Maria came back, smiling and looking refreshed.

"Go, Karl darling, have at least a little wash, and you'll feel better. You have done a marvellous thing. We will be safe here, and you'll see, soon we'll make a new life in this country; we'll have our baby, and everything will be fine."

Karl gave her a rueful smile, took off his coat and jacket and went to the bathroom.

At the agreed time, they went downstairs again. In the bar area, a table had been laid with a white tablecloth and cutlery. A man appeared, almost as rotund as the woman who had greeted them earlier. Karl immediately walked towards him, offering his hand. "I'm Charles Hartman, and this is my wife, Maria."

"Please sit down, Mr Hartman. Glad to meet you. My wife tells me you're from Warsaw. But you must eat before we talk."

Mrs Dickson came in, carrying two plates.

"Roast beef, the usual thing on a Sunday but rare nowadays. We were lucky to get a joint this week. I hope you enjoy it."

After they had eaten, the man reappeared, carrying a book and sat at the table with them.

"Our visitors would probably prefer coffee, Flo," he called out.

"I'm Fred Dickson, the landlord of this inn. My wife is Florence. Now, I need you to sign in here, if you have decided everything is suitable for you. The room with breakfast is five pounds a night. If you want an evening meal, just let us know at breakfast time. As it gets to be dusk, would you be sure to pull down the blind in your room. Part of the war regulations. Is there anything else I can do to help you?"

"Well," said Karl, "I must find work and am not sure how to go about it. I thought I might get something agricultural, perhaps on a farm."

"Oh, I might be able to help you with that. Old Jimmie Cox is looking for help on his farm in Scole. His boy, who used to run it for him, is away in Palestine with the army. It's as much as Jimmie can do to keep the place going. If you like, I'll get a message to him, and perhaps in the morning, you could go and have a talk with him. Scole isn't far from here; you can easily do it on foot in about ten minutes."

"That would be most kind. Thank you, Mr Dickson. We will take a walk now and get to know where we are. Do I need a key for the main door?"

"Yes, I'll get you one. You can have breakfast any time between eight and nine. Just come down, and my wife will take care of you."

Maria and Karl walked slowly around Diss, noticing some very old-looking buildings on their way.

"Well, at least we know it's a Sunday today, the day the English have roast beef for lunch apparently," said Karl with a hint of humour.

"I wonder if we can find a church," whispered Maria, as though this were a shameful thing to be asking.

"Yes," replied Karl, "but it will probably not be the sort of church you want. The English are not Roman Catholics. Look, just up there. There's a church." When they reached it, they read the sign outside. It said, in bold capitals, St Mary's Church, Diss.

"I would like to go in," said Maria. There was nobody inside. They sat in a pew at the back. In a way, the silence was healing. Both Karl, who was not a believer, and Maria felt comfortable in this little Parish church. Maria fingered the Rosary in her pocket. It was a Sunday, and she would like to have heard Mass. It seemed such a long time since she had been able to receive Communion. But she comforted herself with the thought that, under the circumstances, the Lord would accept this quiet time in a little English church as her Mass attendance.

Further on in the town, Maria noticed a long building with, in large lettering, the word 'Bakery' on its façade.

"What is 'bakery', Karl?" Maria asked. Karl translated for her, explaining its purpose as a centre of bread making. Maria was interested in it, of course.

Nearby was a Greengrocer, J Cox.

"Isn't that the name of the farmer Mr Dickson mentioned at lunch?" asked Maria.

Then as the shops and buildings petered out, they walked down a sloping alley and found themselves in front of quite an extensive lake. The area was very attractive. There were quite a lot of people, adults and children, walking by the water, and some families having a picnic. Nobody acted as though there were a war on, unlike the cities, they had passed through on their journey from Warsaw.

"I like this place, Karl. I think we can be happy here."

"Yes, so do I. But Maria, you must try to get used to calling me Charles now. In England, when the country is still fighting the Germans, it's better not to have a German name. Slowly, you must also try to learn some English too. We are in quite a rural setting here, and if, as I hope, I can get work on a farm, we might be able to fit in without arousing too much curiosity."

"But you're a lawyer. Do you know anything about farming?"

"No, I don't. But I will learn. Shall we go back to the inn now? I'd like an early night." Both Charles and Maria slept well.

On Monday morning, Charles wanted to buy an English newspaper and some stationery, so they went again into the town, where this time all the shops were now open. There were quite a few people out shopping, and the atmosphere was pleasantly busy. They passed a school where, through its windows, they could see small children sitting at desks, and after a short walk, they came across a little café where they were able to have a coffee. At the table, as they drank, Charles wrote a short letter to Sikorski, and afterwards, they walked to the post office to mail it. They were beginning to find their way around Diss. The lovely, sunny day seemed to pass quickly.

On Tuesday morning, Charles made his way to the farm at Scole, leaving Maria to explore more of Diss. He told Maria that he would look for her in the market square when he got back.

It wasn't too long a walk, as Fred Dickson had said, and the day was again warm and sunny. Charles was aware that he needed soon to buy some new clothes. He was a little concerned about presenting himself for a job interview in clothes he had been wearing for some days now. A good-sized farmhouse came into view on his right, surrounded by some few acres of land, all given to crops it seemed. He noticed, too, a small cottage, some stables and a long row of greenhouses and outhouses.

Charles walked up the front pathway to the main door and rang what looked like a ship's bell, which hung by the door. A small, elderly man appeared from behind the house.

"Hello, are you Mr Hartman?" The voice was deep and warm, belying the man's small frame. He wore an old trilby hat from which escaped tufts of greying hair. Rolled-up shirtsleeves, somewhat grubby trousers, told Charles that here was a working farmer. Charles thought he was probably not as old as he looked.

"Yes, Charles Hartman. I believe Fred Dickson spoke to you about me? How do you do?"

The men shook hands. Charles continued, "I must tell you Mr Cox, that I am a lawyer by trade and know nothing about farming. My wife and I are refugees from Poland, and I desperately need a job."

"Well, let's walk around the farm, and I can show you what's involved," replied Jimmie Cox. "You desperately need a job, and I desperately need some assistance. Perhaps we can help one another?

"I grow mainly vegetables. There's a small orchard and hens. I have a greengrocery shop in Diss, and once a week, I have a stall in the market there. I need to keep both these outlets supplied. Very few people stop off at the farm to buy directly, although that is something that could be developed when this wretched war is over."

The two men walked slowly along the outer perimeter of the fields. They passed a small cottage, next to the farmhouse but detached and adjoining a long row of greenhouses.

"I can see you have a lot of tomatoes here," remarked Charles. "I suppose you would also be using these greenhouses for starting off your crops?"

Jimmie Cox laughed. "I can see you'll learn quickly. Yes, it's quite a juggling affair and depends a lot on the weather; most crops need hardening off slowly before they can be planted out where they'll grow."

They walked on past quite an extensive pen of hens.

"Eggs are always in demand, in spite of the ration," said Mr Cox. "But the fact that we have them means that within reason we don't have to go without, and the boys can have a few extra too. We're not really troubled much by foxes either, which is a mercy."

"What are these big sheds for?" asked Charles. They adjoined the chicken run and ran down to the back boundary.

"Well, we need to store a lot of produce to see us through the year. Potatoes, for instance. People always want potatoes. Let's go in and have a look."

They went inside, and Charles saw that there was shelving all around the walls, a lot of sacks filled with produce piled and labelled and stacked in an orderly way. Charles began to realise that the job consisted of much more than the simple growing of crops in the ground. Along the back boundary at right angles with the storage sheds ran a block of stables. Behind them and marking the extent of the farm were a long line of coniferous trees.

A horse's head looked out of one of the stables as the two men approached.

"This is Millie," said Jimmie Cox, patting the horse's nose. "She is alone here and getting elderly, like me," he said with a chuckle. "She takes the produce to the shop each day and to the market as well on Fridays. I also use her for helping with the soil preparation."

The men walked on until they came to a narrow pathway on their left, which was the main access to the crops growing in each segmented portion of the field. The pathway ran vertically down the entire length of the fields. Jimmie Cox paused there.

"The barns you see up there," he said, pointing to a long building occupying the rest of the back boundary, "are for the storage of machinery and tools." They started to walk up the centre pathway. Charles was beginning to realise the extent of the work involved as he glanced at the abundance of different crops growing in each area.

"You have gone very quiet," said Jimmie Cox.

"Yes," said Charles, "I am amazed at the amount of work involved here."

"I have ten acres, without the orchard, which you can see over there." Jimmie pointed over to the right. "I grow mainly apples, but I am experimenting with damsons at the moment. Getting fruit from abroad now is almost impossible. That piece of land is not actually mine; I rent it."

Charles was trying to keep track of all the information he was being given and was feeling a little overwhelmed. Nevertheless, he liked this man who was obviously so enthusiastic about his farm and everything concerning it.

"One of the most important jobs is keeping the soil in good condition and winning the battle against all the little creatures that assume the crop is for them. As you can see, we have a lot of composting bins over there, and Millie contributes to them quite considerably." Again came the warm chuckle.

"Your role would not be mainly manual, Mr Hartman. We have young boys to do most of that heavy work. What I need is someone who will help me with the actual running and direction of the business, which includes of course the shop and market stall."

"I think I could do that," said Charles, "but of course, I would have a lot to learn before you could entirely rely on me."

"Well, I think if you shadowed me for a whole year, you would quickly learn the routine. My son was always my right-hand-man, but he was called up, and now he's with the Army in Palestine. I could never understand why his occupation didn't excuse him."

They were now almost at the end of the centre pathway and back in front of the farmhouse. Charles looked back over the farm, thinking how well organised everything seemed to be. He liked Jimmie Cox, and although this was a work totally alien to him, he thought he could manage and enjoy it, following the guidance of his employer.

"Let's go in, Mr Hartman. Oh, I can't keep calling you that. You are Charles aren't you, and I am Jimmie. Let's not be so formal. My wife, who is Ethel, will make us a pot of tea, and we can talk."

They went in and entered a large, bright kitchen. It was everything you would expect of a farmhouse, warm, cosy and welcoming. A big wooden table occupied the centre of the room, and the two men sat at it, opposite one another. Jimmie introduced his wife, Ethel, and asked her if she would bring them some tea. She was what Charles would call a pretty woman, with a rather shy smile, short like her husband but perhaps a little younger Charles thought. She seemed, to Charles, the sort of woman you instantly warmed to. She soon returned with the tea, then left the two men alone.

"Tell me a little about yourself, Charles." Jimmie began to pour the tea.

"Well, as I said, I come from Warsaw in Poland. I practised law there and had my own successful law firm. After Poland was invaded, things gradually became very difficult and unpleasant, to say the least. When my wife told me she was expecting our first child, I knew there could be no future for us as a family in Warsaw. Britain was our ally and had promised help, so it seemed to me that maybe I could build a future here. My wife and I made our way through Germany and France as far as Dieppe. There, we were helped by the French Resistance and were able to travel to England with the Polish Government in Exile. We have been staying with Mr and Mrs Dickson at their inn in Diss. Of course, none of this is remotely a qualification for farming." Charles felt relieved that he had been able to give a believable account of himself without having to tell any lies.

"You must have had a terrible time getting here. You obviously have courage. When is your baby due?"

"At the end of October," said Charles.

"Well, you know, the main thing is organisation. The hours can be long, and the weather often makes things a bit unpredictable. There are certain things you'll need to know about because of Food Regulations, but we can go over that in due course. I think we could work together, and I would be glad to help you and your wife settle down here if you think you would like to take us on. Gradually, I have in mind that Bob would take over from me when he gets home. I am beginning to think about retiring! But I have a few ideas of how we could expand the business, and I would not be at all surprised if Bob didn't want to introduce livestock to the farm." Jimmie looked at Charles to see what his response would be.

"I would like that very much. It would be a complete change for me, but I am interested and happy to learn."

"Good," Jimmie responded. "Now, do you have any plans yet as to where you will live? You probably need to get something settled before you start work.

"Actually" – Jimmie paused a moment – "I wonder if Bob's little cottage would suit you and your wife? I would have to discuss it with Ethel, but it might be a solution for you. You would be near, and although it's not very large, it might be a comfortable home for you, at least until you have time to look around. When Bob comes back, he can easily move in with us; we have plenty of room. Would you like to go and have a look at it?"

The two men went back out and made their way to the little cottage. It was a simple dwelling-place, with a good-sized kitchen and scullery downstairs, the kitchen having a coal-fired range. Off the scullery, there was a somewhat rudimentary bathroom. Upstairs was just one large bedroom. Charles thought it would be adequate, at least for a year or two. He discussed with Jimmie a salary, and they shook hands on it. Charles could not help but wonder at his luck.

"Now, I think you will need a day or two to get registered here Charles. You'll need identity cards, and you'll have to register with the ministry to get a ration book. Perhaps you'll be ready to start work next Monday?"

Charles walked slowly back to Diss, taking notice of the surroundings in a very different way from the one in which he had observed them on his way to the farm. This is where they would live. This is where they would build a new life. Charles felt a sense of warm anticipation. He wanted to tell Maria all about it. He found her in the market square, sitting on a bench. People were wandering around, shopping and meeting friends. You could hardly believe there was a war on. Charles sat down beside Maria.

"Well, how did you get on?" she asked him. Charles wanted to savour the moment. He felt rather pleased with himself.

"Maria, I have a job, and we have a home."

"Oh, Charles, that's wonderful! And a home too?" Maria grasped his arm, not liking to embrace him in public. Her joy was obvious. "Tell me about it. When will you start work? Do you think you'll manage it? What's our house like? Did you like Mr Cox? Oh, Charles, what a great blessing this is."

Charles laughed. Sitting here, in the centre of this little village in England, the sun shining and a possible future opening up, Charles for the first time in many weeks began to feel more himself. He didn't stop to ask himself who he was, though he might well have done. Had he done so, he might have realised that he was now more truly himself than he had been for a long time. The Warsaw experience had been, for him, a very dark time. He knew that there were still many obstacles to overcome, but at this moment, he felt relaxed and full of hope.

He took Maria's hand. "Let's see if we can find a little place around here where we can get some coffee and something to eat. I don't suppose you've eaten since breakfast."

They walked a little way, but finding no café where they were at that moment, they went back to the inn. As it had been on Sunday, it was empty and somewhat forlorn looking. Charles rang the bell, and as before, Mrs Dickson appeared.

"Would it be possible to have some coffee or tea and a little snack, Mrs Dickson?" Charles asked.

"Yes, of course. Would a cheese sandwich do? I can probably make you a small plate of salad. It's not so easy these days."

Charles told her their news and asked her if she could do a meal for them that evening.

"That I can, although it will be simple. I'll go and get you some lunch. Fred will be pleased to hear your news." When Mrs Dickson returned, Charles asked her if there was a Roman Catholic Church in Diss. The smile immediately disappeared from her face, and to Charles, the hostility was evident in her whole demeanour.

"No, I wouldn't know about such a thing."

Charles was very surprised by Mrs Dickson's reaction. He had not thought to encounter such prejudice.

"Is something wrong?" asked Maria as Mrs Dickson returned to the back room. Although Maria had not understood the conversation, she had picked up the change in Mrs Dickson's attitude.

"Well, I just asked if there was a Roman Catholic Church here. Our landlady did not seem to like the question. It is as well that you should be aware that you could encounter some hostility on this subject."

That afternoon, Charles and Maria walked down to the lakeside. Charles wanted to talk to Maria about something that he thought would be difficult. His next hurdle, he knew, was to register with the authorities. He thought that the safest way would be to present himself as a lawyer with connections to the Polish Government in Exile. Charles was, not surprisingly, still thinking like a German.

"Maria, as you know, I wrote to Wladyslaw Sikorski on Monday. I offered him my services as a lawyer. No, please don't question me just yet. Let me tell you how I am thinking. Let's sit here on this bench."

They sat facing the lake.

"We have to register here, so that we have legal residence. We need to be citizens, Maria, not refugees, and I am thinking also about the future of our child. I am willing to do what I can to help Poland, but I am considering first of all, our own needs. If the people here see me only as a refugee, they will probably want details of my background in Warsaw. I don't need to tell you that if we took no steps to register, the police would make enquiries, and it could be very bad for me. On the other hand, if I present myself voluntarily, and I can say that I have a connection with the Polish Government, they may contact the office in London to verify this. When they do, it would be better for me if Sikorski remembers me and has me in view as a legal expert ready to assist his government. His confirmation that I have contact with him could make a big difference to us. It is imperative that I register us with the authorities here this week."

Charles paused as two young people strolled by, also enjoying the afternoon sunshine by the lake. Once again, Charles marvelled at the relaxed atmosphere here, in spite of the country being at war.

"We need to buy food, and for that we need documents. We also both need clothes. I don't want you to be anxious about all this, but I want you to know what I am doing. This may not be an entirely easy procedure." Charles paused.

"We don't know yet how the future will unfold, and of course, we also need to register you with a doctor."

Maria took Charles's hand. She was moved by the extent to which Charles had planned out things for them. She felt a deep love for him and an immense appreciation of all that he had done to ensure a secure future for them.

"Charles, I understand everything you say. It sounds sensible, and possible, to me. In any case, I trust you absolutely to do the best for us." Then her practical mind took over. "But what will you do if Sikorski wants you in London to help him with legal matters? You've just got a full-time job."

"I don't really know, Maria. I think I'll cross that bridge when I come to it. Now" – Charles looked at his watch – "we must go to the police station. We have to register there." He had noticed, on their earlier walks, where the police station was, and quite quickly, they reached it. They went in and stood in a small reception area. There was no one behind the desk. Charles and Maria waited.

"Do you have your documents with you?" Charles asked Maria quietly.

"Can I help you, sir?" A middle-aged policeman came to the desk. He had sharp features but greeted them with a reassuring smile.

"My wife and I are refugees from Poland, and I believe we need to register here."

"From Poland?" The policeman grimaced. "How on earth did you manage to get here?"

He didn't wait for an answer but disappeared for a moment, returning with a file.

"I'll need you to fill in some forms." Clearly, this was quite an infrequent occurrence, and Charles could see that the man was not entirely sure of the procedure as he searched through the file.

"Where are you staying? Oh, I expect you are the couple staying with Fred Dickson. He mentioned you to us."

Charles was immediately on his guard. These people were not to be underestimated.

"Yes, we arrived on Sunday with the prime minister of Poland. I am a lawyer and hope to be of service to the Polish Government in Exile. I have obtained a job and a place to live."

Charles felt like a schoolboy having to justify his behaviour to the headmaster. The policeman pushed over some papers towards Charles. Charles noticed his bitten fingernails.

"You'll need to fill these in and then one of our officers will go over them with you. I'll leave you to get on with it. You have a pen?"

Charles took his fountain pen from his jacket pocket and began to complete the documents. He had only to fill in one set of papers because his wife was included in his own details. It took some time. Maria grew weary, but there were no chairs on their side of the barrier. When he had finished answering all the questions, Charles rang the bell.

A different officer came in, lifted up the desk flap and bade the couple follow him. They were led to an office and asked to take seats. A short time passed and yet another officer came in, taking the chair behind the important-looking desk. Charles handed him the papers he had completed.

"Good afternoon, I am Charles Hartman, and this is my wife, Maria."

The officer merely nodded and took the papers from Charles. Charles sensed this was not going to be easy. The silence, as the policeman glanced through the pages, made him feel uneasy. Maria, he thought, was just glad to be able to sit down. He took her hand momentarily. Every so often, the man looked up, as though appraising these two foreigners sitting in front of him. His expression, when he did so, gave Charles no sense at all of whether this man would be sympathetic to them or not. He looked, to Charles, like your average Englishman: nothing particularly distinguishing about him, except perhaps in this case the lack of any warmth. Since he had not introduced himself, Charles knew neither his name nor his rank. Charles could not help thinking that he would be glad when this interview was over.

"Passports please."

Charles took Maria's from her, and together with his own, handed them to the dour man facing them. Charles hoped that he would not find any reason to question his own fake Polish one. He felt tense again. He waited for questions to be put to him. The officer looked at the documents, comparing them at times with details Charles had filled in on the papers. Charles involuntarily took Maria's hand again, an unconscious attempt to steady his nerves.

"Well, Mr Hartman, I can give you the documents you need immediately, but I shall have to ask you to report to this office every fourteen days until we have completed our enquiries." He handed the passports back to Charles.

"Certainly, I will do that, but I am starting a new job on Monday, at Cox's Farm, and so a time outside of normal working hours would be helpful to me."

The officer looked at Charles, with still not the glimmer of a smile, inscrutable, and it would seem, disinterested. "We know where to find you. Just make sure you report fortnightly." He held the door open for them. "Good afternoon, Mr Hartman, Mrs Hartman. Please wait in the outer office and your identity cards will be ready in a few minutes."

It was over. Charles felt a wave of relief. They stood for fifteen minutes in the little reception area, and eventually, the policeman they had met earlier came out and handed Charles two small identity cards. They were clearly temporary cards. Still, he thought, they will be the entry we need to more permanent documents.

He and Maria went out into the late-afternoon sunshine. They both felt they had had enough for that day and made their way back to the inn to get ready for their evening meal. On the way back, Charles gave Maria her card and told her to be sure to have it with her always.

"It makes you legal, more or less," he said, with a smile.

Maria laughed, probably more with relief at getting out of the police station, than a response to Charles's humour. They both felt thankful that this ordeal was over.

Over breakfast on the Friday of that week, Charles was very surprised when Mrs Dickson handed him a letter that had arrived for him. He saw immediately that it was from Sikorski's office. It asked Charles to ring the office once he was settled. Of greater interest to Charles was the second paragraph, which informed him that they had received an enquiry from the police at Diss regarding the Polish Government's knowledge of him. Charles felt considerable relief. The first big hurdle was over.

After breakfast, Charles suggested they go to the Friday Market. It would be good to see how it worked since he was going to be involved with it very soon. It seemed quite busy. They saw Cox's Farm Stall, with a young man behind it, engaging with several customers. There were joints of pork hanging at another stall and yet another, offering all kinds of ribbon and cottons. The cheese stall looked very inviting. It seemed as though the local traders owned the stalls.

"It would be nice to have a cake stall here," remarked Maria. There was a nice bustling atmosphere in the square, which Maria liked. There didn't seem to be anywhere to have coffee and a snack though.

"If you've seen enough, I'd like to go to the Doctor's Surgery. We should get registered."

"Do you know where it is, Charles?" asked Maria.

"Yes, I think so. I noticed it once when we walked down to the lake. I think it's this way." He took Maria's hand, almost boyishly. Charles was beginning to feel more relaxed. They reached a narrow lane and Charles stopped at a shiny black door with a brass plate bearing the name Matthew William Hall followed by various medical qualifications. There seemed not to be a bell, so Charles pushed the door. They stepped into a narrow passage with a flight of stairs. They went up and found themselves in what was obviously a waiting room. No one was there. They were not sure what to do. Then, a serious-looking man, tall and slim, dressed in quite a formal dark suit, came in.

"How can I help you? I'm Doctor Hall." His smile transformed his face and put Maria and Charles instantly at ease.

"Good morning, Doctor Hall," said Charles. "My wife and I are new to this area, and I am hoping that we can register with you for medical care. My wife is expecting our first child around about October, and we are anxious to make sure that everything is fine."

Doctor Hall extended his hand to Maria, "Congratulations Mrs…? And Mr…? Please sit down." Charles and Maria both warmed to this man, who seemed gentle and welcoming. Charles explained their circumstances.

"So, Mrs Hartman, I assume it could be more than two months since you had a medical check?"

"My wife doesn't yet speak very much English. I'm afraid I shall have to interpret for her."

"Right," said Doctor Hall, "that shouldn't be a problem. I can offer you an appointment on Monday, if that would be convenient?"

"Well," said Charles, "I start a new job on Monday, and since I shall need to come with Maria that might be a little difficult, unless it were in the evening."

"Yes, I could do that. What about seven o'clock?"

"That would be fine," said Charles. Then, feeling somewhat embarrassed, he asked what the arrangements were for payment.

"I send my bills out on the last day of the month, Mr Hartman, and if there are any medications required, you pick them up here. Until Monday then. I'm pleased to have met you."

As Charles and Maria descended the stairs and went out again to the narrow lane, they looked at one another and smiled.

"I like this doctor," said Maria.

"Yes, I think he will be a friend," said Charles.

When they got back to the inn, Mrs Dickson caught them as they were going upstairs.

"Mr Hartman, here is a note for you from Jimmie Cox. He left it for you this morning. You only just missed him." She handed the note to Maria who was following behind Charles. In their room, they opened it.

It said, "Dear Charles, Ethel and I would like to invite you and Maria to lunch on Sunday. We thought you might like to bring your things and get settled in before starting work on Monday. There is no need to try to get a message back to us. We shall expect you about midday. Jimmie and Ethel Cox."

"That is so kind," said Maria, "it will be good to get settled down properly."

Chapter Five
Settling Down and Making Friends

So it was, that on Sunday morning, Charles and Maria said thank you to Mr and Mrs Dickson, paid their bill and made their way to Scole. As they opened the gate to the farm, Jimmie Cox, who must have been watching out for them, came out of the front door and walked up the path to greet them. The grubby-looking farmer had given way to a gentleman wearing a smart shirt, plain blue tie and neatly pressed trousers. Charles realised he was a good-looking man. He turned to Maria and introduced her to Jimmie. They shook hands and Jimmie, still holding on to Maria, said, "Welcome, both of you; we'll go to your little cottage first. Goodness, is this all the luggage you have?" He took the suitcase from Charles and led the way to the cottage.

"Ethel has been here and cleaned. I don't know exactly what she's done, but she was a long time doing it. I expect you'll find most things ready for you. There is clean linen and towels in this cupboard here" – he indicated a cupboard in the kitchen near the range – "and I think you'll find that she has put some basic things in the food cupboard. I'll leave you to settle yourselves in. Please come down to the house as soon as you are ready. I think Ethel has opened a bottle of wine."

Off he went, with a little chuckle of anticipation. Maria noticed a vase of flowers on the kitchen table. She had, of course, not seen the cottage before, but she was appreciative of how their hosts, who were also their landlords and employers, had done everything they could to make them feel welcome. Maria embraced Charles, who it must be said, looked a little lost. For once, it was Maria who took charge and reassured him.

"We are home; everything is going to be all right, Charles. I love you very much and especially for all that you have achieved for us." She kissed him lightly on his cheek. "This is the beginning of our future. Come on, let's unpack our things and begin to make ourselves feel as though we are at home. Who knows, we may return in a state unfit to do much. That's if Jimmie's wine is as good as he seems to think."

Over the next few weeks, Maria saw Dr Hall, found the best way to get into Diss, received ration books and registered with retailers in Diss, signed up at the local library, got all their clothes washed and stood over Charles (more or less) until he burnt the Nazi uniform that was still in the suitcase. The metal emblems, which would not burn, Charles put in a box and secreted in the small loft, not liking to bury them in ground with which he was not familiar. He didn't want one of the farmhands digging them up.

As for Charles, each day was filled with new tasks to be learned, getting the overall timing of each day into his head, overseeing the young staff and generally finding out how to run a farm in line with government requirements during wartime. In the evenings, after eating, Charles had strength left only to collapse into a chair and catch up with the day's news from The Times. Occasionally, their peace would be disturbed by the sound of aircraft overhead, either leaving from, or targeting, the air base a few miles away. On the whole, they were not much bothered by attacks, most of them being aimed at Norwich.

Maria quietly wondered at Charles's adaptability and admired the way he got on with whatever was required of him. Warsaw seemed a long way away. She asked him one day if there was a possibility of contacting her parents. Charles thought not, at least until the war was over.

In July, Charles read of the death of Sikorski in a plane crash. He felt saddened by it. The man had been of considerable help to him. Charles was aware of some political differences between the old regime under Sikorski, and the new prime minister and felt it relieved him of any obligation he felt to contact their office. However, he was reminded that he still owed the Polish Government the money they had loaned him. He was also aware that he had to be careful about what he spent. With him, he had a considerable amount of money in Reichsmarks, but at this time, it was of no use to him. He kept them, hoping that when the war was over, he might be able to change them into pounds sterling. He had opened a bank account on the strength of his monthly salary, but he had no savings. He gave no thought to the property he owned in Warsaw and had abandoned. It was gone, together with his life there. Charles did not allow himself to think about the past. His whole life now was centred on his desire to be successful in his work and to make a happy life for Maria and himself and for the child whose birth they both looked forward to.

On November 1, All Saints Day, Maria was delighted to note, she gave birth to a baby boy, small but healthy. Charles was out on the farm; it was eleven in the morning when the midwife called to him. By the time he got there, both Maria and the baby were clean and tidy. Hard on his heels came Dr Hall. The two men stood looking at mother and child. Dr Hall stayed only to ask Maria if she was all right, to have a look at the baby and speak briefly with the midwife. Then he left, saying he would call again soon.

"Could I hold the baby?" asked Charles.

The midwife took the child from Maria and placed him carefully into Charles's arms. "You have a beautiful little boy," she said. "I'll just go down to do some jobs and then I'll come back."

Charles sat on the edge of the bed, cradling his tiny son, one arm around his wife. "What shall we call him?" he asked Maria. She looked at the sleeping child with tenderness as Charles kissed her on the forehead.

"I should like to call him Gregory, then of course he should have your name and maybe that of my father?"

"Gregory Charles Jan. That sounds wonderful. That will be his name," said Charles, full of pride.

"We must arrange his baptism as soon as we can."

"When you are up and about again, we can contact the church at the monastery. I'll get it sorted out," replied Charles.

Charles put the baby gently into a large drawer by the bed, a drawer from their chest, which they had prepared with linen. As yet, they had no cradle for him.

"I will sleep for a little while if you don't mind, Charles. I had never thought that giving birth could be such hard work!"

Over the next few months, Maria got to know Ethel Cox much more closely and to appreciate her gentle and considerate kindness. Maria watched how she handled the baby and learned to deal with little Gregory herself more confidently. Maria's own peacefulness seemed to transmit to the baby, and he seldom cried. Ethel had made it clear to Maria that she did not in any way wish to interfere, but that she would always be ready to help should Maria need it. She talked with Maria, over coffee in the mornings, when Charles was out on the farm, about her own experience as a mother, when Bob, her only child, was a baby. The two women got on well, and Ethel also helped Maria to speak English more confidently.

A few weeks after Gregory's birth, Ethel knocked at Maria's door one morning with a baby's pram in tow. When Maria came to the door, Ethel said at once, "Maria, Jimmie and I wanted to give you a present to welcome your baby and decided a pram might be very useful to you. If you don't like it or would like something different, please do not be afraid to say so. It can easily be changed or exchanged for something different. It is only a second-hand one, but it's in good condition, and I have made sure that it's absolutely clean."

Maria was almost speechless with delight. "Oh, Ethel," she said, "it is just what we need. It is lovely. Thank you so much; it is very kind of you. I will be able to walk into the village with him. Perhaps you will come with us too sometimes."

The two women hugged. Maria watched Ethel as she walked back to the farmhouse, thinking how blessed she and Charles were to have found such friends.

Likewise, on the farm, Charles was getting to appreciate Jimmie's qualities. Jimmie was pleased that Charles seemed to pick up very quickly the principles of how to run the farm, and he noted that the young employees accepted his authority without question. On Charles's part, he grew greatly to respect Jimmie's handling of things and looked forward to the day when he, Charles, would be competent enough to allow Jimmie to take a little more time off.

Jimmie was in his early sixties, and gradually, Charles noticed that he tired quite quickly. Running a farm in wartime was not a straightforward thing, to say nothing about the handling of the shop in Diss. He looked forward to being able to relieve Jimmie of some of the burdens the business entailed.

Maria felt happier, and more settled, once she discovered through the information desk at the library that there was a Mass centre in Diss. It was just a room over one of the larger inns there, where a priest came from the nearest Catholic parish so that local Catholics could hear Mass. It was a very common arrangement when there was no Roman Catholic Church nearby. Maria joined the congregation, which numbered between ten and twelve people and was able to join them most Sundays to hear Mass. She was surprised to notice Dr Hall amongst the regular attendees. They said hello and talked a little about the baby's progress. Maria wondered whether she could ask Dr Hall if he would stand as godfather to little Gregory.

One day, a week or so before Christmas, Maria was working in the kitchen when she noticed an officer on a bicycle dismount at the farm's gate, stand his bike at the fence and walk down the path to the farmhouse door. Maria thought he was a police officer, but actually, he was from the post office, delivering a telegram. Maria was not sure what was happening but felt a little anxious. She saw that Ethel opened the door, that something was handed to her, and then the officer walked back up the path, mounted his bike and rode off. Maria thought it was strange.

A few moments later, she heard the ship's bell being rung, the usual way of communicating with the men when they were out in the field. Shortly after, Jimmie arrived, followed by Charles. When Charles came into the cottage, Maria explained to him what she had seen.

"Oh dear," said Charles, "that was almost certainly a telegram for them. It might not be good news. I will wait a little while and then go down."

Charles allowed half-an-hour to pass and then went down to the farmhouse. After about ten minutes, he returned. "It is as I thought, Maria. Bob has been killed in action. I couldn't do very much. They are terribly distressed."

Maria jumped up. "I must go to them. Please watch the baby." Then she was out of the door and hurrying to the farmhouse, entering with a knock at the back door. She heard the 'Come in' and went through into the sitting room where Jimmie and Ethel were sitting side by side on the settee, a framed photograph of Bob in Ethel's hands.

"Oh, I am so sorry. This is terrible news." Maria sat, hardly knowing what to say.

Ethel spoke. "At least he died very quickly without suffering. That's what the telegram says. It is difficult to believe that our son, our dearly loved boy is…" Ethel couldn't say the word.

"May I look?" asked Maria, indicating the photograph in Ethel's hands. She saw a fresh-faced young man in army uniform, like so many other young men, husbands, sons and brothers, who had gone off to fight for their country. But this was not any other young man.

"He's very much like you, Jimmie. Do you want to tell me a bit about him? Or perhaps you'd rather not? What if I go and make you a pot of tea, then if you want to talk, you can. I think a hot drink would be good, if you haven't had one. You've both had a shock."

"No, we haven't had any tea. That would be kind of you, Maria," said Ethel in a flat and lifeless voice.

When Maria came back in with a tray of tea, Jimmie and Ethel were still sitting in the same place, the photograph on Ethel's knees. The couple seemed frozen in time, stunned and hopeless.

Maria took the photograph gently from Ethel. "Where would you like me to put him whilst you have your tea?" she asked. As Jimmie indicated, Maria placed the photograph on the windowsill facing the settee. Bob was like a fourth person in the room.

Jimmie began to express his thoughts as Maria poured the tea. "He was always such a good boy. He never caused us any trouble. And such energy! He loved the farm and would really have liked us to have branched out into rearing stock. I never thought I could manage animals and dissuaded him from it. Perhaps I should have listened to him."

"He played for the local Cricket Club, and we often went to watch the matches," Ethel reminisced. "He wasn't really a great sportsman, but he was popular with the others in the team. Do you remember, Jimmie, that time he scored fifty runs, the best he ever did? He was so proud. We were too."

Maria sat quietly with Jimmie and Ethel as these past events came to them, like flicking through a photograph album and one or two of the pictures immediately lighting a little flame of memory. She didn't question but was a sympathetic presence for the two, ready to support them if they fell into silence and sorrow again.

After a little while, she thought perhaps she should leave. She rose and said, "I must go back now, but if you would like to come up to us in a little while, when you feel ready, perhaps you would have some lunch with us? I don't suppose you feel much like preparing anything, but you need to eat."

It was Jimmie who replied. "We will do that. Thank you for asking us. But first, I must go out and finish what I was doing on the farm."

"Please don't do that, Jimmie. Charles will take care of things. You are not even to think about anything to do with work today. This is time for you and Ethel to be together, remembering and loving your son. Let us help you, please, as much as we can." Maria embraced each of them and left.

When Maria went indoors, Charles was rocking Gregory in his arms. Maria told him that Jimmie and Ethel would be coming up shortly to have some lunch with them.

"We'll have the soup and the bread I made yesterday, and if they feel able to eat more, I can serve the vegetable pie with the rest of the cold meat." Maria went on talking as she busied herself getting things ready for the lunch. "I told Jimmie that you would finish off on the farm today. And whilst they are here, I think we should not make too much of the baby. They have just lost their son. I can't begin to imagine what they must be feeling."

When Jimmie and Ethel arrived, almost the first thing Ethel did was to go to the baby, now propped in the easy chair.

"May I hold him?" she asked. Ethel took the sleeping child in her arms and sat with him in the chair. The baby didn't stir.

Charles asked Jimmie what he had been doing and what he still wanted done with regard to the farm, and assured him that after lunch he would take care of everything. The time passed with gentle, sporadic conversation. During coffee, Maria asked the couple if they thought a little Bob-garden somewhere on the farm would be a nice thing to make. If they chose some of Bob's favourite plants, Ethel could then have them in the house as well. Neither the cottage nor the farmhouse had a garden as such, but when they talked over the suggestion, there were plenty of ideas about where to situate such a plot and how to arrange it. Ethel, at her insistence, helped Maria clear away the dishes, and then she and Jimmie took their leave with hugs and thanks. Maria could not help noticing Jimmie's ashen face and realised she was more anxious about him than Ethel. Ethel seemed to have more inner strength than Jimmie, Maria decided.

She watched them walk across the path to their door. They faced a different future now from the one they had envisaged. Maria thought how difficult it would be for them not to have a funeral for Bob, nor a grave in which to place his body somewhere near to them, at home in England. That's why she had suggested the garden for Bob. She thought too about the thousands of other young soldiers, German, Canadian, American, Polish, whose parents faced the same grief as Jimmie and Ethel. It was a terrible business. Surely, it must end soon, she thought. When it does, we must work hard for a peace all over the world. We have given our beloved sons, who lie now in foreign soil, just as our enemies have given theirs, surely, we can learn to be friends again?

These were Maria's thoughts as she watched the couple return to their home. When she went back into the kitchen, the baby was slumbering contentedly, and Charles went out to get on with his work on the farm.

As good as baby Gregory was at home, when it came to his Baptism, he protested vociferously. Matthew Hall, Jimmie and Ethel Cox stood around the font in the entrance porch at the Benedictine Church, together with Maria and

Charles. A couple of the young lads who helped on the farm had also come, which greatly pleased Charles. Maria was happy to notice that although they were not in the body of the church, the porch area was warm. The officiating priest, Fr. Paul, spoke the Latin quite quickly, but as the baby was screaming and crying, the little group only wanted to get the ceremony over with.

Matthew Hall, as a practising Catholic, was the accepted godfather, with Jimmie and Ethel Cox welcomed too as adults who would have a special role to play in the child's upbringing.

Afterwards, the group, together with Fr. Paul, went back to the farmhouse, where Ethel had prepared a celebratory tea. Maria had, with the help of rations from the Coxes, made a beautiful cake for the occasion. As is so often the case, once away from the church, the baby stopped crying, and the afternoon passed happily. Maria was pleased to see that Ethel and Jimmie seemed able to enjoy the afternoon, and when Matthew Hall asked Maria about the name Jan, she told him a little about her parents in Warsaw and how she had learned her cake-making skills from them. They talked about the two grandparents who were present at the ceremony only through the name given to the baby. Maria found it a lovely thing to be able to talk a little about her parents. She realised how much she missed them and was grateful for Matthew's interest. The tall, serious doctor they had first met was becoming to both Charles and Maria, as they got to know him better, someone they knew they could always rely upon. Maria could not help wondering why it was that this very good-looking and charming man was without a wife.

And so, for Cox's Farm, life began to settle down, as the staff got to know Charles and he got to understand the workings of the farm. Preparing for the Christmas Season now occupied Jimmie and Charles. Charles would learn that winter was one of the busiest times on the farm. But he was happy. Maria noticed the gradual change in him. The rather stern and serious man she had known in Warsaw was becoming, she couldn't think of a word, more human. He was relaxed and even at times displayed a sense of humour. Consequently, Maria too felt more at ease. England, she thought, suited them. Everything seemed to be working out for them.

However, Maria remained a little concerned about Jimmie. She talked over her worries with Charles. He agreed that Jimmie was doing less work on the farm, but Charles thought that might be because he felt more able to leave some things to him.

"Yes, maybe you're right," she said and put it out of mind.

About the middle of June 1944, soon after Charles and Maria noted they had been in England for one year, news began to appear about the Allied Invasion of Normandy. Everyone's hopes soared that this was surely the beginning of the end of the war. Maria had been deliberating for some time about how she might set up a small business using her bread and cakemaking skills. Now, she thought, she might be able to bring this project to a reality. Her first problem, she knew, would be to obtain the ingredients needed for bulk cookery in this time of rationing. Then, she was unsure what attitude Charles would take towards her ideas. He might say that she had a baby and husband to care for and that it was his job to be the breadwinner. Maria thought it would be best to start with a stall in the Friday market, keeping the expenditure low. If it turned out to be successful, she had in mind a small teashop in Diss. She knew that was only a future possibility and kept it at the back of her mind. No, the market was the best place to start. She thought she could probably enlist the support of Ethel where baby minding was concerned. However, Maria soon realised, as she made tentative enquiries, that with rationing likely to continue for some time, the difficulties of such a project would be insurmountable. She put it to the back of her mind.

In August, Charles heard on the news that an uprising by the Polish Resistance in Warsaw, against the German occupiers, had taken place. It had led to the Germans, under the direction of Himmler, razing the city to the ground, probably because they knew the Russian army was advancing.

Charles knew that for Maria this would be devastating news. He told her about it as carefully as he could, knowing that she would probably have to face the likelihood that her parents might have died. He thought it possible that, in fact, they may have been transported to one of the extermination camps, along with so many other Poles, but decided not to mention this to Maria. Charles watched the colour drain from Maria's face as he related these events to her.

"These Poles were very brave, Maria. They wanted, I think, to try to regain power of their own country again before the Soviets got there." Charles put his arm round Maria and held her close to him, as she sobbed.

"But I am afraid, darling, that Russia will fill the void of the destruction before too long, and poor Poland will find itself under the heel of another tyranny."

"We should have brought them with us" Maria managed to say.

"Yes, Maria, if only we could have done that. But at the time we were ourselves in great danger, and I could think only of us and our unborn child." Charles continued to hold his wife. "I am sorry, darling, but I think we will have to accept the probability that your parents are lost."

"Oh, Papa! Oh, Mama!" Maria trembled and cried in Charles's arms.

They sat in their embrace for some time, until Maria quietened and felt able to face the day ahead.

It took almost a year before the war in Europe was brought to an end. When victory came, Maria and Charles looked at the pictures in The Times of the king and queen on the balcony of Buckingham Palace with Mr Churchill and caught the joy and feeling of liberation expressed by the hundreds of people gathered there. The day the war ended became known as VE day, standing for Victory in Europe.

In Diss, they held a street party for their own celebration, as in fact most people were doing throughout the country. Maria was gathered into the planning and designated cakemaker in charge. Because of the shortage of ingredients, she kept the recipes simple but tried to vary things as much as she could. However, nothing could dim the joy of that summer of 1945, when the people of Diss and its surrounding areas came together for this great undertaking. For Maria, it meant that she got to know other women from the area, and she enjoyed sharing in the cake making with them, although in her heart she carried the destruction of Warsaw and the loss of her parents as a constant sorrow.

The actual VE day was, luckily, warm and dry. In Maria's memory, it would always remain predominantly a noisy and muddled cacophony of chatter but more importantly an occasion of happiness and relief. Everyone, in their different ways hoped that life would now return to normal. The children ran around the market square, in and out of the tables, waving streamers of red, white and blue. Union Jacks hung from every building. Ethel walked down with Gregory in his pram, and he demanded a streamer too. On that party day, not one of the adults present envisaged the hardships that would continue to limit their lives for some years to come. They embraced only the feeling of freedom, joy and hope. Diss had not suffered any destruction, and the market square looked as it always had, except that now it was festooned in the country's colours and accommodated tables with food for everyone, in spite of rationing.

Gregory, in that summer of 1945, was growing rapidly. He was alert, walking even if a little unsteadily and expressing himself in baby language. His most remarkable physical characteristic was his very blonde hair and contrasting dark brown eyes. He was a happy child who seemed specially to like visits from strangers. He exhibited a curiosity about people, without a hint of shyness. Ethel was not a stranger of course, and he clearly loved her, but when occasionally Matthew Hall dropped by, Gregory chortled and laughed at him and was quite happy to be picked up and whirled around by him.

Matthew was a single man, kept busy by being a very popular doctor around Diss. He became, as time passed, a friend of Charles, for which Maria was grateful. Charles didn't make friends that easily. In some ways, the two men had similar characters, both quite serious, very reliable and dedicated to their work. Gregory called Matthew Uncle Matt and the little boy became an important part of Matthew's life. In a very real and permanent way, Matthew Hall became a part of Maria and Charles's life too.

Matthew was alone in the world. He told Charles and Maria one day that his parents and younger brother had died in a car crash. Matthew had been twenty-one at the time and was almost halfway through his medical studies. His parents had died instantly, but his younger brother survived for a few days. It was his brother's fight for life that had made Matthew determined to complete his studies and devote his life to healing.

"But you have never wanted to marry?" Charles asked.

"Well, somehow or other I've always been busy and haven't met anyone with whom I would wish to share my life." Matthew gave a rueful smile.

Early in 1946, Charles was sitting at home one Sunday morning reading that day's copy of The Times. Maria had gone to Mass and Gregory was on the floor playing with the railway set he had been given for Christmas.

On one of the inside pages, Charles read about The Nuremberg Trials then taking place. He was immediately taken back to that day late in 1941 when Himmler had visited Warsaw and discussed with Hans Frank the plans for the eventual extermination of the Jews and unwanted Poles in that area of the General Government. He remembered too, the visit of Himmler intended to expedite these measures in 1943, just before he and Maria had escaped. Immediately, he felt on edge. He saw again the starving people of the ghetto, for whom he had really had the responsibility. The dying child he had passed by one day came again into his memory. For Charles, at this moment, reading the report of the trial, it was as though the boy was still lying there, waiting for him, Charles, to help him. But Charles had walked on. Charles began to feel confused, unclear of the sequence of things. Although sitting at home with his own little boy at his feet, he felt as though he was actually in the Warsaw Ghetto, a little Jewish child dying in front of him.

Charles looked at the picture in The Times, which showed the major figures in the Nazi hierarchy at the trial. Goering was there in the front row, and the article in the paper described the legal figures hearing the evidence of the accused. The latter's actions were being considered as crimes against humanity and war crimes. It seemed that the sentences of those found guilty would be imposed not by a single judge and jury but by a tribunal. Absolute fairness! Actions being measured! Punishment meted out!

Charles became aware that he was finding it difficult to breathe.

Yet he was drawn to the pictures in the paper. What ordinary-looking men were there, sitting in that front row ready to defend themselves. One or two looked defiant and angry, as though it was an affront that they should even be questioned; others just sat, only Goering was seen, in one picture, to be smiling. For those found guilty of crimes against humanity, because of their participation in the deliberate and systematic murder of Jews and others, the article suggested that the death penalty was inevitable. Justice demanded it.

Charles felt all his peaceful and happy life slither away from him. He suddenly felt cold and desperately alone. How was it, he thought, that he had been able to put all these terrible things so completely out of mind? He could be one of those men sitting in that front row accused of murder. No, he thought, not could but should. Was Hans Frank there in that courtroom?

Charles was unable to differentiate between the genocide in which these men had been involved and his own involvement in maintaining the ghetto. Deep in his mind, he was convinced that he was as guilty as these men facing the judges.

The paper slid from his grasp and lay on the floor. Charles felt nauseous and he was aware of that old knot in his stomach that he had not experienced for a long time. He was confronting once again the central problem of his life, which he did not know how to handle.

Then two small hands were placed on his knees.

"Papa, are you sad?"

Charles pulled Gregory up onto his lap and kissed his cheek.

"Not when you give me such a lovely cuddle," he said.

And that was how Maria found the two of them when she returned. She took off her coat and went to the larder to get out what she needed to prepare lunch. She knocked over a bottle of milk, which spilled onto the floor.

"Oh Chwist," exclaimed Gregory, as he jumped down from his father's lap and stood looking at the puddle of milk.

"Gregory," said Maria quite sternly, "I don't know where you heard that language, but it is not nice, and I do not want ever to hear it again."

But at least the tension and sadness that she had felt present in the room when she returned was dissipated. Later, both Charles and Maria laughed about it and came to the conclusion that Gregory must have heard one of the boys on the farm use the expression.

Later that year, Charles read that Hans Frank had been hanged for crimes against humanity. He did not discuss it with Maria, although he knew that she must also have read the item. But he went on turning over in his mind all that had happened in Warsaw and the Nuremberg trials. Maria saw the subtle change in him and guessed it was connected with the news of the trials in The Times. As always, she left it to him to talk about it. But he never did.

Chapter Six
Changes and a Happy Reunion

During 1946, many of the long-planned changes that the people of Britain had waited for began to take shape. There was to be the establishment of a Welfare State where the life, particularly of the poor, would be changed for the better. A National Health Service Act was passed, which planned health care for all citizens, to be paid for by taxes to which all the employers and employed would contribute. However, the citizens of Great Britain still had to endure many years of shortages, including unemployment, as men returned from the war and found in many cases their jobs taken by women who had no desire to give them up.

It was about this time too that Maria brought up with Charles the possibility of trying to make contact with her parents. "We don't know for sure what happened to them" she said to him, "couldn't I just write to their old address and see what happens?"

"I am a little concerned about the danger of doing it," said Charles, "but of course, you want to know what has happened to them. I understand that."

"I want to tell them about Gregory; he is their only grandchild and I know they would be delighted. Perhaps we could get a photograph done and send it."

"Well, let's do it. The political situation in Poland is not good, with the Soviet takeover. You'll have to write to the only address you have and hope it will reach them. Be careful about what you write, Maria. I shouldn't say anything about politics and perhaps it would be better not to say too much about our situation here. You mustn't be disappointed if you don't get a reply." In his heart, having seen the pictures of the utter destruction of Warsaw, Charles thought it highly unlikely that any good could come of it.

And so a few days later, Maria went to the post office in Diss and mailed her letter, together with a picture of Gregory, now a small boy with a head of very blonde hair, almost three years old. She felt very strange as she handed over the envelope; it was a feeling of real contact with her parents, their names printed boldly and clearly, and she was parting with it. Jan and Irina Swoboda. How stupid, she told herself. If you don't send it, there is no possibility of their getting it. She said a little prayer as she left the post office, that they would receive it and that she would soon hear from them and know that they were alive and well.

As the weather began to warm up in May 1947, so welcome after a winter of heavy snow and bitter cold, Charles suggested to Maria that they have a day out.

"You've got something in mind, haven't you?" she said.

"Well, yes. I'd love to go to London Zoo, and I think Gregory would like to see the animals. What do you think, Maria?"

"I think it would be a lovely day out. How would we get there?"

"I think we can get a train from Diss to London without having to change. The zoo is in Regent's Park, so I imagine we would be able to go by underground from the main station to the park. I'd have to check that that is correct. Do you know, Maria, I have never been to a proper zoo. I used to go, as a small boy, to a restaurant where the owner kept a few wild animals, and I loved it. I must say, though, that I'm not sure whether keeping these creatures in cages is right."

Well, all misgivings put aside, Charles, Maria and little Gregory set out one Tuesday morning for a day at London Zoo. Gregory, getting on for four now, was very excited. Maria had bought him a picture book of wild animals and had tried to explain to him the fact that he would have to travel to different countries if he wanted to see them roaming around freely. She had made a mental note that maybe an atlas would be a good thing to get him soon.

Gregory loved the train. His nose glued to the window; he watched the countryside flashing past. As they got out at Liverpool Street, Charles explained to him that they would now be travelling on a train that was under their feet.

"But how will we get on it?" he wanted to know. "The mole in our field, he lives underground, doesn't he?"

"Yes, he does. Look, here is a map. You see all these coloured lines? They are the different trains that all travel underground. We will get on here" – Charles pointed to the Liverpool Street stop – "and we go to Baker Street on this yellow line, and there we change onto a red line, which takes us to Regent's Park. That's the stop for the zoo."

Maria, who had never done this before either, was glad of the simple explanation. They went down to the platform, and Gregory was first to jump on the train when it came in.

"But I can't see anything," he exclaimed as he peered through the window.

"Well, Gregory, if you think about it, you know why that is." Charles looked at his son.

"Because we're underground, Papa."

The day was a great success. Gregory hardly stopped talking, so full of questions was he. When Charles asked him which was his favourite animal, he thought for quite a few moments before shouting triumphantly, "The monkeys!" Maria thought that Charles had enjoyed it just as much as Gregory.

For Cox's Farm, the death of Jimmie Cox in 1948 was an almost unbearable event amidst what seemed to be a turmoil of change going on in the country in these early years after the war.

They had had no real warning that Jimmie was at all unwell. Until the evening of his death, he had done most of his usual jobs around the farm, although slowly. It was March, and everyone was beginning to look for the coming of spring. Ethel and Jimmie decided to retire about ten o'clock on that Saturday evening. Jimmie had some difficulty getting upstairs. He seemed unusually short of breath and kept having to take little pauses. He was sitting on the chair on the landing when Ethel, having put out the lights downstairs, came up. Jimmie smiled at her ruefully but did not speak.

"Come on, luv, take my arm," said Ethel and helped Jimmie into the bathroom and then into the bedroom. "Let me hang up your clothes for you. You just get yourself into bed."

By the time Ethel had done this and prepared herself for bed, Jimmie was snuggled under the feather quilt. Ethel joined him and picked up the book she was reading.

"Do you mind if I read for a little while?" she asked him. Jimmie gave a little shake of his head, smiled and closed his eyes. Ethel picked up her book and began to read. Only a few minutes had passed when she heard Jimmie give a strange little cough. She knew at once, although it had not been even remotely in her mind that Jimmie had died.

She touched his face. "Oh, my darling, oh, Jimmie."

She knew it; she knew that he was now beyond her reach but could not believe it, and afterwards, she was sure that her words and actions were done in the hope that he could still hear her. She once more touched his face. "Jimmie, darling, Jimmie."

Then she got quickly out of bed, threw on a dressing gown, unlocked the front door and seeing the downstairs lights still on in the cottage, ran quickly down the path and knocked.

Charles opened the door. It was about 10:15, and of course, he knew that it must be an emergency of some kind. He called out to Maria that he was going down to the farmhouse, took Ethel's arm and went with her. He thought maybe Ethel had made a mistake in her anxiety for Jimmie, but when he went to the bed and felt Jimmie's pulse, he was sure that he had died.

"I am sorry, Ethel. He has died. It must have been very peaceful. If I may, I will use your telephone and ring Matthew. Come downstairs with me, and perhaps whilst I use the phone you will put the kettle on."

Within twenty minutes, Matthew was there, and he confirmed Jimmie's death. He was almost certain, he told Ethel, that his heart had failed and that he had known nothing about it. He just, as it were, stopped going and fell into a sleep. Matthew was very gentle in the way he spoke to Ethel and did his best to comfort her, realising that she was in a state of shock.

Ethel did not weep but sat shivering in the chair. In later days, when she went over these events in her mind, she couldn't remember any other details of that night. She did remember, always, that Maria came to the farmhouse and that they both slept in the guestroom because Maria insisted that she was not to be there alone. There was a vague memory of someone coming and carrying Jimmie's body away, and gradually these vague memories were overtaken by the deep feeling of gratitude that he had not suffered. What better way to die, she thought. In his own bed, with me beside him, warm and comfortable, no fear. Death had come silently like a little cloud passing over the sun.

Just over a week later, Jimmie's funeral took place at St Andrew's Church in Scole. The church was crowded, witnessing to the fact that Jimmie Cox was a well-known figure in that part of Norfolk. Flowers were those of springtime and Jimmie's farmhands, at their request, carried the coffin into the church. Charles and Matthew did a reading, and Ethel very beautifully and calmly talked about her husband. Although he was only four years old, both Charles and Maria thought it right to take Gregory to the funeral. They had carefully explained to him in simple terms what it was all about, and he knew that Auntie Ethel was very sad and that he must be very good in the church. When Ethel returned to her place in the front pew, having spoken about her life with Jimmie, young Gregory wriggled out of his seat between his parents and went straight to Ethel.

He tried to hug her as he squeezed into a space beside her. It was only then that Ethel began to weep.

Over the next few weeks, slowly things began to change at Cox's Farm. Effectively, Charles was in charge of the business, but he always deferred to Ethel. About a week after Jimmie's funeral, Ethel and Charles sat down together in the farmhouse to discuss the way forward. Ethel told Charles that she and Jimmie had talked about what should happen when Jimmie died, not thinking at the time that it would be so soon. Jimmie had wanted the farm to pass to Charles. After the loss of Bob, both Ethel and Jimmie thought that that was what they wanted. Ethel said it should be done properly, with a lawyer drawing up the documents required to make Charles the legal owner. She wanted only the right to remain in residence. Then came another big surprise.

"Charles, I would like to suggest also that we swap homes. This farmhouse is too big for one, especially when next door you three are squeezed into a dwelling, which was only intended for one. Gregory is growing up, and you badly need another bedroom and more space generally. I would be very comfortable and happy in the cottage. In fact, I don't like being in this house without Jimmie. What do you think?"

Charles did not know what to say.

"Ethel, you and Jimmie are very dear to us, like our family really. And you will always have a special place in our lives. Jimmie put his trust in me by taking me on when I knew nothing about farming. And now, you tell me that you want the farm to be mine." Charles paused, trying to read in her eyes Ethel's true feelings.

"I can't find the words properly to say thank you, which in any case is utterly inadequate. I would love to continue with the farm but on condition that you would always remain a part of the planning and decision-making. I think big changes are coming as we begin to re-shape the country, and the farm must change too."

Charles hesitated. He didn't want to offend Ethel, but he wanted to protect her from too hasty a decision.

"However, Ethel, I think it is too soon for you to take such a major decision about the farm. It is a very big step, and I should hate to think that you would come to regret it. Let's wait a little while and make sure that you are comfortable with what you are proposing." Charles deliberately turned to more practical matters.

"I do think, though, that we should now promote young Michael Collins. We are a man short, and I think Michael shows a lot of ability and interest. If we promote him, gradually to learn the job I originally had assisting Jimmie, we could employ another young man to help with the manual work."

"Well, Charles, that sounds very sensible, but these are now your decisions. You must be free to do whatever you think is good for the business. Naturally, I will always be interested to hear about your plans. And if it makes you more comfortable, Charles, we will wait a week or two before I sign over the farm to you."

Ethel placed her hand on Charles's. "But there is no reason why we cannot change houses. It makes perfect sense, and we should get on and do it. Now go and tell Maria about it. If she is happy with a change of dwelling, we could start to move as soon as you feel ready."

"Well, Ethel, if you are to live in the cottage, there are things I would want to do to it. For one thing, I must put in a telephone for you. Then the bathroom needs some attention. Generally, it would be good to decorate, so that it is nice and fresh for you. I should like to be sure you would be comfortable there."

"All in good time, Charles, now do go and tell Maria all that we have talked about."

And so, over the next month or two, everything was done as Ethel had suggested. Charles decided, without a second thought, that the business should continue to operate as Cox's Farm; Michael Collins was promoted; a new hand was taken on, and Ethel and Maria exchanged homes. A firm from Norwich was engaged to update the bathroom in the cottage, and a telephone was installed for Ethel. Another local firm came in and decorated throughout. Perhaps most importantly, in the next month or so Charles Hartman became the owner of Cox's Farm, Scole and its associated shop in Diss.

When the family first moved into the farmhouse, Gregory did not like the idea of having his own bedroom. Charles had to persuade him that big boys, especially those who would soon be going to school, always had their own room because they often had a lot of things to do for school and needed a desk to work at. The thought of having a desk seemed to catch Gregory's attention, and he warmed to the idea. "Will I be able to do whatever I like in my room?" he asked.

Charles must have given some acceptable reply for Gregory soon occupied the second bedroom quite happily and gave his father no peace until a small desk had been installed there for him. Gregory himself chose a few of his favourite storybooks to begin to fill the shelves above the desk.

Charles and Maria had decided on the new primary department at the Church of England School in Scole for their son. They had told the head teacher that they were happy for Gregory to take part in all religious teaching and events, explaining that he would receive particular Roman Catholic doctrine from the church they attended.

For some time, Gregory had been 'helping' on the farm and having a lot of fun with the boys, probably more of the latter than the former. He liked looking after Bob's garden and would sometimes sit on the bench there with Ethel, looking at the flowers and reading to her the latest book he had borrowed from the library. Ethel helped him, from time to time, with words he didn't know. He liked learning, whether it was writing his name or writing his numbers.

But as the summer advanced, Gregory wanted also to sit with his father and ask him all sorts of questions about what he did when he was at school. He also wanted to know about the other children that would be there. He did not seem to be at all nervous about this new experience.

"Papa went to school when he was a little boy, and I have to go too," he told his mother quite seriously. "I'm a big boy now, and I'll be in Miss Milner's class."

Just a week or so before Gregory was due to start school, Charles surprised Maria by suggesting that they took a couple of days to go to Dieppe. Maria felt that he had been thinking about this for some time. It was not a sudden idea, she thought.

"We have never properly thanked Pierre and his wife for the help they gave us. It would be good to be able to do that, don't you think?"

Maria agreed, and they made their plans for two nights in Dieppe, travelling by ferry from Newhaven. Of course, neither of them knew if Pierre would still be able to be found at the little cottage where they had stayed with him, but they agreed that even if they couldn't find him, a day in Dieppe would not be a waste of time, and Gregory would surely enjoy the ferry and the beach at Dieppe. It would be their last day out before Gregory started school.

The journey took most of the first day, and when they got to Dieppe, they went straight to their hotel. The next morning, they set out for the harbour, retracing the steps they remembered having taken in 1943 and found the little cottage they thought was Pierre's.

Sure enough, and remarkably, it was Pierre who opened the door. For a moment, he did not recognise Charles and Maria, perhaps confused by the little boy with them. But as soon as Charles mentioned the escape with the Polish Prime Minister, he remembered.

"Come in, come in," he said. Just as they had done before, they sat in the little front room, now bright with the sunshine streaming in through the small window.

"Excuse me, will you have coffee? And you, young man, what would you like to drink?"

"Pierre, my name is Charles, my wife is Maria and my little boy is Gregory. When we were here last, I didn't tell you my name. We wanted to come back and say thank you for all that you did to help us. Without you, I don't think we could have made it to England. Our lives there have worked out well, and we are very happy."

"I'm so pleased to hear that. But let me go and make some coffee. I won't be long."

"I will help you," said Gregory, following Pierre. As he marched out behind Pierre, Maria and Charles heard him saying to himself, "I'm in France now."

In a few minutes, Pierre came back carrying a tray, Gregory following with a plate of biscuits.

"We would like to invite you and your wife to have a meal with us. We are only here today. Would you be free to do that, or perhaps I should say would you like to do that?" said Charles.

"Thank you. My wife died during the Normandy invasion, so I am alone here now. It would be very nice to have a small meal with you, but nothing grand, I am a simple man." Pierre suggested a little place he knew. "I need to change, so why don't you take your son down to the beach for a little while, and if you come back in about an hour, we could walk around the harbour to the little café."

And so it was that Charles, Maria and Gregory spent the day with the man who had played such an important part in getting them safely to England.

When they got back home, Charles and Maria felt that it had been a very worthwhile trip, although they felt sad that Pierre was now alone in his little cottage. Gregory was very proud that he had learned to say 'Bonjour'.

As September came around, Maria was occupied with getting Gregory's school uniform together, buying him a little satchel and generally preparing everything for him. Gregory was getting very excited.

When the day arrived, Maria and Gregory set out together for school.

"I want Papa to take me," Gregory protested, as Maria put her coat on. "I'm sorry, Gregory, your father is busy at work; you'll have to put up with me," was Maria's reply. She left him at the school entrance amongst a small group of other four and five-year-olds shepherded by Miss Milner.

"Either I, or Auntie Ethel, will be here to bring you home at lunchtime. Be a good boy and have a lovely time." Maria kissed her young son and left him. She felt upset as she walked home. It was quite a milestone. Gregory was no longer a baby. He was beginning his education. She wondered about his development, what he would be interested in, if he would make friends.

When Gregory got home at lunchtime, he was full of information about what he had done and all the new things he had been told. "Do you know, Mama, there are girls there? And I don't have my own desk like at home. I have to share with three others. There are two girls and another boy. That makes four," said Gregory, checking it off on his fingers.

As the beginning of November loomed on the calendar in the kitchen, Maria wondered about having a small fifth birthday party for Gregory. The first of November was a Monday, not a very good day for a party, she thought. She decided that the previous Friday would be better. Yes, Maria thought, that will be best. Surely, Matthew would try to be free, and maybe one or two of the farmhands would be able to pop in too. She wondered if Gregory had been long enough at school to have made any friends yet. She asked him first if he would like to have a party and then if there was anyone he would like to invite. His reply surprised her.

"Oh, that's good. Raff will come. I want Raff to come. Can we have lemonade?"

This was a new name to Maria. "Who is Raff?" she asked.

"Oh, Mama, he's my best friend."

Maria duly bought some bright little invitation cards and gave them to Ethel, Matthew and the boys. The card for 'Raff' she gave to Gregory to give to him. In the evening, she received a telephone call from his mother. The two women had not met.

"Mrs Hartman, hello, I'm Sara Neuberger. I'm Raphael's mother. Thank you so much for the invitation to Gregory's party. Raphael is very keen to come. He tells me Gregory is his best friend. There is just a little problem about it being on Friday for us. You see, we are Jewish, and it is the beginning of our Sabbath."

Maria had not reckoned on this, but her suggestion that she changed it to Sunday afternoon in view of the fact that Raphael was actually the most important guest in Gregory's eyes was met with gratitude from Mrs Neuberger. So it was fixed. It would be on Sunday afternoon October 31. Maria thought about Gregory's friendship with a little Jewish boy and wondered how Charles would react to it. When she returned to the sitting room, she mentioned it to Charles.

"Charles, the little boy that Gregory calls Raff and says is his best friend, comes from a Jewish family. Their name is Neuberger. I've just spoken to Mrs Neuberger, and because Friday is the beginning of their Sabbath, I have agreed with her that we will have the party on Sunday afternoon instead. Is that all right with you?"

"Well, that's a surprise. Sunday is fine with me. I am glad Gregory has a little friend. I must say, though, that I feel a little uncomfortable about it being a Jewish family. If they knew my background, they wouldn't want to have any contact with us. I expect they are German too. I'm not sure I feel easy about it. I don't like the feeling of making a friendship with a family on the basis of having to hide my true identity."

"Well, darling, we have had to do that ever since we arrived in England. It hasn't worried you with Matthew or the Cox's."

"No, but they aren't Jewish, that makes all the difference."

Charles said no more, and Maria hoped that the friendship of the two little boys would be a bridge that would help Charles to feel comfortable at being friends with a Jewish family. She knew that Charles had nothing against the Jewish community; what she was not aware of was that his problem stemmed, once again, from Warsaw but particularly from the association there with another little Jewish boy.

Precisely at three o'clock on Sunday, a car drove up to the farmhouse and out jumped a small dark-headed boy. Mrs Neuberger followed close behind. Maria opened the door to them, and Gregory squeezed forward, excited to have his friend come to his house.

"Please come in," said Maria. Raphael had already disappeared with Gregory.

"If you don't mind, I won't on this occasion, Mrs Hartman, but I expect as our sons are best friends, there will be lots of other opportunities. I am just on my way to visit my mother who is poorly. Can I pick up Raphael on my way back? What time would be convenient? About 5:30?" And off Mrs Neuberger hurried, a small, plump, dark-headed lady, probably somewhat hyperactive Maria thought.

In the sitting room, the adults sat in quiet conversation.

"The two boys are upstairs," said Charles, "Gregory seemed keen to show Raphael his desk."

When the boys reappeared, they were laughing about some secret they seemed to have shared. Maria was struck by their little guest's beautiful smile. It illuminated the child's face and was the sort of smile that would melt a heart of stone. It rose up into his eyes and made it seem that they smiled too. The two boys were a contrast, Gregory blonde and slim, Raphael dark and a little round. The two were obviously conspirators. Charles spoke to Gregory. "Gregory, you haven't introduced your friend to us yet."

"Oh, everyone, this is Raff; we're both in Miss Milner's class."

Raphael, in quite a grown-up way, smiled and said, "Actually, I'm Raphael, but I'm usually called Raff and that's all right with me."

Matthew leaned forward and put his hand out to shake Raphael's. "Hello, Raphael. I know your parents, but I haven't met you before. I'm Dr Matthew."

"You know the Neubergers, Matthew?" asked Charles a little sharply.

"Yes," was all Matthew said, nodding his head.

A small pile of presents lay on the coffee table. Gregory seemed keen only to escape with Raphael.

"Papa, can I take Raff out and show him the chickens?"

"Yes, but you must both put your coats on. It's chilly."

The two boys quickly disappeared. Quite some time passed, and Ethel wasn't the only one beginning to wonder what the boys were up to. Maria was about to go out when Michael and Ernie knocked and entered the kitchen with the two little ones in tow.

"Look what we found," called out Michael.

"Come in, we are in the sitting room." Maria introduced the young men. Then she looked at Gregory and Raphael, "You two, muddy shoes off and then, Gregory, I'd like you to pay attention to all these parcels here."

Matthew noticed not only the muddy shoes but dirty marks on the seats of their trousers and concluded that it was not only the chickens they had visited.

The boys sat on the floor, and Gregory began to open the parcels that had been brought for him. He couldn't read the writing, so Ethel took over, passing each parcel to Gregory and declaring whom it was from. She quietly reminded him to say thank you. A new locomotive for his trainset, a book which pleased Gregory because he noted that it had more writing than pictures, a warm navy jumper, which probably pleased Maria more than Gregory and a whole set of beautiful coloured pencils. Then last of all came the present which seemed to please him more than any other, a recorder.

"What's this?" queried Gregory, handling it with curiosity. Matthew explained.

"It's a musical instrument, Gregory. You put this part to your mouth and you blow gently. You make different notes by covering these holes. You'll have to learn how to make music."

Gregory put it to his lips, blew, and a loud shrill note echoed across the room. Everyone laughed, and Raphael covered his ears.

The last little package on the table was for Raphael. He was obviously not very impressed when he was told it was some fresh hens' eggs to take home.

"Come on, it's time we had some tea. It's ready in the kitchen." Maria led the exodus from the sitting room.

Gregory's joy was complete when he saw that in the very centre of the table stood a beautifully iced and decorated birthday cake with five candles on it. He was even more pleased when everyone sang Happy Birthday as he blew out the candles.

That night, as his parents tucked him up in bed, he hugged them and said, "This has been my best day ever."

The next day, Maria as usual picked up the post from the doormat. There were one or two business leaflets and a letter from Warsaw. As soon as she picked it up, she felt a surge of despair and disappointment flood through her. She saw that the letter was in fact the one she had sent to her parents, now re-directed back to her. It had been opened and resealed. She realised that it had never reached her parents. The photograph of Gregory was still in it.

Maria sat at the kitchen table for some minutes, the letter in her hand. It seemed to her almost a confirmation that her parents were dead. She was too stunned to cry. She thought that Charles had been right. Then she began to find reasons why this might not be so. The returned letter told her only that it was probably true that their home was no longer there. But they themselves might have escaped and be living somewhere else in Poland. Without having received this letter from her they would have no way of knowing where Maria and Charles were. For Maria, this thought was a small ray of hope. She heard the clock chime twelve, and putting the letter in her apron pocket, she got up to prepare something for them both to eat when Charles came in.

Charles arrived at about 12:30 for lunch. Gregory was now at school until 3:30, so Charles and Maria had a quiet, undisturbed meal together. Maria took her parents' letter from her pocket and passed it to Charles. She said nothing.

"Ah, at last, a reply! Oh, I am sorry, Maria, it is as I thought." Charles realised it was his wife's letter, returned to her. He looked at the envelope again, and gave it back to his wife. "This has been re-directed by the Soviets, and it took them almost two years to deal with it. I don't know what else we can do."

A heavy silence descended between them. They ate without speaking. Charles returned to his work on the farm. Maria noticed that Charles had sounded like the old 'Warsaw Karl' as he commented on the letter. It seemed as though any mention of or contact with Warsaw transported him back immediately to those terrible days from which they had fled. At such times, Charles seemed to be tense and uncomfortable and his manner with her often became sharp and abrupt. She tried hard to understand. She wondered if he would ever be able to free himself from these terrible associations. As she started to clear up, she told herself there was nothing more she could do. She knew how very dear to her was the memory of her parents' love for her. The knowledge of it helped her to bear what she thought she now had to face, the fact that they were beyond her reach, dead or alive.

Gregory had his tea when he got in. It was the day after his party and so actually his birthday. His father stopped work at about five, it being already dark by then. He came in and sat in the kitchen whilst Maria made some tea.

"Now, young man, come here," said Charles to his son. Maria looked over at him, recognising a somewhat stern tone in his voice. "I would like to know what you did on the farm when you and Raphael went out yesterday."

"Well, we looked at the chickens and..." Gregory's face took on a pout, which was rather disagreeable.

"Yes, and what?"

"I showed Raff the storehouse. We had a game of slides." Gregory shifted his feet, clearly uncomfortable about having to reveal this.

"Yes, I have seen the evidence. Those sacks are full of stored food, which I have to sell to people to eat. You made a slide out of them and the pair of you slid down them as though you were on the slide at the park. Much of the food in the sacks is spoiled. You are a very naughty boy, very naughty indeed. Go up to your room and get ready for bed. I don't want to see you again today."

Gregory immediately did as he was told. His face crumpled, and with tears welling in his eyes, he left the kitchen.

"I like you saying I love you best," was all he could manage between his tears as he mounted the stairs to his room.

"Don't you think you were a bit harsh with him?" said Maria. "After all, it is his birthday." Maria's heart was already heavy enough without having this upset to bear.

"No. He has to learn to be responsible about the farm."

"Of course. But he's only five. I expect he was showing off."

After he had finished his tea, Charles went upstairs, ready to put things right with his young son. Maria, downstairs, heard what ensued.

Charles opened the door to Gregory's room and was saying, "Are you sorry…" She heard a loud 'No', young feet running across the floor and the door slam shut.

Charles reappeared in the kitchen, picked up his newspaper and went into the sitting room. Maria joined him; she could see he was upset, so turned the radio on for the early evening news and said nothing about what had happened upstairs.

When the news was over, she went up to Gregory's room. She tapped on the door. "It's Mama, Gregory. May I come in?"

No reply was given, so Maria gently pushed the door open a little wider. Gregory was stretched out on his bed, still in his school clothes, eyes red from crying. Maria sat herself on the bed beside him and gathered him into her arms.

"Papa doesn't love me anymore," he whimpered.

"That is not true, Gregory. Papa and Mama will always love you. Papa had to make you understand that playing with things on the farm is not a good idea. I know you won't do it again."

Maria kissed her small son's damp cheek feeling that she wanted to cry too. How precious, she was thinking, is the time we have with our children.

"Now, I want you to come down with me and say sorry to Papa. There is still some lemonade left and some birthday cake, so we can have another little birthday party together. Will you do that? You know, Papa is very sad too. He doesn't like being angry with you. Will you come down with me and say sorry?"

"Yes, Mama."

So, the two of them went downstairs together. Gregory went straight to his father, stood in front of him, looking at his father anxiously. "I'm sorry, Papa."

Charles pulled him up to sit beside him. "We'll say no more about it, Gregory. You have said sorry, and you are forgiven. Now, Papa wants to give you a very special hug."

The three of them sat on the settee; Gregory had a small glass of lemonade, his parents a glass of wine each, and they shared the rest of the birthday cake.

"Can I stay up a little longer today?" Gregory asked.

"Yes," said Charles, his eyes meeting Maria's, "you can have an extra half-hour, but no longer, because it's a school day tomorrow."

"For how long will it be my birthday?" asked Gregory.

"Each day lasts until midnight, that is twelve o'clock at night," explained Charles.

"So every day we have twelve hours?"

"Well, in a way, yes; there are twelve hours of the day and twelve hours of the night. Do you know what that makes altogether?" Charles paused, but it was a little beyond his son. "It means that every day has twenty-four hours."

"That's a lot of hours," mused Gregory. "Do you love me twenty-four, Papa?" The big brown eyes looked questioningly at his father.

"I love you twenty-four and twenty-four more times twenty-four, and Mama does too. So that makes far too many times to be able to count."

Gregory snuggled down contentedly between his parents. That's all he wanted to know.

The next morning, rather to her surprise, Maria saw Charles come back into the house, as she was getting ready to walk Gregory to school.

Charles took his son's hand. "I'll go with him this morning," he said to Maria. "Is that all right, Gregory?" The child almost visibly swelled with pride. The realisation, that for the first time his father and he would go to school together sent a huge smile over Gregory's face. Father and son walked down the path, Gregory waving goodbye to his mother. And so the little boy, just five years old now, went to school that day, happily secure in the warmth of his father's love.

It was early spring. Maria was still busy in the bakery, but Charles was in the sitting room reading his paper. The doorbell rang. When Charles opened the door, a tall slim man, dark hair with flecks of grey at the temples, stood before him. For a moment, the two men just stood and stared at one another. There was a kind of long-since-forgotten recognition between them.

"Karl?"

"Klaus?"

Charles recovered his senses, although amazement and incredulity washed over him. "Come in, come in. However did you manage to find me? Klaus, it's wonderful to see you after all this time."

The men shook hands. They stood back and looked at one another again, and then Charles embraced his brother, holding him tightly in his arms.

"Come into the sitting room. I'll put some coffee on. Let me hang up your coat."

Over coffee, Klaus told Charles that he was in London for a few days in connection with a property deal. He had had a great deal of difficulty tracking him down, and even as he took the train to Diss, he had not been entirely sure that he was on the right track. The conversation between the two men flowed back and forth, as they caught up with one another's movements over what now seemed a lifetime of separation. Indeed, they had not met since Charles had gone to university. Klaus had not married and had inherited their father's estate when he died last Christmas. He lived now in Frankfurt and was a banker.

"Klaus, how long can you stay? My wife will be down soon, for lunch, you will of course eat with us? By the way, Klaus, I should tell you that I am Charles now. I took the English version of my name when we came here in 1943. Everyone knows me as Charles."

Soon Maria came in. Charles introduced her. Maria was a little hesitant, an inner anxiety for Charles's well-being made itself felt. She had never met Klaus and knew very little about him. Was he a threat, is what she was wondering. She was impressed by how alike the brothers were physically.

"I'll get us some lunch," she said, with a smile. "You're very welcome."

After they had eaten, whilst Maria cleared away the dishes Charles took Klaus out to show him around the farm. The two men felt quite easy with one another; in fact, Charles certainly could not help thinking how sad it was really that all those years had passed with no contact.

"I'd like you to meet our son, Gregory. How long can you stay, Klaus?"

"Well, the day is mine, so long as I am back in London tonight."

"I shall have to walk down to Diss to pick up Gregory from school, very soon. Would you like to come with me?"

The children all came tumbling out into the playground just a minute or two after Klaus and Charles got there. Gregory ran up to Charles and looking at Klaus asked, "Who are you?" It sounded a little rude, although the big, soft, brown eyes looking up at Klaus were merely curious.

"Gregory, this is your Uncle Klaus."

"But Uncle Matt is my uncle." Gregory stared at Klaus, with a frown on his face.

Klaus spoke up. "Well, Gregory, you can have more than one uncle, you know. So, I am Uncle Klaus, and I am very pleased to meet you, Gregory."

By the time they got back to the farm, Gregory was holding Klaus's hand and asking him all about Germany. He also wanted to know if Uncle Klaus had been to the London Zoo. Maria found it very interesting, over the course of the day, to observe the two brothers together. Physically, they were quite alike, but she thought that Klaus was a far more outwardly confident and dominant kind of person than Charles. She thought that Charles was probably much kinder.

After Gregory had gone to bed, the adults sat together in the sitting room, the two brothers still trying to catch up with one another's lives. Charles said very little about his work for Hans Frank in Warsaw but described their escape across Europe to England in compensatory detail.

It seemed that Klaus, too, was not entirely eager to say what he had done during those years, and Charles was very happy not to pursue the topic.

"I envy you your life here, Karl, sorry, Charles. You chose a very beautiful wife" – he smiled at Maria – "and you have a delightful little boy. If I wondered at all what you were doing, over these years, and I often did, I would never have imagined you a farmer. This life seems to suit you. Would you ever come to Germany, to visit me in Frankfurt?"

"But of course if it can be arranged."

"Well, let's try to keep in touch by post until then," said Klaus. "I don't want to lose you again. And now that I know I have a nephew, it's even more important."

Charles walked down to the station with Klaus and waved him goodbye as the train departed. Perhaps, what had always seemed to Charles a tragedy of a childhood for the two brothers, could be mended, thought Charles as he walked back home. Nevertheless, he felt sad as he returned to the farmhouse. It seemed to Charles that Klaus was very alone.

Chapter Seven
Visitors, Visits and Surprising Revelations

As the 1940s passed amidst quite profound social changes and difficulties, Charles became aware that he needed to think about how he ran the farm and consider some modernisations.

He sat one morning with Ethel and Maria, around the farmhouse kitchen table, to discuss his ideas and hear about what they thought might be done.

First of all, he told them, he had read about a new way of selling food that involved one large store from which a housewife could buy everything she needed. Individual outlets would no longer be required if this new method caught on. It might mean that their shop in Diss would be competing with a much larger store. And since it could be more convenient for the shoppers to buy everything in one place, the Diss shop could lose a lot of trade.

Then Maria brought to the discussion an idea which she had had a long time ago.

"You know, I have always wanted to set up a small business, perhaps a little teashop, where we could sell my bread and cakes. Could we do that with the shop in Diss?"

This suggestion met with immediate approval from Ethel. "That sounds good to me. A little teashop in the town could be very popular, especially with fresh homemade bread and cake."

To Maria's surprise, Charles also responded positively. "Yes, that sounds a very possible way forward, although we could also do that here on the farm, especially if we have less call for fruit and vegetables. The possibility is in my mind that we could develop the farm in a slightly different direction, and a teashop on the premises could be a part of that. It would certainly make it easier for you, Maria, to be here at home running a teashop, rather than having to do it in Diss. We have also to consider Gregory's care. He's still very young."

"So, are you suggesting, Charles," asked Ethel, "that we wouldn't need the shop in Diss? If we sold it, we'd have to think about Pauline; she's been with the farm a long time, and I wouldn't like to make her unemployed." Ethel looked at Charles, concerned for the girl they had employed since she had left school.

"Well, we would certainly need more help on the farm, so we could probably offer Pauline work here. Maybe we should concentrate on thinking about what the possibilities could be of developing the site here. Any ideas?" Charles looked at the two women. He had been jotting down notes as they talked and now looked at Maria and Ethel, waiting to hear if they had any other suggestions.

"Well, Charles, it sounds as though the likelihood could be that in the near future we may need to grow less produce. That would give us more space to utilise. But what would attract customers? We would have to find a way of selling that would be more than just going to buy vegetables."

Both Charles and Maria looked at Ethel with respect.

"I think you've hit on the right approach, Ethel. You agree too, don't you, Maria?"

"Yes, I think we should consider this as an option. We could give up our outlet in Diss, expand the farm in a way we're not too sure about yet but perhaps incorporating a teashop. Maybe homemade bread and cakes could be an attraction to customers, apart from a teashop."

"That sounds like a good summary of where we have got to so far," said Charles.

"This is a very big decision we're trying to make." Maria moved from the table to the kitchen. "Coffee, everyone?"

Charles excused himself from the coffee break and returned to the farm. Maria and Ethel sat and chatted about a possible small café on the farm and enjoyed a cup of coffee together.

It was a few days before the beginning of Holy Week 1950, when Klaus rang. He spoke to Maria and asked if they were open to having a visitor for Easter. Maria knew that they had nothing particular planned and told him that he would be very welcome.

"Will you be all right if I put you in Gregory's room?" she asked. "It would be much nicer if you were able to stay with us at the farmhouse."

"Yes, I would like that, so long as Gregory doesn't mind."

"When would you like to come, Klaus?"

"Would Monday be all right? I know you are usually busy over the weekend. I could get an early flight into London and make my way to Norwich, or Diss, by train. Could I stay with you over Easter?"

"Of course. So, we will expect you on Monday?"

It was arranged! Maria had first to find Charles and tell him about it, then her next concern was to speak to Gregory and ask him if he minded sleeping in the little box room whilst Uncle Klaus used his room. Gregory didn't mind at all, so long as his little desk was moved with him. Over that weekend, bit by bit, Maria and Charles prepared for Klaus's visit. By Monday morning, all was ready and young Gregory kept excitedly looking out of the front window to see if Uncle Klaus was coming. Gregory had made certain to consult his atlas to find out exactly where Frankfurt was in Germany. He also had a special surprise for his uncle. Soon after Klaus's first visit, Gregory had insisted that they buy him a model of a little monkey. He thought it was terrible that his uncle had never been to a zoo. And never to have seen a monkey, especially when you were so old, to Gregory was unthinkable. So not without considerable difficulty, they had found a little figure that satisfied Gregory, and now it was placed by him on the little bedside table in what would be Klaus's room during his stay.

Klaus arrived mid-afternoon on Monday. It was Gregory who took charge as soon as the front door was opened.

"Hello, Uncle Klaus. This is where your room is." Gregory took Klaus's hand and led him straight upstairs, giving Klaus no time at all to greet Maria. "And I got this for you." Gregory picked up the little monkey from the table in his room.

"For me, Gregory? Thank you. I bet this little chap comes from the London Zoo." When they came back down, Klaus was properly greeted by Maria, who had of course put the kettle on by now, and they settled down in the sitting room, Gregory occupying the seat next to Klaus on the settee. It seemed that this new uncle was the one to be favoured with the whole of Gregory's attention. Charles came in a little later. Gregory had been told that on this occasion, since it was holiday time, and Uncle Klaus was here, he could stay up to have dinner with them. Gregory had a great deal to ask Klaus, and sometimes it was hard for either Charles or Maria to get a chance at a conversation with him. Gregory was curious to know why it was that Klaus had no children. So the pair of them had a talk about family, and Gregory then wanted to know why he, Gregory, had no brother when his father did.

"Well, Gregory, I think you'll have to ask Mama and Papa about that," Klaus replied, with a quizzical glance at Charles and Maria.

"But not now," said Maria. "I'm going to get dinner ready. Charles, what about opening a bottle of wine?"

The next day, Charles having freed himself from most of his farm duties, the two men set out to wander around Diss. Gregory, at first disappointed at not being included on this outing, was consoled by the fact that he would spend most of the day with Auntie Ethel. As was so often the case, Charles found himself making for the lake. The brothers sat on one of the benches. Charles wanted to ask Klaus about their mother.

"Well, I was only about five when she died, so all my memories are childhood ones. She always smelled delicious. She was probably the opposite of our father. I remember lots of cuddles and treats. She always told me what a good boy I was, and she was patient. I don't remember her setting targets for me, like our father did. She loved me. And I loved her. When she died, I blamed you. I thought it was your fault." Klaus looked at Charles with an expression of regret. "It was Frau Schmidt, when she came to look after both of us, who one day tried to explain to me that in no way was it your fault." Klaus fell silent as he thought of those days of long ago. Then he continued.

"No, Charles, you were not the problem in my life. You may have thought that your life was blighted by being the second son, but being the firstborn was not much fun. Our father was a strict man, and he set almost impossible standards for me to attain. I used to think that I could never please him, whatever I did. But what about you, Charles, how did you find him?"

"The one word I would use would be unloving. I always felt that whatever I did, I had already been judged and found wanting, and however hard I tried, I would not measure up to the expectations he had of me. Not that he really seemed to have any regarding me. It was always very clear that you were the one that mattered. It is strange, Klaus, I don't think I ever bore a grudge against you because of it. You loved me, I think, and I loved you."

The two men sat in silence for a moment, each transported back to their childhood in Posen. Then Charles spoke again.

"I feel rather bad about having spoken so ill of our father. I wonder why he was such a harsh man. Do you ever remember any grandparents, Klaus?"

Klaus didn't. But he told Charles that he thought that going to Munich and escaping his father, as it were, was the best thing Charles could have done.

"I always felt as though I were in a straitjacket, Charles. My father wanted to make me in his own image. But of course, one must remember that the times he lived in were very different from what we enjoy now. History also has its influence on us. When you went away to Munich, I was envious but also glad for you. My father did not make it easy for me to keep in touch. In fact, Charles, I was never told even about your marriage." Klaus was obviously becoming depressed and a little angry. Charles acted quickly.

"But Klaus, we are here now. And you do have a family. We have years left to us in which we can see one another. You have in your life now, a brother who loves you, a sister-in-law and a little nephew who I believe has taken you under his wing." The two men laughed. "Tomorrow, Klaus, you will meet my best friend, Matthew, who will also be spending Easter Day with us. I expect Maria and Matthew will go to Mass on Easter Day with us. You're not Catholic, are you, Klaus?"

"No, I was brought up, like you, Lutheran. Probably like you, I expect, I have no faith now." Klaus paused.

"Charles, I want to talk with you about our father's will. Our father left everything to me, his property, land, cash. Nothing at all was left for any of his servants, no gift for Frau Schmidt and nothing for his second son." Klaus looked ruefully at Charles.

"Please, Klaus, don't be concerned about it. I never expected that I would be included in his beneficence." Charles sounded a little sarcastic.

"But I want to include you in it," said Klaus firmly. "It is a disgrace that you should be left out, and I want to put it right. I want to share the cash and the cash value of anything I manage to sell, fifty-fifty." Klaus swivelled around on the bench to face Charles.

Charles's feelings were very mixed as he met his brother's gaze.

"Klaus, I appreciate your kindness, but I do not need money. I would rather know that your future is secure, and after all, you may still decide to marry and have a family, and they would then be your first responsibility."

Klaus was quiet for a moment, then he said, very quietly, not looking at Charles, "I will never marry, Charles, I feel no sexual attraction to women."

Charles was horrified by what he thought his brother was saying but kept control of himself, although inwardly he felt deeply saddened by what seemed to him a bleak future facing Klaus. He felt compelled to clarify what he thought had been said. He spoke hesitantly.

"Are you telling me, Klaus, that you are homosexual?"

"Yes. But I do not have a partner, Charles. I have learned to live alone. In any case, the law requires it."

"Klaus, you are as you are, and you are my brother, and I love you and want you to be happy. We need say no more about it. To return to our father's will, why don't we just leave things as they are? If it enables you sometimes to treat Gregory, I'm sure he'd love a real live monkey, and if you can afford to come over to see us quite frequently, well, let us just enjoy that."

"All right, Charles. But please remember, that if ever you are in need, I am here. Any help would not be a gift, it would be your right. About the other matter, could we keep it just between ourselves?"

"Of course, Klaus. Now I think it is probably time that we made our way home."

Wednesday evening was a very cheerful event, with Ethel joining the family too. Matthew was impressed by how physically alike Klaus and Charles were. He said they could pass as twins. Whilst Maria prepared the evening meal, helped by Charles, Ethel Matthew and Klaus played 'Snap' with Gregory. It was a lively and somewhat noisy affair.

After dinner, with Gregory in bed, the four adults talked over what they might do with the rest of the holiday. Klaus said that he would like to invite them all out to lunch on Easter Day, and Matthew thought they could all squeeze into his car for a trip to the coast, provided the weather were kind to them.

All too soon, Easter was over, and once more, Charles walked down to Diss station to see Klaus off.

"It was wonderful, being with your family, Charles, thank you."

"Not my family, Klaus, but our family. Have a safe journey home. We'll see you again soon, and don't forget you are always welcome here."

Charles walked slowly home, once again feeling sad for his brother.

When he got indoors, Gregory, full of excitement, rushed to meet his father. "Papa, Papa, there are packages everywhere! Mama wouldn't let me open them until you got home!"

There, on each seat in the sitting room were little packages, with each of their names on them. Gregory tore the packaging away from his rather large parcel and found a beautiful globe of the world, with two tiny paper flags stuck on. One was on Frankfurt and said, 'here lives Uncle Klaus', the other was on Africa and said, 'you are all invited to come with me here'.

"What's yours, Papa, what's yours, Mama?"

"I have an air ticket to Johannesburg, another for somewhere else and a hotel booking voucher for one week on Safari in the Kruger National Park. I expect yours is the same, Maria?"

"Yes, except there are tickets for Gregory too."

"They are from Klaus, a thank you he says. I have to ring him in a day or two to confirm that we would like to go and when we think we could be available. It is very generous of him."

"Papa, what is Safari?"

"It is going to Africa and staying out in the countryside with all the wild animals wandering about. You stay in a little house, and it's like a hotel, because you get all your meals. But the main thing you do is to go out each day to watch the animals. If you look at your globe, you will see that Uncle Klaus has stuck a little flag on Africa so you can see where you will be going."

Charles and Maria looked at one another, both lost for words and deeply moved by Klaus's generosity and thoughtfulness.

"But how can I say thank you, Mama? Uncle Klaus has gone."

"After lunch, we'll help you write a little thank you letter. Then we must begin to think about getting your things ready for school tomorrow."

They decided that either the end of the summer school holiday or the autumn half term would be suitable times, and the next day, Charles spoke with Klaus who said he would see if either time could be organised.

They arranged to meet Klaus, at the end of August, at Heathrow Airport where they all boarded the flight to Johannesburg. Gregory had never flown before. Neither had Maria, except in that little transport aircraft that had brought her from Dieppe to Norfolk. Gregory was full of questions, and on the flight, he decided he would sit with Uncle Klaus, which gave some relief to his parents and enabled them to enjoy a reasonably peaceful flight. At Johannesburg, another short flight in a much smaller aircraft took them to a small airport where they were picked up by a car from the Safari Lodge. Gregory, having had a nap, was now full of questions again, and luckily for his family, the lady driving the Land Rover took on the responsibility for answering them. Their lodgings were tents but raised on a platform with surrounding balcony. They were spacious bedrooms, with showering facilities in the small outside area at the back. The ranger who had picked them up, Jenny, took them to their tents and told them a butler would be along with cold drinks, and she would see them at the main reception area at three o'clock in time for the afternoon safari. Maria decided to stay with Gregory, enabling him to sleep, and Charles and Klaus would do the safari.

Charles returned from the safari to find Maria sitting out on the balcony, and Gregory still fast asleep. "Maria, it is absolutely wonderful. Our rangers are Richard and Jenny, that's the girl who picked us up at the airport. Almost immediately, we saw a large herd of impala and zebra, but the highlight was that we drove very slowly behind three lions! Imagine it, Maria! They took no notice of us at all. Richard told us that these lions are brothers and that they live in the Kruger, but you can't be sure when you'll see them because of course the park is very large. You have to remain sitting in the jeep to be safe."

"Oh, Charles, you sound just as excited as Gregory was. For more practical matters, we meet everyone else at dinner, that's in precisely half-an-hour. I'll wake Gregory whilst you tidy yourself. I think it's all quite informal."

Safari left at six the next morning, but at 5:30, their butler brought them a tray of tea and some milk for Gregory. Maria had decided that showering at that time of the morning, when it was still quite cold was not an option. Klaus was already at the main reception when they arrived, and then they were away again in the jeep with Richard and Jenny. Gregory noticed that Richard carried a rifle. Gregory was sitting in a little raised chair in the centre of the jeep, directly between his parents, with Klaus and another couple called Doug and Hazel occupying the other seats. Klaus and Charles had met the couple the previous afternoon and introduced them to Maria and Gregory. Gregory was only interested in the animals he was hoping to see and at this precise moment in Richard's explanation as to why he had to have a rifle with him.

Just a few minutes after leaving the camp, they passed slowly through a large herd of gnus and zebra and then, driving through what seemed like scrub, a small group of giraffes were seen ahead. Soon after, they found themselves in the midst of a large herd of buffalo. Large, black beasts, their heads low, Klaus said later that he found them much more frightening than the lions they had seen the evening before. Gregory said they were all frowning at him.

They returned to the camp for breakfast at about nine o'clock and the family sat out in the open around a circular table. The restaurant area was on the banks of a riverbed where, Richard had told them, elephants would come sometimes to drink. The family were just beginning their breakfast when Gregory noticed his bread roll had disappeared from his plate. He had been to the buffet table with Maria, and when he got back, it had gone!

Charles, having earlier noticed the monkeys sitting in the trees above them, told Gregory to look up. There, indeed, was his roll being greatly enjoyed by a little monkey! Gregory roared with laughter. After breakfast, they went back to their tents, and Charles suggested Klaus come over to them about eleven o'clock. Charles had asked their butler to deliver some light white wine and sure enough, it was there in the little fridge. Maria explained to Gregory that because their camp was not fenced, he was not to go off their balcony on his own, and at all times, he was to stay with his family. She explained that the small animals wandering around the camp were not dangerous but that nevertheless he was not to wander off the balcony alone.

"Yes," he replied," it's very dangerous, and I haven't got a rifle."

The family slipped quickly into a kind of routine; the days centred around the two safari trips. Maria's favourite day was when they came across a large group of wild dogs with about a dozen young ones. The adults went off hunting and left the group of babies close to the jeep, so they were able to see them close-up and watch them playing with one another. Charles declared his favourite day was when they had seen a leopard strolling along a nearby path. Jenny had stopped the jeep and, keeping quiet, they had all watched it as it went to a nearby water source to drink. Klaus declared his favourite to have been the huge bull elephant they had accidentally cornered. They had had to reverse quite quickly. The adults all looked at Gregory, wondering which had been his favourite animal. "I loved the little monkey that stole my bread," he said.

All too soon, the last day arrived and the family had to return to the little airport to begin their return journey. They all agreed that it had been the most wonderful holiday they had ever had. They said goodbye to Klaus at Heathrow, Charles and Maria both insisting that Klaus come and celebrate Christmas with them and continued their journey home to the farm. Then Maria and Gregory concentrated on getting Gregory ready for his return to school; Charles checked over with Michael Collins what had been happening on the farm whilst they had been away; and then, at last, they could relax at home once more.

The autumn term got under way and life on the farm settled down to its normal routine. Almost into half term, Gregory seemed to flag. One evening, quite unusually for him now, since he was almost seven, he climbed onto his mother's lap, said he had a headache and lay quietly against her. Maria felt his forehead.

"Darling, he feels very hot to me."

Charles came over and felt Gregory's forehead. It was damp and hot. He asked the child if he was feeling unwell. Gregory did not reply. His eyes were closed. Charles went immediately to the telephone and rang Matthew. Matthew was in surgery, but the receptionist said she would get him to ring as soon as he was finished with his present patient. Ten minutes passed and the telephone rang. By this time, Charles was panicking. "He's not really conscious, Matt, and he seems to have a fever."

Matthew was calm, his voice reassuring. "I have one more patient to see, Charles, and I will come straight over. Just keep him warm, and if he wakes, a little water wouldn't hurt. I'll be with you very shortly."

It seemed an eternity to Charles and Maria, watching Gregory, mostly asleep, his eyes occasionally flickering open, unresponsive to their questioning. It was actually no more than half-an-hour before Matthew was with them. "We must get him up to bed, Maria, and I can do a proper examination."

Sitting on the side of the bed, Charles and Maria standing nearby, the anxiety etched on their faces, Matthew carefully checked Gregory's condition. Then he gently pulled the covers back over him, straightened himself up and looking with concern at his friends, said, "I'm afraid, it's meningitis. I must give him antibiotics immediately, and then I will need to take some blood for testing. I need to know what type of meningitis it is. He must not be left alone at the moment." Matthew gave the antibiotics intravenously and then took some blood. "I want to get this test done as quickly as possible, so I'll go now, but I'll be back as quickly as I can. I'll see myself out. Don't be too anxious, we've caught it early." Matthew hurried away.

Maria and Charles just stood there, looking at Gregory. Then Charles said that when Matthew came back, they would all need to eat something but that he would see to it and Maria was to stay with Gregory. Charles went downstairs and got out some fresh bread, cold meats and fruit, put them on the table and covered them with a cloth. He called up to Maria to see if she wanted a hot drink, made a pot of tea and took it back upstairs to Gregory's room. The child was still sleeping, or was he unconscious? That they couldn't say, but they sat by the bed, watching their little boy and trying to drink some tea.

At about seven o'clock, Matthew returned. "The lab will ring me here as soon as they have the blood test results," he told Charles and Maria. Back at Gregory's bedside, Matthew took Gregory's pulse, checked his pupils and said that Gregory was unconscious. "Don't be afraid of that," Matthew said, "it is to help his brain recover. He may sometimes come out of it for a little while, but I do not expect him to recover consciousness in any meaningful way for some weeks. You must be prepared for quite a long haul back to full health."

The telephone rang. It was for Matthew. When he returned to the bedroom he said, "I'm afraid it is bacterial meningitis. It is very serious, and we must expect Gregory to be poorly for quite a long time. I could send him to hospital, or we could nurse him here at home. What would you prefer?" Matthew sounded uncharacteristically curt. Charles recognised at once that Matthew was trying to hide his anxiety for his young patient.

Maria was quick to answer, "I don't know what Charles thinks, but I would rather look after him ourselves, so long as we can give him the help he needs. We would be guided by you, Matthew."

Charles agreed, trusting Matthew implicitly. Matthew said he thought it could safely be done at home. "But," he said, "for the first few nights, I would like to stay here with you, just in case there should be any emergency." Matthew may have spoken more as a godfather than a doctor, but in any event, Charles and Maria were relieved to know he would be there.

"Would you be all right, Matthew, if I made you up a bed in the box room? It's better to leave Gregory where he is, isn't it?"

That was agreed, and leaving Maria to watch over Gregory, Charles and Matthew went down to the kitchen to get something to eat.

Charles asked the question he had been afraid to ask in front of Maria.

"Will he recover, Matthew? Will he suffer any damage from this illness?"

"Charles, with regard to damage, it is unlikely, but I cannot say for certain. I am sure he will recover; we got it very early, and he is a healthy boy. But it will take quite some time. For a long while, he is likely to be unconscious, so the nursing will be mainly keeping him clean and comfortable. I will talk with Maria about nutrition. I intend to stay here with you for a few days, to make sure he is stable. If that's all right with you," he added.

The weeks passed, the routine was dull with little reward for it, for Gregory remained unconscious. Gregory's birthday came and went. Then one afternoon, as Maria sat with him, reading a book, she saw his eyes flicker open. Only a moment, then they closed again. When Matthew called in that evening, he said it was a sign that he was beginning to come out of the coma he was in. "It's a good sign."

A few days later, as Maria sat beside the bed, watching her son, he opened his eyes and very weakly said, "Mama."

And so Gregory's recovery began. As Matthew had warned, it was slow. Trying to get him to eat and drink a little was not an easy task. Then one day, when Maria went into his room, she found him trying to get out of bed.

"I want to see if my legs still work," he said. They did, with quite a lot of support from Maria, but she couldn't help thinking that Gregory would certainly not be returning to school this side of Christmas.

"And what happened to my birthday? I've missed it, haven't I?"

It was the second week in December, and Gregory was now sitting in an armchair for part of the day. Charles and Maria had been ringing Klaus regularly to keep him in touch with his nephew's progress. They had been uncertain about Klaus's Christmas visit going ahead, but now they thought Gregory was well enough to be able to benefit from his uncle's stay. So it was arranged that Klaus would come on 22nd and stay into the New Year. Matthew and Ethel would join them too over the festive days, but Matthew warned Maria that it would not be advisable to allow Gregory to get too excited or overtired.

Then Sara Neuberger rang to see if Gregory was well enough to have a visit from Raphael, who kept asking about him. So on the next Sunday afternoon, Raphael came, with his mother, to spend a little time with Gregory. Raphael was a little apprehensive, but Gregory, sitting in the armchair with a warm rug over his legs, was obviously overjoyed to have this particular visitor. Sara went into the kitchen to have her tea there with Maria, leaving the boys to chat in the sitting room. Raphael told Gregory what they were doing at school but had obviously been told by his mother not to worry Gregory about work he had missed. Raphael had brought him a Snakes and Ladders board game as a late birthday present, and they sat playing it together. Maria brought them milk and some little buns, and Raphael asked her if they could go outside. Maria explained to him that Gregory was not quite strong enough for that yet, especially as the weather was very cold, but maybe they could the next time Raphael came. Raphael was obviously anxious about his friend and did not know quite how to deal with a situation to which he was quite unused.

In the kitchen, Sara had deposited on the table a bag of beautiful peaches.

"Wherever did you manage to get them?" asked Maria.

"David came in with them on Friday morning, saying they were for Gregory, to help him get well."

Sara kept this first visit a short one but promised that she would bring Raphael again. As they were leaving, Raphael whispered something to his mother, who nodded to her son. Raphael went to Gregory, still sitting in the chair, planted a kiss on his forehead and said, somewhat apologetically, "I know boys don't kiss, but it's to make you better."

Klaus arrived on 22nd and settled himself into the little box room. Gregory had wanted to give up his room, as he had done on Klaus's earlier visit, but his parents, and Uncle Klaus, had insisted he stay where he was.

"Well, Gregory," said Klaus, "you may have been ill, but I have never known a boy grow so tall in such a short space of time!" Klaus was right; Gregory did seem to have grown quite tall. But without an increase in weight, he looked also rather thin. Ethel worried herself about this, saying they must fatten him up a bit or he'd never be ready to get back to school.

Christmas was taken in second gear, according to Matthew, but no one seemed to mind. For the first time, Gregory took a little walk around the farm with Matthew, holding onto his arm. When it came to Christmas Eve Mass, Gregory wanted to go, but under pressure from Matthew, he agreed to stay at home with Klaus, Charles and Ethel. The family kept the German tradition of Christmas on 24th, so when Matthew and Maria came back from church, they all sat down for their festive meal. The next day seemed to be dominated by present giving, and the atmosphere in the house was chaotic and noisy. After lunch, as they gathered in the sitting room to open the presents, Matthew noticed Gregory turning rather pale.

"I suggest Gregory takes a little rest, and we all open our presents when he comes back downstairs again," said Matthew. He was aware that this was a young boy still in recovery. "Come on, you poor old thing." Matthew laughed as he accompanied Gregory upstairs.

"No one is to open a present until I come down again," called out Gregory as he mounted the stairs with Matthew.

Well over an hour later, Gregory reappeared, looking refreshed. Then the present opening began. The greatest joy sprang from Gregory when a bicycle was wheeled in for him. He tried it for size, rang its little bell and vowed that by the New Year he would be out in the yard riding it.

"Yes," said Matthew, "I think you will."

For Charles, the loveliest present he received was from Klaus. It was a photograph of his mother in a simple silver frame. She was standing at an open door, a gentle smile on her face. Her brunette hair was wound around her head with a plait threaded through it, and she wore a simple summer dress. Charles, always emotional when it came to anything to do with the past, allowed everyone to look at it, answered briefly the questions that were asked but then went upstairs and placed it on the centre of the chest of drawers in the bedroom. He stood for a little while looking at it and then rejoined everyone downstairs. He went straight to Klaus and gave him a hug.

The year 1951 was duly welcomed in. After breakfast, Gregory put his warm coat on and asked Uncle Klaus if he would come with him into the yard so that he could try out his bicycle. Maria watched them from the kitchen window. Klaus steadied Gregory for just a very short way, and then he was off on his own, steadily cycling along the path to the gate and back again. His face was beaming.

"I can do it. I can do it!" he shouted.

Klaus returned to Germany the following day, and a few days later, school began for Gregory. It had been agreed with the headmistress that for the first week he would attend only in the mornings, but by Friday, Gregory insisted that he would stay the whole day, and there was no persuading him otherwise.

"I am as strong as one of those buffalo in the Kruger Park," he said. And indeed, he seemed to be. He was back to normal, and everyone heaved a sigh of relief.

On June 2, 1953, the country celebrated the coronation of Queen Elizabeth. Fred and Flo Dickson announced that they would show the ceremony on television in the lounge at the inn, together with light refreshments. It was a Tuesday, and a holiday for everyone. Charles and Maria decided to close the farm that day, and they booked five tickets, including Ethel and Matthew, to go and watch the televised event at the Dickson's Inn. Like so many people all over the country, they watched the ceremony at Westminster Abbey, following the BBC commentary with wonder and pride.

"This is history in the making," Charles told Gregory. "This is a very ancient ceremony."

"What's the difference between ancient and old?" asked Gregory.

"I pass this one to you, Matthew," said Charles with a grin.

"Well, it's subtle, Gregory. We usually only use the word ancient to talk about something that is a very long time ago, like you could say giving Christmas presents is an ancient custom. Kings and Queens have been anointed and crowned for hundreds of years, so we say ancient. But, for instance, you could say this bread is not nice, it's old."

"But I wouldn't say that, Uncle Matt. I'd say it's stale!"

"I thank you for correcting me, young man." Matthew laughed.

One day in spring 1954, a letter arrived for Gregory. When he came home from school, his mother passed it to him. It was the first time Gregory had received a letter addressed to him, and he opened it with a certain amount of pride.

"It's an invitation, Mama. I'm not sure what it means, but it's from Raff's parents."

He passed it to Maria. She looked at it and then told Gregory that he was invited to Raphael's Bar Mitzvah on Sunday, April 4. He would have to go to the Norwich Synagogue.

"Mama, I would very much like to be there, but I don't know what this is. A Bar…what is that? And how could I get to Norwich?"

"Well, Gregory, you could simply ask Raphael about this ceremony and what it means. Getting to Norwich is not really a problem. You could take a bus from Diss direct. We would check the times and make sure about the time of a bus back home. If you feel unsure about that, we could always do a little trip together beforehand so that you would know exactly where you were going."

"Yes, that sounds fine. But I should write to Mr and Mrs Neuberger, shouldn't I, to say thank you and say that I will come?"

Gregory went to Raphael's Bar Mitzvah, coping with the bus journeys quite confidently, and when he got home, he was full of excitement about what he had experienced.

"Oh, it was wonderful! He's so clever, Mama; he read from the Scroll in Hebrew. Did you know that you read Hebrew from right to left? And the Jews don't have a Bible like us, but a Scroll. And we had a wonderful party afterwards." Gregory's words were all running into one another in his excitement.

"There was even ice-cream! Raff liked the book you bought for him. And I got the bus, just like you said, almost outside the synagogue, and it brought me back to Diss. That was my first big outing on my own."

Gregory stopped to draw breath. He was clearly pleased with himself, and indeed, he had a right to be, for he had ventured alone into a different experience, a culture different from his own. At not-yet-eleven, Maria thought he had been very brave.

As the summer progressed, the question of which secondary school Gregory would attend occupied his parents' thoughts. The blow came for Gregory when he discovered that Raff was going to a Jewish school and they would be parted. He was almost inconsolable.

"A boarding school, Mama, that means that he lives at school and doesn't come home at night?"

"Yes, it does, Gregory. But there are holidays, and sometimes I think the students come home for a weekend. There is no reason why you can't see one another when Raphael is at home."

"Maybe. But I think this probably is the end," said Gregory. He looked very sombre.

"You may be right, Gregory. But remember that you too will be starting out on new experiences, and you'll make new friends. It happens in life. I think you'll always remember Raphael as your first real friend, and it may be that you will continue to see one another from time to time. Try to cheer up." Maria couldn't help thinking that there was something of an actor in her young son.

It was that summer of 1954 that rationing ended. Now was the time, Charles thought, to begin to put into effect some of the changes that had been discussed. He decided the business would continue to function on its own. He considered that they would not need to produce quite as much in the way of vegetables but would utilise the space gained by making room for people's cars, having a teashop and becoming an outlet for small dairy farmers. He wanted to make a feature of the 'Farm Fresh' idea. Maria's bread and cakes to buy would be a good selling point, he thought. Perhaps one of the storage sheds could be made into a bakery and teashop.

He met again with Ethel and Maria and this time Michael Collins was included. Maria was enthusiastic about Charles's ideas, although she told him that a bakery and a teashop would be a full-time job for her. If she could get Pauline's help with the teashop and maybe one other assistant in the bakery, Maria thought it feasible. Michael sounded a little nervous about the amount of work involved in the reorganisation but liked the 'Farm Fresh' ideas. Ethel always supported Charles and offered her help. She thought she might make a good assistant for Pauline as they had worked together before. And so the shop in Diss was sold and changes began to be made at Cox's Farm, which now had the marketing title 'Cox's Farm Fresh'.

Pauline had been employed by the Cox's since she left school. She lived at that time in Diss with her parents, Tom and Barbara Webb. She finished secondary school with a good report and Jimmie Cox took her on to help Ethel in the shop. After a while, it became obvious to Jimmie that she could manage the shop perfectly well on her own, and Ethel no longer needed to support her. She married a local boy, Mark Cook, and they bought a small house on the outskirts of Diss. Their first child had been stillborn, and Pauline was told that it would be dangerous for her to conceive again. The couple were very distressed at the thought of a childless future and for a while considered adopting. Mark was doing well in his job; he worked for the Water Board, and Pauline enjoyed running the Cox's shop in Diss. So, the years passed and with them, all thoughts of raising a family. Now, Pauline was quite happy to move to the farm itself for her work and rise to the challenge of running a new teashop on the site.

Gregory settled down at secondary school. He grew into quite a tall, lanky lad, but his unruly hair became short and extremely well smoothed down. Maria wondered if he had been teased about it, so insistent was he that he went very regularly to the barber. He proved rather disinterested in science but very gifted with words, whether it was through English language and literature, or foreign languages. In sport, he had no interest at all. Then, one day, to Gregory's horror, his form master told the class that they would be introducing boxing into the sports curriculum. Gregory thought about it and decided that he did not want to participate in this sport. He went to the headmaster's study and knocked on the door.

"Come in," called out Mr Butterfield.

Gregory stood in front of Mr Butterfield's desk. "Good morning, sir," he said.

"How can I help you, Gregory?"

"Sir, Mr Henderson told us yesterday that we will soon be starting boxing as one of our sport activities. I am very much against this sport. I do not like the thought of knocking other boys about. I would like to be excused from it, please." Gregory looked a little anxiously at Mr Butterfield, wondering if he would be in trouble with the headmaster.

"Ah, do I have a pacifist in front of me? Well, Gregory, I will need a letter from your father, asking for you to be excused from this sport, and from you, I want by Friday an essay on pacifism and your views on it. Your form master will tell you what you are to do during the time the other boys pursue their boxing classes. Is that all, Gregory?"

"Yes, sir, thank you, sir."

As Gregory left, Mr Butterfield could not help smiling to himself at the cheek of this young man. It showed spirit, he thought. *I will keep an eye on this boy.* Gregory, on the other hand, walking back to his classroom, wondered if it was worth having to find out about pacifism and write up something for the head, in order to get out of boxing. Still, he thought, this was a sport that had little to recommend it, and he felt quite strongly that the school should not be encouraging the pupils to take part in it.

That evening, when Gregory got home, he found out writing paper and an envelope, and when Charles came in, he put them in front of his father and said, "Would you write a letter to the headmaster, Papa, saying you don't want your boy to box?"

Charles was quite happy to comply with Gregory's request. Gregory did not tell his father that he had been to see the headmaster about it. But all other sport was obligatory, so Gregory participated, it must be said somewhat half-heartedly, in all the other sport on the curriculum.

Gregory spent some time over the next couple of days researching the subject the head had set him. He was surprised at how interesting it was, but he came to the conclusion that learning boxing really had not much to do with it. He said so, in the essay he wrote for Mr Butterfield. When he got it back, the headmaster had written that his argument was not very well balanced and that he should have found a little more to say about those who take a pacifist stance in the face of war. He asked Gregory to write it again and try to give some weight to the view that was opposite to his own. Gregory had expressed quite strongly the view that if a wicked tyrant was invading your country, it was the duty of men to fight to preserve their peace and way of life. He seemed to suggest that pacifists were cowards.

Gregory was none too pleased at this extra work. However, of course, he set about rewriting it, and eventually when it was returned to him, he was delighted to see that the head had given it top marks.

At the end of the first year, Gregory won the English and history prizes. As the long summer holiday began, he was pleased to get a letter from Raff. He told Gregory that he would be spending the summer in Israel and that it was unlikely they would get to meet up with one another. Gregory was disappointed.

In his second year, Gregory opted for Latin instead of German, and Maria was pleased to feel that he was settling down and making new friends. His list of companions was rather changeable. One day, it would be Jack who came home to tea, another it was two girls! None of them reappeared a second time. But as autumn half term loomed, Gregory was overjoyed to get a note from Raphael asking him to spend a day at home with him during their break.

It was arranged for the Wednesday. Mrs Neuberger picked Gregory up at ten o'clock. The two boys were full of life and obviously very pleased to see one another. Both boys were now around twelve years of age. The Neuberger's home was in Dickleburgh, only about five or six miles from Diss, so the journey did not take long by car.

"I've got a den in the garden, let's go out there," said Raphael as soon as they got inside the house. "Oh, isn't it good to be off school for a while! Look, there's a tiny staircase here and a little platform at the top where I like to sit and watch the birds. You go up, Gregory, there's not room for two." Gregory loved this little house and thought what a good idea it was to have a small hideaway.

"What's it like being at a boarding school?" Gregory asked Raphael.

"Oh, well, you get used to it," said Raphael with a shrug of his shoulders. "We have a lot of fun, but it's nice to come home. It's quite strict, so when I get home, I really enjoy sleeping late and doing whatever I want, within reason." Soon, Raphael's mother called them up to the house for a drink and something to eat. She asked them if they would like to go to see Framlingham Castle.

"What do you think, Gregory?" asked Raphael.

"A castle sounds interesting. Is it old?"

Raphael had no idea, but Mrs Neuberger told Gregory that it was built in the twelfth century and had quite an interesting history. They decided it would be worth a visit. Neither of the boys had ever been to a castle before and their visit reignited some memories of when they had learned about castles in primary school. When they got back home, Mrs Neuberger went to the kitchen to prepare the evening meal for them. Gregory and Raff went up to Raff's bedroom.

"We don't have any girls at our school," said Raff. "Do you?"

"Yes, we do," said Gregory. "The girls learn some subjects which the boys don't do, like cooking and sewing, but all the other subjects we learn together."

"I wish we had girls at our school. They make things more interesting."

"Do you think so, Raff? I've never thought about it."

"What do you think you'll do when you're grown up?" Raff looked at Gregory, trying to anticipate his reply.

"Oh, that's easy. I'd like to run a zoo with lots of wild animals. The only thing is I am not too keen on seeing them in cages. Perhaps I could go to Africa and help to run the Kruger Park. What about you, Raff?"

"I'd like to marry a film star."

Gregory's face was a picture. "But you can't make a career out of being a film star's husband. What would you do all day?"

Raff laughed. "I think you're right; it's not much of a career. Perhaps I'll go to the moon."

"That sounds better. I think you'd have to learn a lot of science to be able to do that, but it sounds much more interesting to me."

Soon the boys were called down to their meal. Rabbi Neuberger was away, so there was just the three of them. Mrs Neuberger asked Gregory how he was getting on with his clarinet, and they talked about the still quite new Royal Festival Hall. Mrs Neuberger asked Gregory if he would like to go with them to a concert there the next time they were on holiday from school.

After their meal, Gregory and Raphael helped clear away the dishes and then Mrs Neuberger drove Gregory home, the boys vowing to meet next time Raff was at home.

Gregory was always happy to do what he could to help on the farm. In fact, he also learned to cook quite well and would now often make supper for the family at home whilst his parents finished off the day's business at the Tea Shop. At weekends, he would help with the cleaning of the bakery in the early afternoon when most of the bread making was over. As he progressed through the school, his homework became more demanding and his chances of getting out to help became limited. Sometimes now, he would take his bicycle from the shed and go to Mass at the Benedictine church on a Sunday morning, where of course he had been baptised. The liturgy is beautiful he told his mother.

When Raphael was at home, Gregory would also use the bicycle to get to Dickleburgh to see him. He always arrived in a state of exhaustion but soon got over it. Raphael always teased him about his lack of physical fitness. "You should do more sport," he told him, "and stop poring over books." But Gregory would chide him by saying that he had to wait for his mother to drive him to Scole if he wanted to visit Gregory!

"Perhaps," he told him, "you should get yourself a bike! On the other hand, when you learn how to get to the moon maybe you could visit me on a rocket!"

Over the years, Gregory progressed from his recorder to a clarinet and took extra music lessons at school. In his third year, he joined the school orchestra. Charles and Maria were pleased to see Gregory making good progress and growing into a helpful and thoughtful teenager. Matthew was delighted to support his music studies and always attended the school orchestra performances.

It was just after Easter in 1957 that Sara Neuberger rang and asked Maria if Gregory would like to join her family at the Royal Festival Hall for a concert. She suggested Gregory stay overnight with them since it would be late when they got back from London. The concert Raphael was keen to hear was on Saturday, April 27, and was a Chris Barber jazz concert. It was the end of the Easter holiday, and Raphael would have to return to school the next day. It seemed a good opportunity for the boys to spend some time together. Sara had actually discussed this with David, since it was a Sabbath. He had simply said that he felt sure the Almighty would not punish them for going to listen to music, and that of course they should go and enjoy it. Sara picked up Gregory on Saturday morning and returned him home on Sunday morning. Gregory, like Raphael, was thrilled by this music. Neither of them had heard a great deal of Jazz, or seen a 'blues' singer before, but they both agreed that the music was 'fabulous'. When Gregory got home, he couldn't stop talking about it.

"I don't think I could play jazz on my clarinet," Gregory told his parents. "But I'd like to try."

When he discussed it with Matthew, he wanted to know if he could learn to play this kind of music. Gregory was clearly impressed with what he had heard Chris Barber play, and his appreciation of music had been greatly enhanced.

Meanwhile, changes had taken place for Matthew. By 1957, Matthew was working at a practice in Diss with three other doctors. It was part of the National Health Service and its registered patients came from many villages around about. It meant that Matthew had regular free time, had colleagues with whom he could discuss medical problems and now was not so much alone.

On Wednesdays, it became almost a fixed date that he would spend the evening with Charles, Maria and Gregory. He usually appeared about lunchtime when he had finished morning surgery and would wander around the farm until Gregory got home. The two would talk, very often about the latest scheduled concert for the school orchestra, sometimes about history. Gregory was beginning to think about his 'O' level examinations and even about what would follow.

Gregory valued Matthew's opinions, especially when it related to his studies. From time to time, the two of them would go together to Mass at the Benedictine church on Sunday. Sunday was quite a busy day for the farm, so Maria slipped down to the Mass centre in Diss, so as not to be away from the farm for too long.

The Tea Shop was busy at weekends, often it would seem, with people who came out for a drive, many of them on bicycles. Many workers had only Sunday free, so it became very much a day when families would go out together. The customers would usually visit the produce shed too and buy fresh vegetables and fruit. The dairy produce, which came from a nearby farm, was also popular, but the undoubted success was Maria's bread and cakes and the teashop. For Charles, Michael Collins was an indispensable help. He was reliable and thorough, and Charles could trust him with anything.

Gregory came up with an idea for the farm, which he put to his father. "You know, Papa, I have often seen families having their coffee and cakes in the picnic area, but there is nothing for the little children to do. Would it be a good idea to buy some slides and things, so that they could play?" Charles thought it a good suggestion and told Gregory he would talk it over with Michael and Ethel, and if they agreed, maybe Gregory would help in the choice of what they bought.

For relaxation, the family always enjoyed their Wednesday evening meal with Matthew. Somehow, the family didn't seem complete without him.

Ethel was becoming more frail but still liked to do what she could to help in the teashop. It was noticeable how good Gregory was with her. She was as indispensable to him as a grandmother, although Gregory always called her auntie. He often asked her advice, and when she joined them for a meal, as she often did, he was considerate and courteous. Her little cottage had been updated at the same time as the renovations and rebuilding that had taken place when the farm was altered, and Ethel seemed happy with all that had been done there. Bob's garden remained unchanged. In the summer holidays, Ethel would often sit there with Gregory, as they had done when he was a small boy. What they talked about no one knew, but they spent regular time together, time that seemed to be important to them both.

"I'm worried about Auntie Ethel," Gregory confided to his mother one day in 1957 as summer began to turn into autumn and Gregory prepared to begin his fourth year at secondary school and his 'O' level course.

"Why, what's the matter?" asked Maria.

"I don't know. She seems distant somehow, and she always takes my arm as we walk from the garden back to the cottage. She didn't used to do that."

"I think she's getting old, Gregory, that's all."

But Gregory was right to be concerned. A few weeks later, when Ethel had not appeared to do her usual tasks at the Tea Shop, Maria slipped quickly over to the cottage. She let herself in. All was quiet, the curtains still drawn. Ethel lay dead in her bed.

When Gregory got home and was told the news, he broke down.

"She died alone, Mama, no one was with her. Oh, that's terrible. Poor Auntie Ethel. I should have been with her." Gregory buried his face in his hands.

That evening, they sat quietly in the farmhouse, Matthew came over, and though the four of them were together, as so often they were, a presence was missed, for Ethel had often joined them for a meal on Wednesdays. The atmosphere was heavy with sadness. Then Gregory broke the silence.

"You know, I thought it was terrible that Auntie Ethel died alone, but I think now that she was not alone. We often sat by Bob's garden in the summer, and she told me that Bob and Jimmie were always with her. I think it's me that feels alone, not Auntie Ethel." The adults were silent for a moment, a little astonished and moved by Gregory's reflection.

"I think you are right, Gregory," responded Matthew after a moment's silence. "But when we get over the shock and the missing of her actual presence, I think we will find that Ethel is also still with us. She will always be a part of this farm."

"I must make Bob's garden a little bigger when the spring comes. What were those flowers Auntie Ethel liked, Mama? It would be nice to plant some of those for her. When you think about it, her whole family are now together." Gregory seemed to be consoling himself. "Yes, I'll make it a garden for Bob, Jimmie and Ethel. They'll be with one another. I loved Auntie Ethel. I will always love Auntie Ethel and in the garden, she will be with us too."

It was a Sunday evening. Gregory was working in his room and Charles and Maria were alone in the sitting room. Charles put his arm around Maria, pulling her close to him. He kissed her, full on the mouth.

"My darling Maria, I am happy, and so in love with you."

"Charles…?"

"We have been so lucky. We have a good life here, and we have a wonderful son. I haven't always been the easiest person to be with I know, but you have been the best thing that ever happened to me, and I love you dearly." Charles hesitated.

"Do you remember that day we left Warsaw? I was so terrified, and I don't think I breathed easily again until the day we got to the Dickson's Inn. But I could not have done it without you. You have always been a very big part of what I have managed to achieve, Maria, I know it, but I don't think I have ever told you so. Together, we have made good things happen." Charles took Maria's hand and kissed it.

"Come to bed with me now. I want to hold you close."

Gregory did very well in his 'O' level examinations and his form master recommended he should bear in mind the possibility of applying to Cambridge after 'A' levels. Gregory opted for history, English, religious studies and music for his 'A' level courses and settled down to serious studies as he celebrated his sixteenth birthday that year.

Before school broke up for Christmas, Gregory came home with the news that they were having a dance at school to which the local girls' secondary school sixth form were to be invited in order to boost the number of girls. "There will be live music, and we are expected to dress properly. I suppose that means a suit and tie."

When he came home from this event, his parents could tell that he had thoroughly enjoyed the evening. The music was very lively he told Charles and Maria, mostly modern, and some jazz which he had liked.

"But it wasn't quite up to the standard of Chris Barber," he said. "And I think I might need to take some dancing lessons if we are going to do this again," he told his parents.

Soon after the New Year festivities of 1960, Gregory was up in the loft at the farmhouse, storing things he thought he no longer needed now he was thinking ahead to university. As he rummaged around, he came across a small box, which he opened. In it, there was a metal swastika badge and other Nazi emblems, which looked as though they had belonged on a uniform. They seemed so alien. He couldn't understand why they were there. He went down to the kitchen, holding the swastika in his hand. He found his father in the sitting room.

"Papa, what is this doing in our loft?" He opened his hand, displaying the ugly symbol.

Charles just stood still, almost transfixed. His body tingled with the icy coldness that ran through it.

"What is this doing in our loft? Why have we got this terrible thing?" Gregory was looking at it with disgust.

"Gregory, I must explain."

Time seemed suspended.

"I'll tell you. I'll explain. It was mine. You see, I've never told you, but I was, in Warsaw, a Nazi officer."

Charles flinched inside himself as he looked at his son's face. Gregory was looking at his father with utter disbelief and horror. For a moment, the full impact didn't dawn on Gregory. He stood there, still, with the insignia in his open hand.

"I can't believe this. Tell me it's not true what you're saying. You were a lawyer, a Polish lawyer. These aren't yours."

"I'm sorry, Gregory, they are, or they were, mine."

Charles felt as though a black cloud had descended on him, and he felt both spiritually and physically unbalanced by the admission he had made.

Then, in a sudden fury of disbelief and disgust, Gregory threw the badge at his father, shouting as he did so, "No, no, no."

The swastika hit Charles on the forehead; he fell, smashed his head on the corner of the sideboard and lay still on the floor, blood seeping from a wound on his head. His son had fled.

Gregory, in a mist of tears and uncontrolled emotion, had not fully registered his father's fall. That would come later. He rushed out of the door, up the front path, running wildly, not knowing where he was going, wishing only to get away from this horrific confrontation with the father he loved so dearly. He ran until he could run no more for lack of breath. He followed, unconsciously, a familiar path, although one not usually taken on foot.

When Maria came in and saw Charles lying on the sitting room floor, unconscious, with blood over his face, she picked up the telephone immediately and asked for an ambulance. She called out to Gregory who she believed was at home. When no reply came, she scribbled a note for him and as soon as the ambulance arrived, went with Charles to the hospital.

Gregory, becoming more exhausted physically as well as emotionally, after stumbling on for well over an hour, collapsed at the gates of the monastery whose liturgy he knew and loved so well. He wrapped his arms around his body, trying to keep warm and as night fell, gave in to an uneasy sleep.

It was there that Father Andrew found him early the next morning and took him to their infirmary. And it was at the monastery that Gregory stayed for some weeks.

Chapter Eight
The Truth Revealed, 1960

It was Sunday morning. Gregory tidied himself, went out through the side passage near the turn and into the church. He saw his mother in their usual pew and surprised and delighted, he took his place beside her. No sooner had he sat than the officiating priest, Father Andrew, and the servers processed in, and the congregation stood.

"*In nomine Patris, et filii, et Spiritus Sancti,*" Father Andrew intoned.

The Mass had begun and Gregory could only squeeze his mother's hand as they sat again. When Mass was over, they made their way out. Father Andrew was greeting people as they left. "Good morning, Mrs Hartman." He shook hands with Maria, and then said, "Gregory, would you like to take your mother along to the first parlour next to the turn. One of the brothers will bring some coffee."

"Thank you, Father," replied Gregory and led his mother down the passage towards the turn.

The parlour was overwhelmingly brown in its impression and rather stark. There was a low dividing shelf of polished wood across the centre, and at the side where Maria and Gregory had entered, the space was occupied with four wooden chairs. Neither Gregory nor Maria took much notice of their surroundings because they were lost in their warm embrace.

"Mama, oh, Mama, I am so happy to see you." Gregory released his mother just as a tap on the door on the other side of the dividing shelf was heard. The door opened and in came a young monk with a tray of coffee, which he placed on the shelf. He greeted them and left the parlour.

"Gregory, you look well. How are things with you?"

"Mama, I am fine here, but I miss home. I have had a lot to think about and to be sorry for. The community have been so kind to me. I have a little cottage in the grounds, and I work in the gardens, just like I used to do on the farm with

Papa." At the mention of his father, Gregory paused and then spoke in a quiet and contrite way.

"How is he? I must talk with him and tell him how sorry I am for what I did. Oh dear, I should pour you some coffee. As usual? Milk, just a little?" Gregory poured himself a cup too. "I can't believe I am sitting here with you. I thought I might never see you again." His voice faltered.

"Gregory, how can you be so silly? You must know how we love you. We want you to come back home, as soon as you feel you can. Your father is especially anxious of course, that the pair of you should talk. There is a great deal you do not understand, Gregory, and it is important that you should speak with your father about the past. You should not judge him on the basis of his having loathsome insignia. He is a good man."

"Oh, Mama, I know that. I think it was out of shock that I…that I hit out at him. It was a terrible thing to do, and I wish that I hadn't done it. I want the chance to talk with him and of course to say sorry for my actions. But Mama, I must also understand what he did when he was a young man in Warsaw. Not to judge, no, not to judge, but…" Gregory could say no more for he really didn't know how this whole incident would develop, nor did he have any idea of what he would say to his father when they met again. He wanted things to be as they had been before this terrible event had happened. But he knew that they probably couldn't be. He was anxious and uncertain.

"My dear Gregory, you will make a judgement, but it will be made out of knowing all the facts and from a loving heart. Remember, that ultimately only God can know our heart and intentions, and He can be the only true judge. But you are an intelligent boy, and you know that it has been given to us also to come to a judgement about another's actions. We have law courts and rules, and yes, we have punishments. You will listen to your father's story, and I believe, whatever you think about what he did in the past, you will continue to love him."

Gregory embraced his mother again. "You are so wise, Mama. I will think carefully about what you have said."

Maria stood. "I must go and pick up my bike. It takes quite a while to get back and your father will be expecting his lunch. Come home as soon as you are ready. We will be waiting for you, Gregory."

Gregory walked with his mother to where she had left her bicycle and waved goodbye. He stood watching until she disappeared from view, then he delivered the coffee tray to the turn.

The next day, Gregory felt uneasy and miserable as he woke. He had had some bad dreams. He got dressed, put on his warm coat and went out to feed the hens. He picked up, at the turn, the heavy and messy pails of scraps, which truthfully, he found ugly and nauseating and trudged out towards the chicken pen feeling low and depressed. As he walked into the second of the enclosed gardens, he lifted his bowed head and was confronted with a totally unexpected glory.

On the wall opposite, a little flowering cherry had come into bloom. The small, fluffy, pink and white blossoms covered the branches in an abundance of all that was pure and beautiful. In the dim light of the early morning, it stood out like a radiant vision, everything nearby fading into insignificance.

Gregory stood still, afraid that this loveliness was an illusion. He drank in the shining beauty, like balm for the ugly fears and thoughts he had had overnight. He felt this was a reverent moment, an epiphany, almost a sacrament. He was aware of having been lifted outside of himself, out of the misery to something far higher. He felt tears running down his cheeks. Thank you, Lord, thank you, his inner self breathed. He knew something profound had happened to him.

The glow of it stayed with him as he completed his pedestrian morning tasks.

After lunch, Gregory sat in his small room, the door to the garden open and began to think about what he wanted to do next. He thought that by staying in the monastery much longer, he would be cowardly. He would also be prolonging his father's sense of having been judged and rejected. He knew that it was very important that he should listen to what his father had to say. He tried not to get tense and anxious when he thought about that. He would remember that morning's vision of the little flowering cherry. He must try to reach out to something much greater than his own tendency to judge and condemn. *After all*, said Gregory to himself, *I haven't yet heard the story.*

He walked slowly around to the church and sat in his usual pew. Then he knelt. He had no words. He felt that God had spoken to him that morning and that he must listen. In all his misery, as he had walked into that little garden, Gregory felt that God's love had shone out in the radiance that had confronted him. He did not understand, but he felt different and knew that he must go patiently into the future, listening carefully for what God might want from him.

He thought of that Nazi badge. He thought about what he knew of the ugly wickedness that it represented. Was it possible that God could be found there too? His special people, the Jews, surely God must have been with them in those dreadful days? He thought about his friend, Raphael and the Neuberger family.

But was God with the perpetrators? Gregory felt that he could think no further. He was afraid to follow that thought, knowing that his father may have been one of them. He loved his father and knew that he would always love him, whatever he might hear about his past. Gregory stayed, still and quiet in the shadowy church and tried to let the beautiful vision return to him.

By the time the evening came, Gregory had come to the decision that he would see Father Vincent the next day and tell him that he felt it was time for him to go home. Although nervous about the coming confrontation with his father, he felt at peace with what he had decided. He slept well that night. The next morning, after he had fed the chickens and when he took the eggs to the turn, he rang the bell and asked if he could see Father Vincent. A message came back that the Fr Abbot would come to Gregory's lodge in about ten minutes time.

Gregory's feelings were very mixed. He was surprised by the regret he felt at leaving the monastery but not so surprised that the coming meeting with his father made him feel nervous and apprehensive. He realised that the monastery had been a refuge for him, a safe place from which he had been able to cope with the emotional turmoil that had overwhelmed him. But he also knew, in a way he did not yet understand, that it had been more than just a refuge. Because of these weeks of solitude and the support of the community of monks here and remembering too the counsel of his mother, he felt he had grown sufficiently to be able to make a new start with his father, whatever he might have to tell him. Gregory hoped that the emotional outburst that had severed his relationship with his father would never be repeated.

Gregory took out another chair onto his little porch and soon Father Vincent arrived, and the two of them sat. Gregory took charge of the moment.

"Father, I think I am ready now to go home. I want to say sorry to my father and try to mend things with him. I also want to get back to school. I want to thank you for all that you have done for me; it has been a very wonderful time in a way that I cannot explain. You have all become so important to me that I am sad to say goodbye. But it is time. I will tidy the lodge, and if I may, I would be glad to have lunch as usual, and then I will go."

Father Vincent was impressed by the maturity Gregory was showing. So different, he thought, from the boy of just a few weeks ago.

"Yes, Gregory, I think you are ready, and I am pleased that you have grown into this decision. I will miss you, and I am sure Brother Simon will too. I expect I will see you at Mass from time to time. You will always have friends here, remember that. I am going to ask Father Bernard to drive you home. It's Cox's Farm, isn't it? Shall we say you will be ready to leave at 1:30?" Father Vincent rose from his chair. "Go in the love of the Lord, Gregory. Goodbye."

Gregory watched his mentor return to the house. He knew that they were both deeply moved by their farewells and that the somewhat brusque nature of their conversation covered a sadness felt by both of them. After lunch, the little lodge tidied, and dirty linen delivered to the turn, Gregory waited outside the gates for Father Bernard. As soon as the old Ford appeared, he jumped into it, and they were on their way.

When they arrived at the farmhouse, Gregory said thank you and goodbye to Father Bernard and walked up the path to the front door. He had to summon up courage, for indeed he felt a little shaky and unsteady and in a strange way, embarrassed. He rang the bell. Quite quickly, the door opened and his mother stood there. She made no fuss. "Come on, Gregory, I'm just making coffee. Have you had some lunch?" She gave him a hug. "We are in the kitchen. Your father has just gone out to the chickens. He will be back any minute."

She took Gregory's hand, sensing his awkwardness and led him into the warm farmhouse kitchen.

Gregory went straight to the back door, opened it and called out, "Papa, Papa." He wanted to grasp this moment straightaway, before his nervousness got the better of him and became very apparent.

His father appeared. It was a moment that would be forever frozen in Gregory's memory.

He was just the same.

Charles's tall frame was so familiar to Gregory and roused in him at that minute a feeling of love and sadness. He noticed a red scar on his father's forehead. Yes, that was different; he had never seen that before. Gregory knew nothing about the injuries he had caused; he only wondered why it was that he should expect his father to look different.

Charles also, if the truth be told, felt awkward and apprehensive at the sight of his young son standing at the kitchen door. He realised the brokenness of this relationship. He didn't know what to do with the eggs he was carrying. Gregory stood back, to let his father into the kitchen, and when the eggs were safely, if somewhat hurriedly, placed on the table, Charles turned straight to his son and threw his arms around him. This usually well-controlled man felt tears welling up in his eyes.

Maria broke the moment. She saw Charles's emotion. She had never seen him cry. "Come on, you two, the coffee's getting cold." The two men broke apart, both with tears running down their cheeks.

"I always thought homecomings were supposed to be happy occasions," said Maria as she sat and began to pour the coffee.

"Indeed. And this is a very happy day," said Charles, trying to smile.

"Mama and Papa, I am so glad to be back home with you again. It reminds me of the Prodigal Son in the New Testament, except there is no fatted calf. Still, there is a very nice cup of coffee, and I haven't been out living a life of excess in any case! Yes, please, Mama, just a little milk and no sugar, as usual."

The reunited little family sat down with their coffee. As they finished, Gregory was almost surprised to hear himself ask his father if he would walk with him around the farm so that they could talk.

Charles was pleased to see that his son was wanting to speak with him about the pain that lay between them. He felt that Gregory had matured over the few weeks they had been apart, and he felt hopeful that the two of them could speak like adults.

"Of course, Gregory." They put on warm coats and went out and walked around to Bob's garden and sat there. A place of peace, friendship and memory, thought Gregory. Some of the bulbs were just beginning to bloom. For Gregory, Ethel's presence was very real. It seemed to give him courage. Then Charles spoke.

"I could give you a history lesson, Gregory, and give you facts that you can read about in books. But I think you really want to know if I was complicit with the evil that was at the heart of Nazi Germany under Hitler."

Charles took a breath. He had never spoken about these things to anyone before, not even Maria, although she had lived through many of the events with him.

Gregory, with respect for the gravity of this moment, and with fear for his father's very soul, said nothing. He knew his father was not wanting a reply but was trying to order his thoughts into a truthful narrative.

"I should have to say that yes, I was, to some extent."

Again, Charles paused, trying to steady his voice.

"Joining the Nazi Party was something that was demanded of every man who wanted to advance in his career. Having a Nazi badge meant only that you belonged to the NSDAP, and I suppose, by implication that you supported Hitler. You must understand that I am German, not Polish, and so I too joined the Nazi Party."

Charles stopped speaking. The garden was very silent.

"You probably know that by this time Germany was a one-party state. There were no opposition parties tolerated, so it was a dictatorship. I never wanted to be a part of Hitler's plans to eradicate peoples he considered to be worthless." Charles's thoughts were coming out in a haphazard way.

"Yes, I was responsible to a large extent, under Hans Frank, my old student mate at Munich University, for the way in which we gradually changed the Jewish quarter of Warsaw into a ghetto. I was living in Warsaw when Hitler invaded Poland. I had a legal practice there. I knew that the living conditions in the Jewish quarter had become inhumane, that they could not live on the meagre rations they could afford to buy and that the majority faced only death. Yes, I knew that, and I did nothing to alleviate their suffering."

Gregory felt a tension in his body. He hardly knew how to listen to these things he knew about only as distant atrocities. It all seemed so foreign. It was a terrible thing to be hearing this from his own father, the man sitting beside him at this moment. Yet he realised at the same time how difficult it was for his father to have to relate these long-buried experiences to his son. He felt conflicted by the horror of his father's story and the love and respect he had always held for him. He also found it quite difficult to follow his father's rather muddled account of things.

How could it be, Gregory asked himself, that this tall, kindly man he called 'Papa', whom he had always loved, could be the same person as had been involved in these terrible events? Then, pulling his thoughts back to the present moment, he noticed that when a very difficult thing had to be said, his father would often go off on a tangent, unable to grasp the real issue immediately. Gregory realised again the pain his father felt at having to talk about his past. He tried hard to follow what he was telling him.

"To be absolutely truthful, my politics were, and are, right-wing, but that in itself is no crime. I supported my country's efforts to extend its influence in the world, although you may well ask me, as I have often asked myself since, how a policy that permitted the Warsaw ghetto and much worse, could be thought to advance an influence that could be respected."

Strange, thought Gregory, how beautiful this place is, here and now, as I hear my own dear father talk about these dreadful things. The sun still shines. I see an occasional insect enjoying the warmth. Everything is quiet. Then Gregory tried to pull his thoughts together. *I must not detach myself*, he thought. *I must listen. I must try to understand.*

Charles's voice broke into Gregory's thoughts. "No, I must admit, I was guilty. I was guilty because I remained silent and did nothing. I was guilty of murder because I passively assisted the destruction of hundreds of people, men, women and children."

Charles's face was contorted and white, as though he were in physical pain.

Gregory placed his hand on his father's arm. He shared, in a way he would never be able to explain, his father's agony. He could not believe he was a cold killer. From the way he spoke, Gregory knew that his father regretted the part he had played in these dreadful events, but Gregory felt that he seemed to condemn himself mercilessly. Nevertheless, with a moral stability beyond his years, Gregory couldn't help thinking that, as yet, he had expressed no regret for what he had done. They were just facts put in front of his son.

Charles went on, "It was when Himmler came, and I heard him and Frank planning the Extermination Camps, that I knew I had to get away from it all. It was about that time too that your mother told me we were to have a child. Neither of us wanted to bring up a new young life in that hell.

So, we escaped and made our way to England. We were lucky. People helped us. I presented myself as Polish, as I do to this very day."

Charles paused. His throat felt very dry.

"But Gregory, I am German. Your mother is Polish and you of course are British because you were born here. I have lived on the lie of being Polish ever since we left Warsaw. It won us safety and the possibility of a life together in peace. It was still two years before the end of the war when we arrived here. At that time, I would have been considered an Enemy Alien. That means, that as a German citizen, I would have been deported and almost certainly once back in Germany, executed, not because I was Nazi but because as a Nazi I had deserted. You know, at the Nuremberg Trials in 1946, Hans Frank was found guilty of war crimes and crimes against humanity. He was hanged."

Charles paused again. He had not once looked at his son sitting beside him. He stared into the distance. He was not in the garden with Gregory at all.

"But Papa, those were trials with a judge, and Counsel for Defence and Counsel for Prosecution, I suppose. Am I right in thinking that some of those Nazis who appeared there were found not guilty or were considered less guilty than others? Not all of them were hanged."

Gregory was trying to find a way in which he could suggest to his father that his guilt might be less culpable. Yet, in his mind, he could not help thinking of the many Jews his own father had seen perish without lifting a hand to help them. Jews, like Raff. What would they say? Indeed, did they not have a right to justice? They died. Death is death, thought Gregory, there's not a lesser death to go with a lesser guilt.

Gregory was deeply torn between his love for his father and his sense of what he thought to be right. It could be easy to sit here on a summer's day in England and let all this horror slide away into the past. Perhaps that is what his father had done. But don't we have to accept responsibility for our actions, Gregory was thinking.

Father and son sat side by side in silence. Then Gregory took the initiative again.

"You know, Papa, I think that perhaps a man's life should be weighed, the good deeds against the bad. If that were to be done, I can see clearly that the good you have done far outweighs any bad." Charles could not help smiling at his young son's immature conclusions.

"Yes, Gregory, but who is to measure the weight of each of the deeds when they are put into the scale? I was a part of an evil so dark and horrific that I think it weighs very heavily indeed on your scales. I used to ask myself whether I should go back and face justice. Would it do any good, would it bring back even one of those souls who died in the ghetto? No. But it would surely have ruined your mother's life and yours."

Charles took out his handkerchief and blew his nose. The tall, capable and highly intelligent man seemed to be reduced to a miserable heap.

Gregory could sense his father's feelings of guilt and hopelessness. Hopelessness, because he could see no possibility ever, of erasing the fact of his inaction in the face of unspeakable evil.

Gregory realised what it had cost his father to reveal all this to his son. Gregory too, at this moment, shared the hopelessness. He could not find any means of comforting his father, nor could he think of any way out of this terrible situation. After a minute or two, when the pair seemed lost for further words, Charles broke the silence. He spoke very quietly.

"I would like to be forgiven, Gregory. But that can never be. Only the Jews I allowed to die can forgive me, and they are all dead. No other forgiveness, except theirs, can be real."

There was silence. A blackbird began its song in a nearby hedge. The afternoon was sliding towards evening.

"Well, Papa, I believe God can grant you forgiveness if you are truly sorry for what you did."

Into Gregory's mental vision came again the little cherry tree, simple and beautiful, there, real, a sign of God's love, if only one could see with inner eyes. He was lost, for a moment, in the remembered beauty of that vision. Then he saw that his father was, for the first time, looking directly into his eyes.

"I wish I could believe that, Gregory. Perhaps you are right. How can we poor humans measure guilt? Even if I catch someone in a misdemeanour and his guilt is obvious to everyone, what is the weight of that guilt? It's impossible to measure, because we can't see inside a man's soul. The law wields a blunt instrument. But it's the only one we have. How, I wonder, would my guilt have been measured if I had been before the Nuremberg prosecutors?"

Gregory felt tears welling into his eyes again. It was a moment or two before he could respond. He believed his father would never be able to receive a full answer to his question, and certainly, Gregory knew, he himself did not have the wisdom to be able to answer it, except in the only way he could.

"With love, Papa," he said quietly. "At least by me."

Chapter Nine
Charles Tries to Deal with His Guilt

Over the next few weeks, Gregory got back to school and caught up on the work he had missed. He tried hard to apply himself to his 'A' level studies but he carried the burden of his father's revelations inside himself and sometimes felt the weight of it as insupportable. He felt dragged down by the anguish of his love for his father and the difficulty of accepting his father's complicity in the crimes of which, before this, he had only read about in school.

Gregory didn't speak again with his father about their long conversation in the garden that day but couldn't help hoping that maybe his own suffering in some way lessened his father's pain. He would often bring it into his prayer. Not with words but as a silent unspoken plea. Sometimes he would go to his father and envelop him in a big hug. Charles, when released, would usually ask what he had done to deserve that. Gregory's answer was always the same. "You don't have to deserve it, Papa, it's simply because I love you."

Soon after their momentous conversation, when Gregory came in from school one day, to his utter amazement he found his father sitting at the kitchen table with the New Testament open before him.

"Papa, I never expected to find you reading the Bible," said Gregory with a smile. "What are you looking at?"

"Well, Gregory, I remember you mentioning a story called the Prodigal Son. Both you and your mother knew it, but I did not. I thought it was time I looked it up. But I'm having some difficulty in finding it."

"It's in Luke's Gospel, around about Chapter Fifteen I think."

Later, Charles spoke with his son about the story.

"That is a very beautiful…is it a parable?" Charles asked his son.

"Yes, I love it too. It shows how God is always wanting to forgive us, waiting and watching and even coming to find us to offer his forgiveness and love to us. It's about being lost and being found. The son was lost in his guilt for all the irresponsible things he had done, but when he went to the only place he could for help, his home, his father ran to meet him and folded him in his generous and forgiving love. There was no cross-questioning, just an embrace."

On Wednesday evening, when Matthew was at dinner with them, suddenly to everyone's surprise, Charles said, "Matthew, do you know the story of The Prodigal Son from the New Testament?"

"Yes, I think so," said Matthew, looking somewhat nonplussed.

"What do you make of it?" asked Charles.

"Well, I think I remember how mean and grudging the second son was. He didn't like the fact that his brother, who had been a bit of a tearaway, was being treated so generously when he finally went back home. But I suppose the father is the main character. It's about love, isn't it? A kind of unconditional love? But why are you asking me about this? Gregory is the one who is doing 'A' level religious studies. You should ask him."

It was around about Christmas time that year, a little after Gregory's seventeenth birthday, when Charles became ill. He said little, but it gradually became more obvious that he was suffering with abdominal pain and didn't really want to eat.

Maria mentioned it to Matthew the next time they had an opportunity to be alone together.

"Don't worry, Maria, I'll speak to him." Matthew did indeed take it up with Charles. He approached the matter by making an observation that he thought Charles didn't look very well. They were alone in the farmhouse.

"I think it's my stomach, Matthew," said Charles. "I've had this sort of problem on and off for years, but now I must say that I have quite a nasty pain. It's making me feel poorly. I'm having to leave more and more of the work on the farm to Michael."

"Well, you have no need to worry about that; he's a very capable man." Then, to Charles's surprise came a question he had not expected.

"What are you worrying about, Charles?"

"Worrying? What makes you think I've anything to worry about?"

"All right, I would like to examine you if I may." Matthew asked Charles to lie on the settee so that he could feel his abdominal area. He finished the examination, straightened up and repeated his earlier question.

"I find no evidence of anything that makes me think you have some internal problem. And there is no reason you should have. What are you, not yet sixty,

Charles? So, I have to ask again, what is it that you are worrying about?" Matthew had on his face the look of an authoritative doctor who was determined to get an answer to his question.

Charles straightened his clothes and sat upright again. "It's a very long story, Matthew." He sighed heavily. "I don't know that I should burden you with it."

"I think it has to do with your previous life in Warsaw? About your life there as a Nazi?"

Charles's incredulity was written all over his face. "You have spoken with Gregory?"

"No, I haven't." There was a moment of silence.

"Charles, you are my dearest friend. I bring this up now only because I believe it could be to do with this that you are ill. What you are suffering from, I believe, is not physical. Yes, it has a physical manifestation, but the cause is psychological. You are carrying a heavy load, which you cannot share and it is making you ill. Can you not share it with me so that I can try to help you?"

"How did you find out about it?" Charles's voice was monotone and resigned.

"In a strange and unexpected way, Charles. The name David Neuberger is known to you?"

"Yes, of course. Young Raphael, his son, is a friend of Gregory. They see one another quite often, and Mrs Neuberger has been here once or twice."

"Well, Charles, David Neuberger is an old friend of mine, of long standing, although we rarely meet these days. In fact, it must be a good ten years ago that we last saw one another, although I saw young Raphael at one of Gregory's birthday parties. David mentioned Raphael's friendship with Gregory when we met, and I told him that I knew you and that in fact I was Gregory's godfather."

Matthew paused. He was very aware of the delicacy of the situation between himself and Charles in a matter about which Matthew knew Charles did not wish to speak. He chose his words carefully.

"He told me he was convinced that you were German because your English had Germanic accents, not Polish. As I am sure you know he is German. I told him I thought he was quite wrong. Anyway, to make the story a little shorter, he made some enquiries, rang me a few weeks later and told me he was almost certain that you were the Nazi officer who had been in charge of the Warsaw Ghetto and for whom the Israelis had been searching."

Charles's face drained of colour. When he spoke, his voice was unsteady.

"Did you say ten years ago?" That was all Charles could manage to say, but it expressed his wonderment that Matthew was still a friend after having been told these things.

"Yes. David did nothing more. His son and yours were friends. He could see that you were living a respectable life. He had no wish, no vindictive impulses to see you arrested and deported. We never spoke of it again. He is rabbi of a community of Jews near Norwich, Reform Judaism I think, and he is a very nice man, Charles. You may not know, but he and Sara fled Germany as Hitler tightened his grip on political power. They too are refugees."

"And all this time you've never said anything to me about my past. Not even a question. You remained my friend." Charles's voice faltered as he looked at Matthew questioningly and with a fear that this friendship, so important to him, might now come to an end.

"Oh, come on, Charles. You will always be my friend, I hope. Now, I am only concerned about what this secret you have carried for so long is doing to your health. I don't want to worry you more than is necessary, but I am now just a little concerned about Gregory too. I assume, from what you said, that you have shared these things with him. If that is so, then he is carrying a burden that is too heavy for a young man of his age, especially when he already has the challenge of all these examinations in front of him. I need to do what I can to help you both. That is, if you will accept my help."

"About me, it doesn't matter, but Gregory, if you think he might suffer, then we must do something. You remember when he ran off to the monastery and stayed there for some weeks, that was because he discovered my past and couldn't bear it. When he came home, we had a long talk, and I told him everything. But what is to be done now? I don't want him to suffer because of me. I have anguished over all this, off and on, ever since I arrived in England and I don't know what to do. I haven't even been able to talk about it with Klaus either. He knows nothing of any of this."

"That is why you are ill now. But after this evening you have another person to help you with this load you've been trying to carry alone all these years. Charles don't keep things hidden from me. And where is Maria in all of this? Do you talk things over with her? No, I thought not. No wonder you are ill. Charles, you have allowed me to be a part of your family. Can't we try to tackle this as a family? All three of you are affected by these memories you carry, and each of you suffer separately, without the support of one another."

Matthew looked at his friend and saw the defeat on his face. But Matthew had a possible plan in his mind of how he might be able to help Charles.

"I need a day or two to think about what I want to suggest to you. In the meantime, I am going to write you a prescription for your digestive discomfort. I'll get the chemist to make it up tomorrow, and I'll drop it off to you after evening surgery. Please try to relax. We are going to work together, as a family, to make things easier for you all. You don't have to bear it alone, Charles. I'm off now. I'll see you tomorrow."

As promised, Matthew arrived the next evening with Charles's medication. Charles was sitting with Maria and Gregory, around the kitchen table, having recently finished supper. The atmosphere was a little sombre.

"I have some pie and vegetables left over, Matthew, would you like to eat?" asked Maria. He declined but said he would love a coffee if she was going to make some.

The four of them went through to the sitting room.

"Am I right in thinking that you both know about my talk with Charles yesterday?" Matthew glanced at Maria and Gregory as he put this question.

"All right. Oh, dear, you all look as though you are going to a funeral." This little bit of humour had no effect, so Matthew went on. "I want to make a suggestion to you, which I beg you to think about. Your first reaction may be negative, but I want you to consider it. I think it may be a way forward to making you all more comfortable with who you are."

"I don't need to be told who I am," muttered Charles, a little aggressively.

Matthew, aware of the three of them sitting each apart from the other, desperately wanted them to come together, closer, not just physically, although he thought that in this delicate situation a hand held, a touch, would help. He realised that Maria and Charles did not easily share their problems with one another. He went on, choosing his words carefully.

"I think we all know that there is no absolute cure, sorry for the word but I am a doctor after all, and I will continue to use this analogy. There is no absolute cure for your problem, Charles, Maria, and Gregory. What is done, is done and cannot be changed. I am looking for an ointment for your wounds, one that will ease the pain and give you all peace." He paused. "I want to suggest to you that we include David Neuberger in our search for that balm. He is a Jew and could represent, in a way, all those Jews whose deaths you agonise over Charles. He is also a wise and thoughtful counsellor."

Maria got up from her chair and sat herself on the settee close to her husband, circling her arm around his waist.

"Yes," said Charles quietly, "I don't know how, but it seems to me that this balm you talk of, Matthew, can only be found inside myself. Maybe David Neuberger could help us find it. I don't know. I'm willing to try. We can't go on like this."

Maria looked across the room to where Gregory sat. "What do you think?" she asked him.

"Well, I'm thinking of the Prodigal Son. He had to make the journey home before he could make a fresh start. For me, the key is being profoundly sorry, and that I know you are, Papa. The trouble seems to be that you can't forgive yourself. Maybe if Rabbi Neuberger were to talk with us and was able to offer friendship and acceptance, your feelings of guilt would fade away."

"Well said, Gregory," was Matthew's response. "Maria?"

"The decision really belongs to Charles, but we are all together in this and so long as he feels comfortable with what you are proposing, Matthew, I am with him. I want us to do what is right and to be able to live happily, and as far as is possible, with clear consciences. How do you think this can be managed?"

"Well, of course, I would have to talk with David about it. If he is willing to help us, I suggest we all have lunch together at my place and see how we get on. If you want to go ahead with it, I will speak to him, and if he is willing, I will make all the arrangements. I think I would have to ask you to help me, Maria, with getting a meal together for us. A doctor I am, but a cook, well, that is questionable."

"It's very kind of you to offer hospitality, Matthew, but if I am to help with the cooking, wouldn't it be easier if we all meet here?"

"Yes, you're right, Maria. We'll do that if it's all right with you."

Gregory sat in his chair, calm and looking like a wise sage. He was smiling. "Thank you so much, Uncle Matt, I feel good about this." And looking across at his parents he said, "Papa, Mama, I am sure Rabbi Neuberger will help us all to feel better soon."

"It's not a small thing," said Charles quietly, still looking a little glum.

But no one took notice of Charles's pessimism, and they began to clear away the coffee cups.

Cox's Farm was doing well in its new form. The star attraction was definitely Maria's bread and cakes and the fact that customers could enjoy them in the little café or picnic site with a pot of tea or coffee. Gregory's suggestion of a play area for children had been acted upon and got a lot of use. Even in the winter months, people came, particularly at weekends, to enjoy the café. Charles had managed to keep on all the young boys although one or two had to be retrained. Millie had died of old age and been replaced with a small mechanised version. The stables remained available, but Charles and Michael, in spite of having several ideas about alternative uses, decided that for the meantime they should stay empty. Maria took on a cleaner to look after the housework at home, a chore for which she now had very little time. Pauline settled down and seemed to enjoy making the café a welcoming place for their customers. Yes, the changes had worked out well.

Charles and Maria felt financially secure again. Charles was able to take a little more time off work, but Maria, on the other hand, was probably a little overburdened. Even having a son who now did not need a lot of looking after, and a cleaner who ran the house, Maria didn't have enough time always to be able to be with Charles when he was off duty.

To Maria and Charles's joy, as Gregory broke up for the Christmas holidays, his last long holiday before his 'A' level examinations began, he told them that he had a conditional offer of a place at Cambridge University to read theology and philosophy. He explained that he had to get at least a B in music but an A in each of his other three subjects. Charles tried to hide his disappointment at his son's choice of subject for university studies. He couldn't really see of what use theology and philosophy could be to him.

Gregory, being no fool, read his father's thoughts.

"Papa, I expect you would have preferred me to have opted for English or history. But it is theology that really interests me. I must find out what the Prodigal Son story is really about. No one in this family will have a moment's peace until I do." They all laughed.

"And talking of the Prodigal Son," said Charles, "I spoke to Matthew this morning and David Neuberger will have lunch with us next Thursday."

Then Maria gave Gregory a big hug. "Congratulations, my clever son, I am so pleased for you."

"Yes," joined in Charles, "It's a wonderful achievement, Gregory, and one that you deserve. I am very proud of you."

"Papa, Mama, I'm not there yet! There's the big hurdle of the exams to be got over."

"You'll do it," Gregory's parents said simultaneously. They all laughed again. It was a long time since they had all been so happy and optimistic.

The following Thursday, about midday, David Neuberger arrived for lunch. It was a crisp, sunny day. He carried a bunch of flowers, obviously bought from a florist and handed them nonchalantly to Maria when she opened the door to him. A small man, a little overweight like his wife, Maria thought, but obviously the origin of the beautiful smiling eyes that she remembered as a characteristic of Raphael. His manner was confident and easy. He greeted Charles and Matthew, and when he faced Gregory he said, "I always remember you as a young lad at Raphael's Bar Mitzvah. You were so impressed by the observation you made that Hebrew is read backwards. Greetings, Gregory." They shook hands. Gregory wanted to ask about Raphael but stopped himself, thinking this was perhaps not an appropriate time.

They went into the sitting room. David Neuberger continued to chat easily. He politely refused the wine offered by Charles and said he would prefer water. He asked Gregory what he was studying and the two of them talked about the clarinet and their favourite composers for this instrument. Soon, Maria announced that lunch was ready.

The five of them sat at the kitchen table and the atmosphere over lunch remained light and relaxed, even when the conversation turned to more serious matters.

"Now tell me, Charles, where is it you come from?" David Neuberger put the question quite casually to his host but continued on without waiting for a reply. "I hail from Hamburg; I was born there and spent all my life there, apart from my years at university. I love that city. It's not really so very far from your home, is it, Charles?"

"No, not really. I was born in Posen, in Prussia as it was then and grew up there. My parents were German, my father a landowner in Posen. I went to university in Munich but chose Warsaw to try to establish myself as a lawyer."

"What was Warsaw like in those days? I suppose we are talking about the period between the wars?"

"Well, I am sure you know it was never a very peaceful part of the world. Germany, even then, as I set up my practice, regarded that part of Poland as rightfully hers and wanted to retrieve it as extra German territory or 'Lebensraum' as it was termed. Parts of Poland had been taken by us and then taken away again in the Versailles settlement. Russia also had its eyes on Polish territory. Racially, it was quite a mixed bag. There was a large community of Jews, but forgive me, David, I am never too sure whether to regard the Jewish people as a race or a religion."

"Me neither," said David with a laugh. He continued, "I don't know how you felt, Charles, but when Hitler began to show his intentions for Germany, that was when I realised the future for my family, being Jewish, was not only dangerous but impossible. I left and came to England."

The others sitting around the table continued with their meal. Maria offered David more fish, which he accepted. "This is delicious," he remarked.

"Matthew, Charles, Gregory?" Maria helped Mathew and Gregory to a second helping, but Charles declined. The vegetable dish was passed around.

"So, Charles, what happened to you when Germany became Nazi?" David gently, but firmly, encouraged Charles's narrative.

"I am rather ashamed to say that I paid little attention at first. I was too absorbed in my legal work and trying to establish myself, to take too much notice of the political scene. Then I met Maria, and she captured me with her loveliness." Charles smiled intimately at Maria, sitting next to him.

"It was of course after Germany invaded Poland, that it all escalated into a nightmare. As a professional man, it became obligatory that I join the Party, and I did, without any objections because I thought I would be able to continue with my legal practice without interference. How wrong I was. I think it might have been Hans Frank, who I had known at Munich, that gave my name to Himmler, and suddenly, I was catapulted into the Nazi uniform and given a lot of the responsibility for the 'Germanising' of Warsaw."

"What did that mean, Charles? What did it entail? You're talking, I think, about the Nazi plans to rid Poland of the people who had lived there for generations but who were regarded under the new regime in Germany, as 'untermenschen', racially and socially inferior. Were you aware that that was your job?"

Gregory looked anxiously at his father.

Maria stood. "May I suggest we move to the sitting room? It will be more comfortable there, and we can have our dessert with coffee a little later."

"Good idea, Maria," said David and followed Maria across the passage into the adjoining room. The others followed.

David took up his question again. "So, Charles, you got caught up in this 'Germanising' of Poland. Try to tell me what it entailed for you and how you felt about it."

"I remember that the Jewish people had always lived separately in a particular area of Warsaw, just like many people with a different culture do here in England today. We were used to that and paid little attention to them. Gradually, as Hitler's policies became more clearly defined, the life of that community became more difficult. I had to implement these policies. At first, it didn't concern me too much. Things happened gradually. First this right, then another would be taken away. I know it is no defence to claim I was only carrying out orders, but truly, I think every officer in a position of power was, in a way, himself a captive of Hitler. Still, the majority of us voted him into the chancellorship, so we all share the responsibility for what was done in his name."

Charles's head was lowered as though he was talking to himself.

"It was when I had to build a wall around the Jewish quarter that my conscience was awakened. I knew it was a way of forgetting these people and their sufferings. But I let it happen. No, that's not true. I wasn't passive, I organised it."

Charles was beginning to break down. His voice became strained.

"I knew that behind that wall families were slowly starving. Then typhus took hold."

Charles couldn't go on; tears began to flow down his cheeks. Maria started to speak, but David stopped her with a warning shake of his head.

"Charles, do you not see that your very distress at this moment, and the moral sensitivity you show, is your salvation?"

David noticeably slowed down. He wanted this lesson to go deeply into Charles's subconscious.

"You care deeply for all those poor families who suffered so cruelly behind that wall. Do you think that Himmler, or Frank, or the controllers of Auschwitz or Bergen-Belsen would have reacted the way you have when confronted with their actions in this systematic destruction of a people? Did you ever see a picture of one of them, ranged in those rows of accused at Nuremberg, sitting there weeping? No, but you saw Goering smiling, even laughing."

David's voice had once again become strong and insistent. He was determined to force answers from the man he was trying to help. He would not let go until he had made Charles acknowledge everything openly. The wound must be opened and cleansed before it could be healed.

All eyes were on Charles. Only he and Rabbi David Neuberger were in this room. It is possible that present too were hundreds and thousands of emaciated, dying, men, women and children. Certainly present was one small, dying, Jewish boy. Not one of them had a voice. David Neuberger spoke for them. He remained strong, unemotional and firm in what he was demanding from Charles, but never was he without compassion.

"Well, Charles, your tears tell me all I, and my people, need to know. Yes, it must be acknowledged that you bear some guilt. But I can understand the impossibility of your situation in that hell that was Warsaw. I have told you that I left Hamburg right at the beginning of the Nazi regime. I did not want to be on the receiving end of those evil policies. What did you do, Charles, as soon as you could? What did you do?"

The tension in this little room, in a small market town in Norfolk, was like a knife cutting through the hearts of each of those who sat there.

"I left. I got as far away from it all as I could."

David's continuing questioning seemed almost cruel. Gregory was not the only one in that room that longed to embrace his father and stop this relentless inquest.

Matthew, friend and doctor, watched Charles's slow disintegration into pain and discomfort. He knew that what Charles was going through was necessary, like a surgeon's knife is necessary to cut out a diseased area, but he felt deeply for his friend.

And Maria? Why, Maria did as she always did. She kept silent; but her deep love of Charles wanted his pain to be over as quickly as possible.

"And why did you do that, Charles?" This man was like a retriever dog with its quarry.

"I heard about the plans Himmler had for these camps where all the Jews would be taken. The purpose of them" – Charles hesitated, for even now it seemed an unthinkable thing – "the purpose of them was simply to kill every person they put there. I was utterly horrified and immediately began to plan how to escape. It wasn't a situation where you could simply hand in your notice."

There was silence in the room for a moment. The others present there began to feel thankful that this was perhaps almost over. But it wasn't. David pressed on.

"So you, like me, distanced yourself from these heinous crimes. Like me, your moral sensitivity was enraged by the Nazi policies. Like me, you came to England. You undertook journeys that no doubt were dangerous for you, but you wanted a new life, away from all that horror in Warsaw. Charles, both of us did the same; we firmly stepped aside, saying 'no' to Hitler and his murderous plans. For you, unlike me, it was difficult because you were already caught up in the web."

David Neuberger paused, his face softening.

"Charles, my friend, neither of us can change the past. We can live only in this present moment. Yes, I agree with you; you were, for a time, involved in dreadful crimes. What you did, or what you failed to do, cannot be erased. But as I said earlier, your salvation is your regret and your longing for forgiveness. In this case, forgiveness must be an intangible thing, for those who could grant it are dead. But I believe, and I beg you to believe it too, that a truly repentant human heart gives birth as a natural consequence, to a forgiveness that is healing and wholesome. Take hold of it, Charles. You are a good man. You don't need me to tell you that." David paused. The room was still and silent. Then David spoke again, deeming it right to break the tension now.

"He doesn't beat you does he, Maria?"

Maria laughed, everyone smiled, even Charles managed what could be called an almost-smile. Gregory picked up on the change of tone. He wanted to save his father any further agony.

"Could we have some dessert; I am absolutely longing for something sweet?"

Maria went out to the kitchen, and Matthew followed her, saying, "I'll help you, Maria."

David stood, stretched and said, "Whew, we've had our own Nuremberg here. Are you all right, Charles? Have you come through?" David slapped a hand on Charles's shoulder.

Charles actually was exhausted. "Yes, but I feel as though I have been torn to shreds. Thank you, David, thank you." Gregory went over and sat beside his father.

"You've served your time, Charles," said David. "These, twenty years almost, of carrying those heavy loads have been payment for the wrongs you did. You can go free now. Live your life, I beg you, be happy."

"Gregory," David went on, "I want you to be sure that your father relaxes over the next day or two. Don't let him think too much; just help him to recover from the battering I've given him. He will be fine in a little while, and don't let him forget to take the medicine Matthew prescribed."

And so the afternoon ended. David drove Matthew back to his surgery where his evening patients awaited him. Gregory excused himself, to get on with his studies, although he really wanted to stay with his father. Almost an adult now, he was sensitive enough to feel that his parents needed time alone. He went up to his room feeling a little lonely.

He had participated in his father's anguish every moment of that interrogation. He too felt spiritually exhausted. He sat in his easy chair and closed his eyes.

Downstairs, Charles and Maria were left alone.

"Shall we take a stroll around the farm, darling?" Maria suggested. "It would be good to get some fresh air."

They were surprised when late that evening Matthew reappeared.

"I had to come back," he told them. "I couldn't rest without being sure that you are all right, Charles."

Chapter Ten
A Happy Christmas Holiday, 1960

Over the next couple of weeks, Charles did gradually get better. His digestion settled, the pains disappeared, and he began to become once more, Charles at his best. Klaus joined them again for Christmas, and the family enjoyed a relaxed and happy time together.

Soon after Christmas, and whilst Gregory was still on holiday from school, the Hartmans received an invitation to dinner from the Neubergers. A little note was scribbled at the bottom saying that Raphael would be at home and was looking forward to seeing Gregory again.

And Gregory had another treat in store. Matthew had asked permission of Charles and Maria to take Gregory to London for the day, before school started and enveloped him in academics once more. It was a Christmas present. He planned to take Gregory to Mass at Westminster Cathedral, then lunch and afterwards a quick look at parliament before hopping on a bus to the Wigmore Hall. A performance of Carl Nielson's Wind Quintet was to be the highlight of this excursion.

"We'll have to make an early start," warned Matthew, "if we are to make it to morning Mass."

"I presume the wind quintet means that a clarinet will be one of the instruments?" Gregory had actually only been once before to a live concert, and that had been at the Royal Festival Hall with the Neubergers.

The day was a great success. Gregory was almost overwhelmed by the soaring and awesome atmosphere of the cathedral, and when Mass ended, he wanted to sit quietly soaking up the beauty of the experience. Matthew whispered that he would leave him alone for five minutes and see if he could buy a postcard of the interior to take home to his mother.

When they approached parliament and Big Ben, they had time only to look at the exterior and had to move straight on to find somewhere to eat.

The Wigmore Hall delighted Gregory. "Its entrance is so small, you wouldn't think it could be a concert hall," he remarked.

"Well, I agree. But then, it doesn't have great big orchestras here. The works are mainly chamber music, and it fits the lovely intimate atmosphere of the interior. You'll see. The acoustics are good too."

On the train back to Norfolk, Gregory turned over in his mind everything he had done that day.

"Uncle Matt," he said, "this has been a red-letter day for me, and I don't know how to thank you enough. I have never heard Nielsen's music before. It wasn't easy, but I liked it, especially because of its being only wind instruments. The way the instrumentalists listened and responded to one another, playing as though they were one instrument, was so very beautiful. I should like to hear much more chamber music. I'm not sure about Nielsen though, I'd like to hear more of his work to see if it really appeals to me. I can't help comparing it with the jazz I heard at the Festival Hall. I prefer classical music, and I think chamber music may be my favourite of all. I love being able to hear each individual instrument at the same time as hearing the overall melody they make. It is very beautiful."

"Well, who knows, Gregory, maybe one day that will be you, playing your clarinet in a quartet or quintet at the Wigmore Hall."

Gregory's voice was serious. "I don't think so, Uncle Matt. I have other things to do."

Matthew said nothing, but later he thought, and wondered, about Gregory's words.

The day before Gregory's return to school, the family squeezed into Matthew's car and made their way to the Neuberger's home. It was quite a spacious house, even elegant, with a half-circle drive where they parked. They did not need to ring the bell for as the family stepped out of the car, David Neuberger opened the door. The warm golden lights of the interior flooded out onto the early-winter darkness of the drive. It was very welcoming.

"Come on in," said David. He took their coats and ushered them into a large front room, which seemed to be a library as well as a sitting room. Books lined one wall, and a fire was burning in the grate. Several bottles of wine, both red and white, and glasses, sat on the coffee table. Charles placed with them the bottles of champagne he had brought. Sara came in and running footsteps were heard coming down the stairs. Raphael burst in and the greetings all merged into almost a maelstrom of hugs and 'hellos'.

When they sorted themselves out, they all sat down and David turned his attention to wine. Although there were plenty of formal sitting spaces, the boys sat on the floor either side of the fire and quietly engaged in their own conversation, a long time overdue. Matthew couldn't help thinking how glad he was that he had brought these two families more closely together. Everyone was relaxed and happy and the conversation flowed easily, punctuated by laughter.

"Red or white?" David went around the group offering wine. "Sara, please would you put this champagne into the fridge? The main course is salmon by the way, just in case you are fussy about drinking the right colour wine with the right food." David grinned.

A voice from the fireplace piped up, "White, please. I'm fussy." It was Raphael, with his smiling eyes. To everyone's surprise, his father picked up a glass, poured a small amount of white wine into it and handed it to Raphael without any comment. "And you, Gregory?"

Gregory glanced over at his mother before answering, "Yes, please. And I'm going to be fussy too."

The evening passed as it had begun, a group of people who could now be called friends, comfortable with one another and enjoying being together. It was Raphael, as they were seated around the dining room table, who then addressed everybody.

"Do you know, it's really quite a miracle, but Gregory and I have both applied to Cambridge. If we get there, we'll be reading in different disciplines, but just think, we'll be at the same university. We end as we began. Together! That's if we make it through our 'A' levels," he said with a grimace.

"Goodness me" – David laughed – "this could be the end of this revered institution. Raphael and Gregory. Double trouble for Cambridge!"

Gregory thought he would pitch into this medley of jokes.

"Not at all! Perhaps just a Double First for Cambridge! You know, Rabbi Neuberger, if you had not become a rabbi, you would have made a very good comedy actor." Everybody's laughter, including that of the rabbi himself, seemed to indicate that they all agreed with Gregory's observation and probably also, his joke.

Dessert, a beautiful almond cake, was served with the offer of a glass of champagne to accompany it. "You can't do better," said David, "It's Krug, courtesy of our guests. Now, I have to make a confession." For a moment everyone thought that something serious was about to be declared. But no. David went on, "It is, I think, entirely my fault that young Gregory here has opted to read theology. It was the Bar Mitzvah that did it. He couldn't get over the fact that Hebrew is written from right to left or backwards as he saw it. Now he has decided to learn how to read it too."

The following Wednesday, as usual, Matthew arrived at the farmhouse about half-past-four and took the opportunity to stroll around the farm with Gregory as soon as he got in from school. The weather was too cold to be out long so they went indoors and sat together in the sitting room. Matthew was glad of the time alone with Gregory, for what his godson had said about having 'other things to do' had stayed with him and an unexplainable anxiety accompanied its remembrance. Matthew loved this boy and wanted him to be happy. He asked Gregory about what he had meant.

"Well, Uncle Matt, I haven't discussed this with anyone at all yet, but for a long time now, I have been thinking that I would like to join the Benedictine Community at Quidenham. In fact, I have been thinking about it ever since I stayed with them."

Matthew felt shocked but tried to remain calm and not show Gregory his true feelings. "You want to be a monk?"

"Yes, Uncle Matt, I do. I feel called to the religious life, perhaps also to the priesthood. I feel as though it's the very best thing I could do with my life. It's a certain kind of feeling, a certainty inside me that brings a sense of wholeness and peace. I expect it's hard for you to understand."

"Not really, Gregory, it's not unlike my own commitment to medicine. But of course, the religious life is a very special undertaking, because you embrace a life without a wife and children. That is a massive thing to commit yourself to, a huge loss. I understand completely your fascination with theology, but living a monastic life is another matter. It's a big step. It must be a hard way of life. You are very dear to me, Gregory, and I want you to have a happy and fulfilled life. If that is to be by way of the rule of St Benedict, you would certainly have my blessing. And that is on one condition."

Gregory's face showed a little apprehension.

"Please, go to Cambridge, or wherever, and complete your studies. Pray, reflect, consider carefully the vocation to which you feel yourself called. After these three years, if you feel the same, then you must go ahead. May I suggest,

Gregory, that you do not tell your parents until you are quite sure about that decision. I think it will be hard for them to accept, particularly your father." Matthew embraced his godson. "I am privileged to have been told these plans of yours, Gregory. I will keep you in my prayers."

"Thank you, Uncle Matt, thank you for your understanding. I have every intention of completing my studies. I feel sure, anyway, the monastery wouldn't take me unless they felt confident that I had thought and prayed about it for quite some time."

Chapter Eleven
New Horizons

Examination time came around. Gregory returned from his music paper feeling quite content. "I was able to write about the Nielson Quintet," he told his parents. A few days later, and he came into the farmhouse with a rather glum face. "I think I messed up the question on the community and the individual. It was not until the last few moments left to me that I realised what the question was really about, and I scribbled another paragraph, which I think hit the mark. But it may not have been enough. I've messed up the religion paper."

Gregory was glum and obviously disappointed and annoyed with himself. His mother tried to console him. "Put it behind you, Gregory. You may have done better than you think. Just concentrate now on your next paper. It's English, isn't it?"

When the day came for this subject, Gregory returned seeming quite happy about what he had done. When it came to history, the last of his papers, he told his parents it had been very difficult. "I very much doubt if I've got the grades I need for Cambridge," he told them.

The summer wore on and the day of the results came around. Gregory went into school with a somewhat heavy heart. He returned to find his parents sitting in the kitchen, a long white unopened envelope on the table. Gregory couldn't manage to keep a serious face as he had planned.

"I've done it, Papa. Mama, I've done it. I got four straight A's. I can't believe it." For a few moments, there was a chaotic scene in the kitchen, with hugs and kisses all around and in some cases, a few tears of joy.

"Perhaps I had better open this letter," said Gregory, when order was restored. "Maybe school got it wrong." He opened the envelope, then nodded with a smile. "No, it's true."

After lunch, the telephone rang. "It's Uncle Matthew," said Maria, handing Gregory the telephone. Soon after, it rang again. This time, Gregory picked it up. Maria and Charles heard only one side of the conversation.

"Yes. Oh, that's wonderful. Congratulations. Your parents must be pleased. Yes, me too. Yes, four straight A's. I am absolutely amazed. Yes, that would be nice; let's do it. Okay. Bye for now."

Maria asked him to whom he had been speaking. "It was Raff," said Gregory, "and we are going to plan a day together in Cambridge, to get a feel for the place. We both got four A's, so that's where we are heading. Cambridge, here we come!"

"Don't forget to write to Uncle Klaus and let him know your results, Gregory. You promised him you would."

"Yes, Mama, of course I will."

Towards the end of the summer, Michael Collins and Charles started to consider once again, how they might make use of the stables. Michael had the idea that ripping out the stalls, putting in good flooring and heating, having new windows, would make an exercise space.

"Yoga is becoming all the rage," Michael told Charles. "Mostly, women go to these classes once a week, and no doubt they would stop for refreshments afterwards and maybe do a little shopping. It's worth thinking about."

Charles said he would find out what the changes to the building would cost. Michael pointed out that they would have to consider whether or not to employ a teacher or to let that person run the classes and pay a hire fee for the premises. When Charles talked it over with Maria, she said that she liked the idea of making use of the stables but that they should also consider other possibilities for it.

"Like what?" was Charles's question.

"Well, another possibility would be an art studio, or you could even do cookery classes, although you would have to install quite a lot of furniture and equipment. It might not be economically worth it."

In the end, they decided on the yoga, which they had realised also needed the building of a toilet block. They thought that at the same time they should build an extension to the Tea Shop, for the extra activities might bring more customers for tea or coffee. Maria had already taken on a young woman who she was training in the art of bread and cake making. She thought they might need to get some help for Pauline, for she'd lost Ethel's help and was now going to be asked to do more. In the end, they decided that it might be better to wait and see how things developed before committing themselves to another member of staff. Their new plans would be quite expensive to carry out. It was a risk, thought Charles. On the other hand, it would provide employment in times which were still not very easy for people.

The following Wednesday morning, Charles got a call from Matthew. He wanted to know if he could bring a guest with him to their usual evening meal together. Charles said that would present no problem but immediately went over to the bakery to tell Maria, in case it caused her any catering difficulties. Maria said that she could cope with it, but together they both wondered who this extra guest would be. Matthew did not arrive early as he usually did, but his car drew up at the farmhouse at about six o'clock. To come by car was also unusual. All was explained when a woman got out of the passenger seat. Maria opened the door to them.

"This is Jenny, Maria. Jenny, may I introduce you to Maria." Matthew beamed, not only with the pleasure of introducing his friend but in the knowledge of the surprise he was causing.

"Please come in both of you." Maria took them into the sitting room. "Charles will be in in a few minutes."

Maria put her head out of the door and called up the stairs, "Gregory, Uncle Matt is here." A rush of feet banging down the stairs, followed by Gregory almost falling into the sitting room, heralded his appearance. He pulled up short, and in a slightly more restrained manner, he greeted Matthew.

"Gregory," said Matthew, "I want to introduce you to my friend Jenny, actually Doctor Jennifer Sullivan. And also to give you a special hug for your 'A' level results."

"Congratulations, Gregory, I'd like to hear about your study plans a little later." Jenny also gave Gregory a hug.

Just then, they heard the opening of the back door, and in came Charles. A huge beam spread over his face as he was introduced to Jenny.

"Well, Matthew you have quite a lot of explaining to do. Where have you been hiding this beautiful woman?" Indeed, the adjective suited her. Slim, almost athletic in build, with short, beautifully cut auburn hair, Charles thought she was probably at least twenty years Matthew's junior, if not more.

"I'll just see to some wine," said Charles. "Don't say anything until I get back. I don't want to miss any of this Matthew."

When Charles came in with the wine and glasses, Matthew explained that Jenny had joined the practice a month or so ago, and they found that they got on well.

"Matthew, I don't think that will satisfy your friends." Jenny smiled at Matthew. "I know a lot about you, Charles and Maria, and of course Gregory, so it is right that I should tell you a little about myself. I come from Bressingham, where my parents still live, and where at the moment I am also staying. I did my medical training in London. I specialise in paediatrics and when I heard that the practice here was wanting to add a specialist in childcare to its staff, I applied for the job. I've been here now…how long have I been here, Matthew?"

"Oh dear, does it already seem like a lifetime to you?" Matthew smiled questioningly at Jenny.

The intimacy of their smiles convinced Charles that either Jenny had been in Diss for quite a while, or that they already knew one another rather well.

The evening passed happily, and when Matthew and Jenny left, the family sat looking at one another, each waiting for the other to say something. It was Charles who broke the silence. "Well, that was certainly a surprise; something I'd never imagined would happen."

"I hope they will be happy together, Papa. Uncle Matt is such a dear man."

Then Maria gave her view. "I liked her very much. They seem to me to be ideally suited, although there is quite an age difference. Still, it's the right way around. It is wonderful that Matthew has found someone to share his life with. He deserves to be happy. Charles, I think you should ring Matthew tomorrow and say how much we enjoyed meeting Jenny and that she is welcome to come to our usual Wednesday evenings with him. In fact, I think you should say that we'll expect her next week if they want to come."

"Now he's got Jenny, Uncle Matt might not want to come every week to be with us," said Gregory.

"I think he will," said Charles.

About the middle of September, the farm was invaded by workmen beginning to carry out the changes Charles had decided upon. As the bills came in at various stages of the operation, Charles began to wonder if he would regret this decision. Sometimes he found himself thinking about Ethel and wondering what she would have said about the new developments. Maria thought about the extra work it might cause for the bakery but managed to convince herself that the new girl she was training was proving competent and increasingly creative, and that they would cope. Michael Collins did an excellent job in organising the various stages of the work, whilst Charles made enquiries about a yoga teacher. Charles was actually doing much less work on the farm these days because Michael was taking on more responsibilities.

At this time, just before Gregory was due to leave for Cambridge, a letter arrived from Germany for him.

"It's from Uncle Klaus." There was silence as Gregory read it and a moment of silence as he closed the letter back into the envelope. Maria waited to see if he was going to share its contents with her.

"Mama, he is sending me money; he says to be sure I will be all right if any emergency arises whilst I am in Cambridge. I have to let him know my bank account details, and he will transfer one thousand pounds into it. One thousand pounds, Mama! I don't know what to say. Have I got a bank account? It is so generous." Gregory stood, looking at the envelope in his hand.

"Gregory, it is more than generous. How very thoughtful of him. When your father comes in, we'll tell him, and he will advise you about opening an account, which you should have in any case, now that you're going to be away from home. What a very kind man."

"I must write straightaway and say thank you."

Maria was thinking how wrong she had been in concluding, when she had first met Klaus, that perhaps he was not as kind a man as Charles.

When Charles came in for coffee, Gregory handed him the letter. Charles read it.

"That is more than generous, Gregory. You're a lucky young man."

Charles advised Gregory to go to the bank in Diss and open an account. He gave Gregory fifty pounds as an initial deposit and Gregory went into Diss that afternoon and did all that was necessary to have a bank account in his own name.

"I'm someone to be reckoned with now, Papa, would you like a loan?" They all laughed, but both Charles and Maria were glad to know that Gregory was starting out on an independent life with some money in the bank.

Life at Trinity Hall seemed to suit Gregory very well. He immersed himself in his work, loved learning Hebrew and Greek but made time for recreation too, often with Raphael who was reading sciences. Raphael took up rowing, Gregory joined the Music Club, and they both signed up for the Debating Society. Raphael, to Gregory's surprise, turned out to be quite a socialite although the fashionable company he kept seemed mostly to be of the feminine variety. Quite often, Gregory would see him with a girl and not very often the same one twice. He seemed a very popular student.

It was at the Music Club where Gregory met his first girlfriend. Lucy played the oboe and was actually a music student. She and Gregory became good friends. Lucy lived just outside Cambridge and sometimes Gregory would be invited to her home to share in Sunday lunch. In the holidays, Lucy sometimes went to Diss to spend a few days on the farm with Gregory and his family. They certainly made a good pair, and it is likely that both families waited to see if anything permanent would develop. Matthew was pleased to see the pair of them happy and relaxed together but kept his counsel.

A little before Christmas, one Wednesday evening at dinner, Matthew and Jenny told Charles and Maria that they had decided to marry. Maria wanted to say that she hoped they were sure, that they hadn't known one another very long, but when she saw their obvious joy, she could only join with Charles in heartfelt congratulations. Jenny had slipped so easily into the family, that it seemed a natural development that she should become Matthew's wife. Jenny told them that on Sunday they were going to have lunch with her parents and would tell them the news then. She said she hoped that, as Matthew didn't have parents living, Charles and Maria would soon afterwards meet Mr and Mrs Sullivan.

"I know Matthew regards you both as his family," she said.

"Perhaps you could invite your parents here, Jenny. We could have our usual Wednesday evening with them, if that were convenient." Maria glanced at Charles who nodded his agreement. The happiness around the table that evening could not be doubted.

"Where will you be married? Have you fixed a date yet?" Now came all the practical questions. But, in a way, these were questions that didn't matter. All four of them were so happy, that Charles and Maria could only rejoice in the love that was so obvious between the couple. They were both so pleased that Matthew had, at last, found someone he loved with whom to share his life.

Matthew tried to answer the questions. "We'll be married at the Benedictine Church, although Jenny isn't Catholic. We have seen Father Andrew, and we've to meet with him regularly before the ceremony, but we haven't fixed a date yet. We won't do that until we have told Jenny's parents. It is possible that her father will not give his permission." Matthew made this last point quite seriously, although no one else took it as such.

"How could he possibly refuse? His daughter is marrying the most good-looking man in Norfolk," Charles said this with a twinkle in his eye.

"I'm not marrying him for his looks," retorted Jenny. "They're just a bonus." Everyone knew she meant it.

Then Matthew, planting a kiss on Jenny's cheek said mischievously, "But I am certainly marrying the most beautiful woman in the country, for her looks but also for all her other wonderful attributes."

Maria pretended to look hurt. "Ah, well, that tells me where I stand." They all laughed.

"Will you tell Gregory when you next speak with him?" Matthew asked. "It would be lovely if he could come when Jenny's parents are here, but I don't suppose that would be possible."

"Of course, we'll tell him just as soon as we can get in touch with him. I'm sure he will want to come to meet your parents, Jenny, but we'll have to settle the date with them first and then see if he can make it. Of course, he'll soon be home for Christmas, so as that's not so very far away, we might be able to arrange for us all to be together to celebrate when he gets home. What do you think, Maria?"

That night, lying awake in bed, Maria told Charles how very happy she was that Matthew had found someone like Jenny to love. "He deserves this happiness, Charles. I hope they will be as happy as we are."

Charles rang Gregory the next day, leaving a message with one of the students whose rooms were on Gregory's corridor. When Gregory rang back later that afternoon, Charles told him Matthew's good news. Gregory was amazed and delighted. Charles told him what they were planning with regard to a meeting with Jenny's parents. He asked Gregory that if they made it at the beginning of the Christmas vacation, so that he could be present, would he like to bring Lucy.

When Charles reported their conversation to Maria, he said, "When I asked him if he would like to bring Lucy to the dinner with the Sullivans, he said no because she isn't family, and he would not want to mislead her regarding his intentions towards her. I was rather surprised. I thought he liked her."

"Well, Charles, he does like her. But that doesn't mean he wants to marry her." In her heart, Maria was pleased that her son showed such consideration towards his friend, but a small seed of anxiety sowed itself within her mind.

It was not possible to make the meeting with the Sullivans before Christmas, and because Matthew and Jenny had fixed their wedding for January 20, the two families met for the first time at the ceremony. It seemed that almost everyone from the surgery at Diss had turned up, but even so, it was not a huge event. Maria found herself thinking of Matthew's parents and brother. Charles was Matthew's best man and Mr Sullivan gave his only daughter away. Jenny wore a simple white dress, ankle-length, with a coronet of fresh flowers in her hair. She carried a similar flower arrangement as a posy. She looked beautiful and radiant, her shining auburn hair complementing the crisp white of her dress.

After the ceremony, Dr Matthew and Dr Jennifer Hall received their guests at a lovely old farmhouse hotel near Bressingham, close to the bride's family home. Matthew and Jenny had decided to postpone a honeymoon because in the winter months it was hard for the practice to spare two of its doctors. So, after the reception was over and everyone had had plenty of time to talk, the couple slipped away to Matthew's home, now their home, looking forward to a couple of days alone. They would be back at work on Monday. However, on the following Wednesday, they knew they were expected, together with Mr and Mrs Sullivan, as guests of Charles and Maria, together with David and Sara Neuberger. Both Gregory and Raphael would be there too.

Back at Trinity, as 1962 got underway, Gregory found the work he was doing that term on the Dead Sea Scrolls difficult but fascinating. It fed into work on the period when both Judaism and Christianity were defining themselves each against the other. He wished he could read Aramaic and wondered about taking it on as an additional subject. His tutor thought not in his first year. Gregory spent a lot of time just sitting and thinking. He found the course so stimulating and interesting that he began to mix socially less and less. He had found a niche in the Catholic Chaplaincy but at the expense of time spent in the Music Club. Consequently, the meetings with Lucy were not so frequent. Sometimes Raphael would come and drag him out to make up a foursome; occasionally, he and Raphael would take a stroll along the river and stop somewhere for a beer. Gregory did not arrange his life with any conscious consideration of what he hoped to do when he finished at Trinity. But as he matured, he felt secure in his sense of vocation. He felt that as much as he was enjoying his studies, there was always present the knowledge that above all he did, there hovered a higher purpose.

As the summer months came around, work at the farm neared completion. It began to feel like a real centre for excellence. The yoga studio was beautiful, and gradually, the frequency of its use increased. Maria was proved right in thinking that women would come to the Tea Shop after class for refreshment and business here increased too. Charles had decided to give fresh fish a try, and a man came twice a week and set up a stall with all kinds of fresh fish available. It proved popular. Fruit and vegetables remained a good selling range, along with the dairy produce, so the farm continued to prosper. Charles now left most of the daily overseeing to Michael and just kept the accounts up to date. He began to interest himself in garden horticulture, utilising one of the greenhouses for his seedlings and gradually designing and building small plots around the picnic area. Bob's garden, with its bench, remained exclusive to the family, but Charles took it on himself to grow the plants with which he wanted to stock it.

Matthew and Jenny kept up the routine of dinner at the farmhouse on Wednesdays, except that occasionally Matthew would come alone because Jenny needed to be at the surgery. On one of the occasions when they were there together, looking particularly happy and excited, they told Charles and Maria that they were expecting a baby early in the autumn. Naturally, this was a cause for much celebration. Jenny told Maria that she would work only part-time once the baby was born, hoping her mother would be able to help out a bit with baby-minding when she needed to be at the surgery.

That summer, Gregory went off to Italy with Raphael. Neither sets of parents heard much from them, just an occasional postcard would arrive telling Charles and Maria that they were in Venice, and a week or so later, David and Sara would ring Charles to say that their boys were apparently now in Rome. Gregory actually wrote a letter from there telling his parents about his attendance at a public audience with the Pope. To have seen John XXIII, even from quite a distance, was obviously for Gregory a highlight. They returned with a little time to spare at home before they were off once again to Cambridge to start their second year. For Gregory, a large part of his work this year centred on textual studies. One week, his tutor set him Luke Chapter Fifteen on which he was required to give a detailed exegesis. *At last!* thought Gregory. *Just wait until I am next at home, the family is going to hear all about this! I can now claim to be an authority on The Prodigal Son!*

On September 30, Jenny gave birth to a daughter, the arrival a little earlier than expected. There were a few difficulties at first with the child's feeding, but gradually, these were sorted out and the new parents began the long process of getting to know their little girl. They called her Emily, and in due course, another family gathering was arranged for her baptism at the Monastery Church. Jenny said that having married in the Catholic Church, she thought it quite appropriate that the baby be baptised there too. The couple had agreed that she be brought up within the Catholic tradition, very much Jenny's decision, because she had no strong feelings against it and was happy to go along with Matthew's wishes. A little over a year later, a baby brother arrived for Emily, still of course very much a baby herself. They called the little boy Sebastian.

Charles was amused. "They aren't wasting any time," was his observation. Jenny now gave up work for a while but was assiduous in keeping up with ongoing research in child development.

With so much attention being paid to these two new little ones, time passed quickly. In the early summer of 1964, Gregory graduated with an Upper Second, whilst Raphael stayed on to pursue further studies. Gregory was impressed that Raphael seemed to be taking seriously his childhood desire to go to the moon. He was going to study astrophysics. For a while, Gregory explored what was happening on the farm and helped his father with the new gardens. He went to Sunday Mass at the Monastery Church, sometimes with Maria. Inevitably, after a few weeks, the subject turned to what he intended to do next. It happened to be a Wednesday evening with Matthew and Jenny present, when the question arose as they sat at dinner. Charles broached the subject in a light-hearted manner.

"Well, Matthew and Jenny, Maria and I are waiting to hear from Gregory what he plans to do next. Neither of us has picked up any hints; I don't know if you have." Matthew smiled but made no comment.

Charles continued his interrogation good-naturedly, "Well, Gregory, can your mother and I let your bedroom out or not?"

Gregory thought it best to be direct. "It will no doubt come as a surprise to you, but I have decided, in fact I decided a long time ago, to seek entry to the Benedictine Community. I know it will come—"

Gregory was cut short by his father's reaction. "You've decided what? You want to be a monk?" Charles's hands gripped the edge of the table. For a second, Matthew thought he was going to overturn it.

"Yes, Papa, that is what I want." Gregory's voice was even and gentle.

"Did you know about this?" demanded Charles, glaring at Maria but not waiting for an answer. "So, you spent all that time at Cambridge, just to end up a bloody monk." The tone was disparaging.

"Charles, please calm down," pleaded Maria. "Gregory, I hope you have thought about this very carefully. You know, it is a big step to take. You'll not be able to marry. I believe it is not an easy life. Are you sure you are suited for it?"

"Easy life," snorted Charles. "What could be easier? No responsibilities. No duties. What do they do all day in that place?"

Charles pushed back his chair from the table, making a scraping noise on the tiled floor. The others thought he was going to walk out. Actually, Charles did not know how to deal with this. He remained seated, but he glared at everyone.

"As Gregory's godparent, may I be allowed to say something?"

Matthew looked at Charles and Maria. He went on. "Gregory is an adult now, and I do not think we should be telling him how he should live the rest of his life. He is very greatly loved by us all, and of course, we want him to be happy, whatever he does. But it is his life, Charles, not yours. So long as he has thought very carefully about it, I think he should have our blessing."

"He gets no blessing from me." Charles reached for the bottle of wine and poured himself another glass, still glowering at everyone.

"There's a whole wide world out there, with opportunities for a young man with your qualifications Gregory. Please." Charles's voice trembled with emotion, and softened. "Please don't waste your life." His plea to his son was heartfelt and deeply moving. It was Jenny who placed her hand on Charles's, whether in solidarity or compassion it would be hard to tell.

"Papa, Mama, Uncle Matt, Jenny, I know, yes, I understand very well that it seems to you like a waste of life. It seems that way to you because you are not called to it. But I feel that I am, and I must test it out. I love you all very dearly, and certainly, this will be a difficult break. I'll not see much of you, nor of my new little" – Gregory stopped, genuinely nonplussed as to his relationship with Matthew's offspring – "well, let's just say Emily and Sebastian. But you see I feel that it is God that has called me to this way of life. I must respond to that call."

"Gregory, I do not think it is a waste of life, my son." Maria was looking at Gregory with tender love. "My only concern, except my sadness at what will inevitably be the loss of you, is that you are as sure as you can be that this is right for you. If you think you have that certainty, then you will go with my blessing and many tears." Maria got up from her chair to embrace her son. "Why don't we go to the sitting room, and I'll bring in some coffee."

Matthew, Jenny and Gregory moved, but Charles stayed with Maria in the kitchen.

"Did you know about this?" he asked in a rather demanding tone.

"No, Charles, I didn't, although I have had, from time to time, the feeling that Gregory was not going to follow any ordinary path through life."

"Well, he has knocked me for six. I am disappointed, a bit angry, and frankly, Maria, I just don't know how to deal with it."

"Maybe, Charles, we deal with it by letting Gregory guide us through it. For both of us, it is almost totally unexpected and an unknown." Maria picked up the tray. "Let's take the coffee in."

In the sitting room, Matthew, not himself without sadness and disquiet, embraced Gregory. "You know, Gregory, that you have my blessing and my love, always. No matter what you do. Be gentle with your father; it is hard for him to understand this. He'll come around, in time."

Jenny hugged him. "I admire you, Gregory," was all she could say.

Maria and Charles came in with the tray of coffee and some chocolates. They all sat and looked at each other. Matthew broke the silence as Maria poured the coffee.

"The four of us have come a long way together; it began a long time before you came on the scene, darling." Matthew glanced at Jenny. "You weren't around either, Gregory; well, I suppose you were in a way. But you weren't yet born. I remember our first meeting at my private practice in Diss. I was very impressed by your determination, I remember, Charles. Maria, you had no English then. Just think of what you have accomplished in these twenty odd years. And the greatest thing is to have reared this wonderful boy here."

"Yes, he is a young man to be proud of," said Charles, trying hard to be positive but meaning what he said. "But I have to say, Gregory, that I am deeply disappointed by what you have told us this evening." He paused and then asked the question that he really dreaded asking, "And when will you go to the monastery?"

"It is arranged that I enter on August 6. That's tomorrow week, Papa."

"The Feast of the Transfiguration," mused Maria. "Oh, Gregory, that's not far away."

"Why don't we try to make this next week a very special time? Let's plan to spend as much time with Gregory as we can and do some things together that we will always remember." Matthew was trying to bring something positive to the evening, understanding at once how difficult this last week with Gregory could be for all of them. To his surprise, Charles took up the suggestion immediately.

"We should do that. We don't want to mope around and waste the last few days we have together. Obviously, Gregory has made his mind up. I shall always regret it, I know. I am sorry, my son, if I reacted badly, I had such high hopes of you, and I can't see the value of the life you are planning. But I must accept it. As Matthew said, it is your choice. Now, what do we want to do over the next week? Can we arrange some time off, Maria? And would somebody please pass those chocolates, or are they just for decoration? Come on, Gregory my lad, tuck in, you might not get much chance of such frivolities in the future."

They all laughed and Maria passed the chocolates around, wanting to hug Charles for the effort he was making.

They decided that by tomorrow the four of them would have arranged some time free of their normal routines and would let each other know the time they could be available.

"Do you think it would be a good idea to ask Gregory if there is anything special, he would like to do?" asked Maria.

"Mama, just being with you is special. But I would like to see Rabbi Neuberger, and if we could spend an afternoon at the sea, I'd love that. A day in London again? Could we do that? And I would like to spend some time with Emily and Sebastian if Jenny can arrange it. Perhaps one afternoon we could all have a picnic tea in Bob's garden? And do you know what I would really love to do? I'd like to go to the zoo again, just to see what I might have done with my life!" This last request brought laughter from everyone, for they all remembered his childhood wish to be a zookeeper.

They all thought that on Sunday they could be free and would go to Cromer to spend the day by the sea. Jenny would bring the babies, and Maria said she would make up picnic baskets. Gregory would spend most of Monday with David and Sara Neuberger if they were available, and with Maria busy in the bakery on Saturday, it was agreed that Gregory, Matthew and Charles would go to London for the day. Matthew told Charles he might have to put up with a visit to Westminster Cathedral, which he felt sure Gregory would want to see again, and he would book tickets for a concert at the Royal Festival Hall for the evening.

"Mama," said Gregory, "could you be free either tomorrow or Friday, to go to Bressingham with me? There are some lovely gardens there I'd like to see. We could go just for the morning, or afternoon, so you could still do what must be done for the Tea Shop." Gregory wanted to be sure to have some time alone with his mother. He wanted to tell her how very much he appreciated the quiet but unwavering support she always gave his father. Gregory had grown to understand that without her, his father's life might have been very bleak indeed. He knew that she was really the strength that had enabled his father to achieve success in his work and contentment at home.

"There can be no debate about what we'll do on your last evening at home," said Charles. "It's a Wednesday, isn't it? So, we'll all be together here for our usual dinner." His voice began to crack.

He got up abruptly and left the room, obviously upset.

"I should leave him," said Matthew as Maria was about to follow him. "He's doing very well and trying hard to cope. Now it seems to me that we have quite a lot arranged. If I were you, Gregory, I would speak to David as soon as you can about Monday, because he'll be busy over Sabbath, and you might not get him on the telephone."

Charles came back in, now under better control. Gregory embraced him, and they stood together facing Matthew, Jenny and Maria, Gregory's arm around his father's waist. Gregory looked at them.

"No one could have a better family than I have been blessed with. Thank you all for the way in which you have each tried to cope with what has been a very difficult Wednesday evening. Let's try not to be sad. When I go next week, you will each go with me and remain with me, in my heart always. My beloved family."

"You will, after all, only be just up the road." Then Maria realised what a silly remark that was, for he might just as well be in Australia.

Thursday, August 6, came around very quickly. It had been arranged that Matthew would drive Gregory to the monastery but that neither Charles nor Maria would go. Gregory hugged his parents, bidding his father take good care of his mother. Then it was into the car and away. The journey was not a long one. Gregory was feeling nervous, not knowing quite what he would face once he went through the big wooden gates that bounded the monastery's private gardens. As he got out of the car, Matthew walked around to him and embraced him.

"May God bless and keep you, dear Gregory." Matthew found it hard to breathe evenly, so deeply touched was he by this separation.

"Thank you, Uncle Matt. Please will you keep an eye on Mama and Papa for me?"

Gregory resolutely walked away, a small case in his hand, went to the big gates and knocked soundly. As Matthew drove away, he saw the gates swing open and Gregory disappear inside.

Gregory walked through the gate and saw only a group of the community standing there ready to welcome him.

Chapter Twelve
A Bleak Day

After Gregory's departure, Maria and Charles tried to make sure that they had things to do each day. Their feeling of loss brought them closer and lifted the love they had for one another from the everyday to something very special. They would sometimes just lie on the settee together, mostly silent, each being the comfort and support of the other. When Charles was busy, Jenny made sure she asked Maria to go over to help her with the children, and when Maria's presence for long hours in the bakery was necessary, somehow or other Matthew managed to arrange his time at the surgery so that he could be with Charles for at least a part of the day.

Matthew continued to spend Wednesday evenings with them, and very often, Charles went to Sunday lunch with Jenny and Matthew, Maria coming later in the day when the Tea Shop was quieter. Maria was always delighted to be able to play with Emily and Sebastian on these occasions, and their presence helped both her and Charles.

Maria found that when she was alone, sitting on the bench in Bob's garden was a calming thing to do. She remembered how as a little boy Gregory had loved to sit there with Ethel.

For the first few weeks, Maria could not bring herself to go to Mass at the monastery and went to the Mass centre instead. Matthew too was there. Each understood but did not talk about the reason for their presence there, rather than at the monastery.

Then, early in September, a letter came addressed to Mr and Mrs Hartman. It was from Gregory. It is likely that never had a letter been received by them both with such joy. He told them a little about what he was doing and how he was finding life in the monastery, and he said that he was missing them. But for both Charles and Maria, it was the feeling it gave them that there was still a contact between them and their son that gave them the greatest pleasure. It eased the pain of separation they had been experiencing ever since they had said goodbye to him.

"Do you think we are allowed to reply?" Charles asked.

"Of course. He's not in a prison. He has written to us, and we will reply. But not too soon. Let's just enjoy the anticipation of it."

At Christmas, Charles and Maria spent the holiday with Matthew and Jenny. Klaus had told them that he would be spending a few days at The Sacher Hotel in Vienna enjoying the opera. The presence of the children at Matthew and Jenny's home kept the atmosphere busy and full of fun. Mr and Mrs Sullivan were there too on Christmas Day.

Soon after, David and Sara Neuberger invited them to dinner. Maria was glad that Raphael was not there. Charles, sitting with David and Sara, a glass of wine in his hand, a roaring log fire in the grate, felt relaxed and comfortable. He could not help reflecting on the fact that this Jewish couple were friends, and that although they knew his background, they were still happy to spend time with him. David probably knew more detail about his past, he thought, than any other person. Yet, like Matthew, they were friends. Charles felt that he did not deserve it.

As Charles and Maria left, Charles, obviously maintaining only the most fragile of holds on his emotion, faced David and after a moment gazing at him, embraced him.

"Thank you, David," he whispered, "thank you, Rabbi David." There was a noticeable stress on the word rabbi. "Thank you for your friendship when you might so easily have shunned me."

When Sara and David closed the door behind their guests, David, his arm around his wife, said, "Charles is a man whose emotions go deep. I think there is still much healing to be done there."

As the New Year began, both Maria and Charles felt thankful to have some peaceful time at home again, although they were appreciative of all their friends had done to help them through their initial feeling of loss at Gregory's departure and his absence at what was usually a family occasion.

It was one morning early in January, a somewhat bleak and dreary-looking day, that Maria, washing up the breakfast things in the kitchen, looked out of the window and saw two men, dressed in city suits, walking up the pathway. Charles was in the sitting room. As the doorbell rang, it was Charles who was first to get to the door and open it.

"Karl Hartmann?"

Charles immediately felt as though every drop of blood was drained from his body. It was like a sudden shutting off of all his strength. He knew at once that these men were hostile.

"Karl Hartmann? Are you Karl Hartmann?" The voice demanded an answer.

"Yes, I am."

Maria came to the door. She had heard the name spoken by the man. The instinct to protect Charles rose immediately.

"What do you want with us?" she asked.

"Can we come in? We'd rather not talk on the doorstep."

Charles opened the door fully, and the men followed behind Charles into the sitting room, the second man staying at the rear and closing the front door behind them. They all remained standing. The men were amazingly alike, almost bald, stocky and not very tall. Their English was good.

The same man spoke again. "We are here on behalf of the Israeli Government and the Simon Wiesenthal Centre. We have a warrant for the arrest of Karl Hartmann."

"On what charge?" demanded Maria, her voice full of fear, though controlled and firm.

"Crimes committed against the Jewish people of Warsaw. Please pack a few essentials. You must come with us."

Only one of the two men did the talking. The other just stood there, a menacing presence.

"Where my husband goes, I go. I will come with him." Maria moved closer to Charles. She took his arm.

"You cannot do that. Mr Hartmann, please get your things together. We must go. Mr Hartmann, your things please. Stay here, Mrs Hartmann." The voice was insistent.

Charles gently removed Maria's arm from his, and the second, silent man, immediately took hold of it very firmly and prevented her from following Charles upstairs.

Charles was soon downstairs again with a small bag and his coat. He took Maria in his arms, dropping the bag and coat on the floor. He kissed Maria as though he would never see her again, which is what he was thinking was likely, and as he gathered up the case and coat, the silent man clamped handcuffs on and they left. Maria often wondered afterwards how she had just stood at the door watching Charles walk away with these two men, without running after him and holding on to him. She watched. The silent one, to whom Charles was handcuffed, pushed Charles into the back seat of the car and got in beside him. The other took the driver's seat, slammed the door and drove away. They were gone. Charles was gone. The grey day was silent. Maria felt as though she was the only person left in the world, a block of stone standing on her doorstep surveying a bleak landscape.

She was in shock and confusion. She remained standing at the door for some minutes. Then she began shivering, not only from the cold of the morning. She went back to the kitchen and started doing the wiping-up. *What am I doing*, she thought, *I must tell someone. We must get him back.* Panic was beginning to set in. Where was Gregory? The house was empty. She looked at the clock. Eight o'clock. Matthew would still be at home.

Later, when Matthew recalled the events of that morning, he remembered only the despair and incoherence in what Maria told him on that desperate telephone call. It was lucky that he had no surgery until the afternoon/evening slot, so he called out to Jenny that he was going to the farmhouse, jumped in his car and drove out to Scole. He knew only that Maria was in serious trouble.

When he got there, the front door was open. He found Maria sitting at the kitchen table, clean dishes and a tea towel in front of her. She was cold and still and made no move to greet him. He saw that she was in a state of profound shock, her eyes vacant and lifeless.

He put his arm around her. "I'm here Maria. I'll help you, but first we must get you warm. Do you have a hot water bottle?"

Matthew quickly located one from Maria's silent gesture towards the cupboard and put a kettle on. He looked at her. Her face was white. She made no attempt to speak; she did not look at him and was still as a statue. Matthew took her hands in his and gently rubbed them. She made no response. Matthew began to feel very anxious about her well-being.

"Try to tell me what has happened, Maria. Where is Charles?"

This was like opening floodgates. Maria let out a scream, which was piercing, then burst into wild tears, expressing the anguish built up in her ever since Charles had been taken away.

Matthew held her in his arms, holding her head against his chest, thankful for the ending of the unhealthy stillness and silence he had witnessed in her before. The kettle began to whistle. He filled the hot water bottle, wrapped it in one of the clean towels hanging by the sink and taking Maria's arm, guided her into the sitting room. He sat her in one of the easy chairs, placed the hot water bottle in her arms and sat on a little stool close to her.

"Try to tell me what has happened, Maria."

Maria, for the first time, looked at Matthew properly. She told him, with long pauses, what had happened that morning.

Matthew was utterly shocked. It seemed unbelievable, until he looked at Maria's face and saw what it had done to her.

"Maria, I understand what you are telling me. You said Israeli Government? And did they let him take anything with him?"

Matthew was building up a picture of what they were dealing with. He looked at Maria, wondering how much he could tell her.

"I think the person to help us is David Neuberger. I don't think it's too early to ring. Will you sit here and keep warm whilst I telephone him?"

Matthew went to the kitchen and dialled David's number. He was greatly relieved when David answered. Matthew told him what he knew of the morning's events. David asked a few questions. Matthew told him what he could. "I can't let you speak with Maria just now, David. I am a bit concerned about her health. She's had a terrible shock."

"I am going to ring the Israeli Embassy and find out what is going on. It is likely that Charles will be taken to Israel today. He must be properly defended by someone who knows him. I shall do that. Don't worry, Matthew, I will do whatever I can to get Charles out of this. I'll ring you and let you know what I find out. Will I telephone you at home or at the surgery?"

Matthew went back into the sitting room where Maria was still sitting holding the hot water bottle. A little colour was coming into her face. And now she looked at him.

"What can we do, Matthew, what can we do?"

Matthew's heart ached as he looked at her. She was lost in a web of complexity not of her own making and could see no way forward. He spoke very gently to her.

"Maria, David is going to contact the Israelis. As a rabbi, I think they will give him the facts about what is happening to Charles. Remember, Israel is a modern democratic country. We are dealing with civilised people. There will probably be a trial, and I think we can count on David to go over to Jerusalem to defend Charles. There is not much more we can do at the moment. But I can get you something to drink. Would you like tea or coffee?"

He ignored Maria's protestations and made some tea. When he came back with the tea, he told Maria she was to drink at least one cup, and whilst she did so he would go over to the farm buildings and speak with Michael and Pauline and make sure that the day's work would go on, if necessary for the whole day without her.

Matthew gave no details to the staff, saying only that Maria was unwell, and they assured him that they would cope. Matthew was also, in the back of his mind, trying to think what was best to be done for Maria. His instinct was to take her home to Jenny and keep her with them for a day or two. Then what should he do about Gregory? He should be told of the situation at the very least.

But first, Matthew thought, he must take care of Maria. When he got back to the farmhouse, Maria was in the kitchen, washing the cup she had used. Matthew told her that the staff would be quite all right and that he would like her to come with him to Jenny. He didn't want her to be alone.

"Matthew, thank you, thank you. But I must be here. Maybe Charles will come back. I must be here in case he does. He'll need something to eat. The business must be seen to." Maria's voice trailed away. She still seemed a little confused and not in touch with reality.

"All right, Maria, but I will stay with you until I need to go to the surgery. Is there anything that has to be done in the house?"

"Yes, I will go upstairs and make the bed. What was that?" Maria jumped as the letterbox rattled. Matthew came back from the hall with Charles's copy of The Times. For a moment, both of them silently looked at it. Then Matthew took it into the sitting room.

"Maria, why don't you go and tidy upstairs whilst I use the telephone again? I ought to let Jenny know what I'm doing."

Maria had to steel herself to go to the bed. She climbed on it and lay with her head on Charles's pillow as though it were the most precious thing in the world. Then, knowing she must move forward into whatever was going to happen, in a strangely reverent way she made the bed, folded Charles's pyjamas, putting them under his pillow and went downstairs. *I will do what must be done each day, until he comes home*, she told herself.

Matthew had deliberately sat himself down with the newspaper. He wanted to make things as normal as possible. He'd opened The Times but was not able to concentrate on reading it. Matthew felt a little reassured when Maria came into the kitchen. Some colour had returned to her face, and she was moving more normally. He wanted to help her do things in a normal way, not like the automaton she had been when he arrived. At the same time, he knew he must help her face reality. But Maria was already there.

"I should think about what we will have for lunch," Maria said.

"Why not keep it simple, Maria. What about some of your lovely bread, with some cheeses and perhaps a bowl of soup as it's so cold? You know, this range needs some fuel. Shall I see to it for you?"

But Maria's mind was not really with these practical matters. She looked at Matthew, her earlier resolve seeming to melt, an unspoken plea on her face.

"Let's go and sit comfortably. You want to talk about Charles, don't you?"

They went into the sitting room. "Matthew, what will happen to him?"

"Well, Maria, I don't really know, but I expect he will be flown to Jerusalem today and will be kept under close observation." Matthew did not want to say the word 'cell'. "And they will get together an indictment against him and gather witnesses. I am not sure legally how Israel stands about this. They have arrested a German, in England, for crimes committed in Poland, to be tried in Israel. But I am not a lawyer. Don't worry about Charles's safety, Maria. He will not be hurt. I think that we will all need a lot of patience, Charles too. These things can take quite a time." Matthew was pleased to see Maria beginning to engage in normal conversation. Matthew continued.

"Our strength will be in David Neuberger's testimony. We are fortunate that David already knows a lot about Charles's past and will have time to make the best defence he possibly can. I will speak with him again this evening and let you know what he has to say. But you must accept, Maria, that Charles is not going to walk through that door again for some time. Don't expect it. He is going to be away for some months, and we all have to carry on as best we can." Matthew paused again, looking at Maria with affectionate compassion.

"Do you feel like a little walk with me up to the bakery to see how everything is going on there?"

"Yes, all right." Maria rather mechanically got up and walked to the front door.

"Maria, you need a coat."

They walked up to the bakery, going through the Tea Shop where Pauline was tidying and where as yet there were no customers. Pauline was obviously surprised to see Maria and asked her how she was. In the bakery, the two girls there were working hard, and it smelled very comfortingly of warm bread. Cakes stood cooling on wire racks, and everything seemed under control. They didn't go into the Yoga Studio, but they could see through the window that the teacher was there warming up before the day's class began.

As they slowly made their way back to the house, a car drew up. It was David Neuberger. Once they were indoors, he immediately embraced Maria, held her away from him and then embraced her again.

"My dear Maria, I am so sorry this has happened to Charles. But fear not, we are going to go to his aid." David sounded like a medieval knight preparing for battle. Matthew began to think that David was never going to let Maria go. She had now begun to weep again. David, holding her by the arm, led her into the sitting room. He ignored the tears.

"Well, I have had a word with the embassy, and being a little early in the morning, there was nobody there to whom I could speak about Charles's case. They have promised to ring me back. Sara will ring here, Maria, if they telephone whilst I am with you."

Matthew made his way to the kitchen. "I'll make a pot of coffee."

"Maria," said David, taking her hands in his, "we must be realistic. At the moment, I can offer you no comfort. I can only assure you that I will do everything I can to help you.

"If you want me to, I will go to the trial and will speak in Charles's defence. I am not a lawyer as you know, and you may decide you want to appoint a qualified legal person to do the job. Either way, there is one thing I need to know now. Did Charles take British citizenship?"

"Yes, he did. I think it was around about 1950. He has a British passport. I believe he has dual citizenship because of course he is German, although born in what became part of Poland."

"Could you check for me, Maria, is his British passport still here or did he take it with him?"

"I doubt that he took it with him; it was all so quick. I'll go and see if it is where it normally is."

In a minute or so, Maria came back into the sitting room with Charles's British passport in her hand.

"Here it is," she said, handing it to David.

"May I take down some details, Maria? I may need to contact the foreign office."

Matthew appeared with the coffee. "David, Maria and I are going to have a little lunch together before I go off to surgery. Will you join us? Is that all right, Maria? I have to be at work by 1:30 so it will be an early snack, some fresh bread and cheese and some hot soup."

David, characteristically immersed in the problems at hand, merely nodded. The telephone rang. Maria made no move, so Matthew went to answer it.

"It's Sara for you, David." He was not long gone.

"The Israeli Embassy has no knowledge of any of this, or so they say. Their opinion is that the men who came here were probably Wiesenthal agents. It makes little difference. I'll contact them again tomorrow. They will be obliged to get the information. I shall also ring the foreign office and let them know what has happened. Charles has a right to the protection of the British Government."

Maria got up abruptly and went upstairs, saying nothing.

David took the opportunity. "Matthew, I don't want Maria to hear this, but we may have to contend with some publicity. I'm thinking a bit ahead I know, but we might have to think about the possibility of the business being affected. And have you given any thought to letting Gregory know what has happened?"

"Yes. With regard to Gregory, I think the best thing to do is for me to ring Father Andrew and give him the facts. Publicity, well, what will be, will be. Yes, it could have a very adverse influence on the farm. I can't worry about that just now. I am, though, thinking about what to tell the staff. If you think there might be publicity, it would be better to tell them the facts ourselves."

Maria came in. She had changed her clothes. "I am going to do what has to be done, every day, until he comes home," she announced.

"And now I am going to get the lunch prepared." Maria's characteristic bravery had surfaced.

At the monastery, Gregory was getting used to his new routine. As a postulant, during the six months of this period he was being gradually introduced to the life of prayer and work that he would follow. He had a small room, generally termed a 'cell' by the monks. He wore a long black tunic over his usual clothes. His formation took place under Father Andrew who was novice master, and at first, Gregory learned how to find his way around the Breviary, the book from which the monks recited *The Divine Office*. It didn't take Gregory long to get used to starting the day at a very early hour, and he loved the silence which was the constant background to everything the monks did. He seemed, Father Andrew thought, to be a young man very used to listening, and not listening to but listening for. Father Andrew raised an eyebrow when Gregory selected from the library, *The Divine Milieu* by Teilhard de Chardin for his private reading. Gregory noticed the raised eyebrow, but since the Jesuit's writings were on the shelf, he could see no reason for ignoring them.

His work was an assignment to the gardens, of which, of course, he had a little knowledge already. Gregory was always pleased when the evening recreation time came around. He enjoyed getting to know the other monks and especially the older ones. During this hour in the community room, the monks were free to engage in conversation with one another, and if there was any important item of national news, Father Abbot would tell the community about it. The monks did not have access to newspapers.

As Gregory looked forward to starting the Novitiate proper in a few weeks' time, one morning he was asked by Father Andrew to join him in his office. It was not usual to sit, but Father Andrew asked him to do so. Gregory could not help but wonder what he had done wrong. It seemed that something serious was afoot.

"Brother Gregory, I have some upsetting news to tell you. Dr Hall has contacted me because there has been a totally unexpected event at the farmhouse and both he and I think you should know about it."

Gregory, listening calmly to Father Andrew, now began to feel anxious. He was aware of his breathing quickening.

"It seems that Israeli officials have taken your father away to answer charges against him in relation to his activities in Warsaw during the War. Dr Hall tells me that he and his wife are supporting your mother and that Rabbi Neuberger is working on your father's defence."

Gregory felt his stomach lurch. He said nothing but waited for Father Andrew to continue.

"The rabbi will in due course go to Jerusalem to assist your father, but Dr Hall is concerned about your mother. My question to you, Gregory, is whether or not you wish to go home to give succour to your mother. You know that as a postulant, or even if you were already in the novitiate proper, you are not yet under vows and are absolutely free to go. Only you can decide this."

"Father, this is a very difficult decision, and I cannot determine what to do without some time in prayer. Although I am not yet under vows, I am spiritually committed to my life here. And yet, I can imagine my mother's distress, and I would like to comfort and take care of her. May I speak with you again tomorrow?"

Gregory wanted to get away and think about what was the right thing to do. The news had been unexpected and frightening. He needed time and quiet to reflect on the best way he could help and time too to deal with his own shock and fear for his father's wellbeing.

The next morning, he went again to see Father Andrew.

Gregory went straight to the point. "Father Andrew, I have decided that I should stay here in the monastery, to which I have already committed myself. I am deeply aware of the distress in which my mother now finds herself, and I share in her agony. I love my father, but I must entrust his freedom and, I hope, his speedy return, to Rabbi Neuberger. My mother I must entrust to God and to Dr Hall and others who I am sure will support her."

For a moment, Father Andrew was silent.

"Brother Gregory your decision surprises and moves me. It is not one I would have expected from a postulant." Father Andrew paused. "However, the community wish to give you two days' leave of absence to visit your mother. We think this is the right and proper thing to do, and it will in no way affect your formation here. You will, I know, return to us and resume your normal routine. Just let me know which days you would like to take. A note in my letterbox will do. I am sure I do not need to tell you that the prayers of the community are with your family at this time."

The next morning, Father Andrew found Gregory's note telling him that he would leave on Monday after early morning Mass and would return the next day before the Great Silence. Father Andrew rang Matthew to let him know and asked him to confirm with him that Gregory's mother had no other arrangements for that Monday or Tuesday.

After the busy weekends on the farm, Maria usually occupied herself on Monday mornings with the general tidying of the house, little jobs she would not expect the cleaner to do. If the weather was nice, she would also do some weeding in Bob's Garden and check the new gardens that Charles had made. On this Monday, she had decided to tidy out her wardrobe and put aside for charity some of the clothes she no longer wore. So it was that she was upstairs when the doorbell rang. She knew it would not be one of the staff and thought perhaps it was the postman. As she went downstairs, she felt a strange sensation of anxiety, which gave way when she opened the door, to disbelief mixed with even more disbelief. She was silent. Before her stood a smiling young man with a mop of blonde tousled hair.

"Mama, darling Mama," Gregory whispered, also overcome with emotion. "It's me. Are you going to let me in?" Maria threw her arms around her son, and they stood on the doorstep hugging one another.

"Come on in. Whatever are you doing here? Oh, Gregory, it is so wonderful to see you." Then she looked at the small bag he was carrying.

"Yes, Mama, I am here until tomorrow afternoon. Father Andrew told me a little bit about what has happened to Papa, and I have been given leave to be with you for a while. If you can bear to talk about it, I would like to know what happened."

"Did you have breakfast? Oh, Gregory! Let's sit in the kitchen then and we can talk whilst I get you something to eat. Tell me, is everything all right with you? Are you happy?"

"Mama, I am fine, you do not need to have any worries about me. Yes, tea would be good. If that's your own bread, I'd rather not have it toasted. Just as it is, with some butter would be great. Now, come on, Mama, you must please tell me, if you can, everything that has happened in the last few days."

Over the next hour or so, Maria told Gregory everything, from the two men walking up the path to the front door, to their departure with Charles in handcuffs. She told him how Matthew had come immediately and that David Neuberger had also driven over that same morning. She explained what she knew about the forthcoming trial and told Gregory that she was almost certain that David would present Charles's defence. She told him also, what he already knew of course, that she thought they had the best friends possible in Matthew and David.

"Have we any idea what we might be looking at with regard to a sentence?" asked Gregory.

"I don't think David has any idea, at least not that he has told me. He has said that the process could take quite a few months before the trial even begins. Already almost a week has passed, Gregory, since your father was taken. It seems like an eternity, and sometimes I don't know how I am going to get through it. But I try to keep going, doing the things that need to be done." Maria hesitated. "I told the staff the truth of where Charles is and what is happening to him. Everyone has been very supportive. And I am glad I told them myself, because if you go into the sitting room and pick up the paper, you will see an article on page three reporting his arrest. No doubt next weekends' local papers will make it into headlines. But I have a lot to do. I must make sure that the business continues to function, do the jobs I usually do in the bakery, do the accounts which your father always did…"

Maria's voice sunk into silence. Then quietly she said, "It's a lot to handle, but I want Charles to find everything in order when he comes home."

Early that evening, Matthew rang to ask if he might come over for a little while to see Gregory. When he arrived, a lot of the talk was about the children, and Matthew wanted to hear something of Gregory's life as a monk. Eventually, this easy conversation gave way to the situation with Charles. Gregory did not want to ask too directly, the question that was uppermost in his mind.

"Do you think the sentence is likely to be a long one?" he asked.

"Well, Gregory, we have no way of knowing, but David is of the opinion that they have no grounds at all for imposing a severe sentence. He will go to Jerusalem a few days before the trial begins so that he can talk with your father about the way he intends to proceed. At the moment, we can only wait. And during this time, you know that Jenny and I will take good care of your mother. I must say I have been very impressed with your manager here on the farm. In fact, all of the staff has been marvellous. Don't worry about your mother; we are all trying hard to support her."

Matthew looked over to where Maria was sitting. "And now I will leave you. Gregory, I am so pleased you came. It has meant a lot to your mother to have this time with you."

"Thank you, Uncle Matt, thank you for everything. I think this family would fall apart if it were not for you."

The next afternoon, Gregory returned to the monastery and things at the farm continued much as they always did but with Maria relying quite heavily on the managerial skills of Michael Collins. She had already spoken with him, since Charles's arrest, about his responsibilities and her intention to adjust his already-generous salary accordingly. He was, at this time, indispensable to Maria. They discussed together the idea Michael had of turning the unused cottage into a staff centre. He told Maria that he needed office space, and he thought the upstairs room would be ideal. The downstairs kitchen, scullery and bathroom could be a centre for the staff, where they could have their lunch, hang their coats and have access to their own toilet. Maria thought it a good use of the property and gave the go-ahead to Michael.

The next thing Maria felt she had to do was to let Klaus know what had happened to Charles. She rang him and told him the events of the last week. She did not know how much Klaus knew of Charles's life in Warsaw.

"I can hardly believe this, Maria." His voice sounded incredulous. "What can I do to help you?"

Maria explained that David Neuberger was defending Charles, and she reassured Klaus that Matthew and Jenny were looking after her. She told him that Gregory had been home as well. Although Klaus wanted to come over to support her, Maria persuaded him that it was better for her if she tried to carry on as near normal as possible. They promised to ring one another regularly.

At the weekend, the local paper's headlines carried Charles's story, as David had suggested they would. Nazi farmer was the headline in bold capitals on the front page, but the story that followed was not as bad as had been feared. Over the weeks that followed, one or two minor incidents happened at or in front of the farm, but on the whole, it seemed that the business was not seriously affected, at least for the moment.

At the end of February as Maria sat grappling with the accounts, she noticed a payment she had seen the previous month on the bank statement and had not recognised. She felt that she should not pass it over once again, so rang the bank manager to check. She was able to get an answer fairly quickly.

"Oh, yes, Mrs Hartman, this is a payment your husband has made monthly for some years now."

"But who is this C Klein?" was Maria's question.

"It's a charity for Jewish children, Mrs Hartman."

"Can you tell me for how long this payment has been made?"

"One moment. Yes, here it is. Your husband began this donation on the last day of June 1948, and it has been paid on the last day of every month since then."

"So, for over sixteen years he has been making this payment?"

"Yes, that would be right. I can print out for you a copy of his instruction if you need it."

"No, that won't be necessary, Mr Horner, thank you for your help."

When Maria put down the telephone, she sat at the table looking at the entry she had made on the accounts. Never before had she bothered to look at bank statements, never before had she known that Charles was doing this. She wanted to hug him. Instead, for the goodness of him, and for the danger he was now in, she put her head down on her arms, laid over the accounts and wept.

Another revelation was to come to Maria.

During the course of the foreign office's enquiry about Charles's arrest, David was told that the Wiesenthal agents had got the connection to his address in England through the Soviet authorities in Warsaw. After careful thought, he decided to tell Maria the full circumstances, so far as the foreign office knew them and to tell her that her parents were dead.

Maria thought that she could give in to feelings of guilt that her letter to her parents was the cause of his being discovered; she could allow herself to collapse in grief for the loss of her parents, or she could keep going day by day as she had vowed she would do, until he came home. And of course, that is what she bravely did.

But that night when she went to bed, she clasped Charles's pillow and cried into it, for the loss of her parents and for her beloved husband who was not there to comfort her. Before she drifted off to sleep, she realised that blaming herself for being the cause of Charles's arrest was useless and could only hinder her efforts to persevere until he came back. What has to be done, every day…Maria fell asleep.

It was at the beginning of May that David Neuberger received notice from the court that the trial of his client would open on Sunday, May 9. He made arrangements with a rabbi from a nearby congregation to stand in for him, rang Maria and bought his ticket to fly El Al to Jerusalem on Wednesday May 5.

He saw Charles in an interview room the next morning. Although pale, he seemed to David to be not much altered. After telling Charles, quite briefly, how things were at home, he got down to the matters in hand.

"We work only with the truth, Charles, and most of the material I shall use is what you gave to me yourself some years ago. There are one or two points I need to clarify with you, the first being your working relationship with Hans Frank. Then I need to know about payments to someone with the name C Klein. I know that the prosecution has only two witnesses to call against you, and I expect they will be former residents of the ghetto. I'd like to hear, as far as you can, what contact you had with these Jews.

Let's start with the first point. By the way, Charles, I shall come again tomorrow morning, but it will be fairly short because of the Sabbath. I'll not see you again until we meet in court. Now, Hans Frank…"

It was when David got to the question of Charles's contact with the Jews in the ghetto that Charles broke down and for some while could not speak. David gave him time.

"Try to tell me what troubles you so much, Charles."

"I shall always remember this little boy. I had to go into the ghetto to check on an official, and as I walked down the street, I saw a small boy lying on the pavement against the wall of a house. He was dying or perhaps already dead." Charles paused, trying to control the horror and sadness he always felt when he recalled this incident.

"He wore a brimmed cap that was too big, and the face under it had very big staring eyes, wide open. The child was emaciated and obviously starving. He looked no more than seven years of age. I walked past. How could I not have gathered up that little child into my arms and taken him to safety? Why, oh, why didn't I do it? It is like a nightmare vision. It comes to me whenever I think about those days."

"I presume," said David gently, "this little boy is the inspiration for your contributions to the Jewish charity?"

"Yes, it is utterly inadequate, of course, but I feel that it is some small way I can try to make up for what I didn't do to help that little boy I saw that morning. How did you find out about that?" Charles looked quizzically at David.

David ignored the question.

When Charles walked into court on that Sunday, he felt calm. He was convinced that he would, at the very least, get a long term of imprisonment. In his heart, he felt it was right that he should be here, being weighed and measured with regard to the guilt he bore. Therefore, he could not feel anything but resignation. He had only half listened to what David had told him about the main points of his defence, for he felt already that the outcome would be 'guilty'.

The courtroom was light and airy, and there were very few people occupying the public gallery. Then it began. Charles represented an almost noble appearance. He was polite and to the point when he was questioned.

When the prosecution called its witnesses, they were two men, probably in their thirties. Their accusations were fairly general. Neither was able to say that Charles, or Karl as he was called here, had personally inflicted suffering on them. David underlined this point when he questioned them. In fact, when he pressed home the point that they had had no contact with Karl Hartmann, they could only say that they had seen him occasionally and knew that he was in charge.

When Charles himself faced the prosecutor, the questions and accusations again were general. Charles answered clearly and politely.

David's summing up was short.

"This man is a victim! He is not guilty of murdering anyone personally. He was a lawyer, dragged into the net of the Nazi machine until he was able to free himself from it. No, Karl Hartmann is not an Anti-Semite."

David looked around the court, timing his defence for the fullest impact.

"For more than sixteen years, he has supported from his income, a Jewish charity for children, and I, a rabbi, am one of his closest friends and have been for some years. This man should be acquitted. The evidence, and his testimony, demand it." David's last sentence was firm but without arrogance.

After a recess, the trial resumed to hear the decision of the judge. A small, elderly man, with piercing black eyes, he called for silence.

"It is my opinion, after hearing all the evidence, that this trial should never have been called. This man, Mr Karl Hartmann, has in this court today been correctly described by his defence as a victim. In no way did he actively seek out membership of the NSDAP. In fact, it is my opinion that not only was Karl Hartmann a victim of Adolf Hitler, he was also a victim of Hans Frank, who having known him at the University of Munich, got him appointed by his boss Heinrich Himmler to the overseeing of the Jewish population in Warsaw. What did the accused do as soon as he heard about the plans for the Final Solution? He embarked on a dangerous escape with his wife, away from Nazi-controlled territory to Great Britain, then fighting with all its might against the Nazi tyranny. This man is not guilty of the crimes of which he has today been accused. Before he goes free, however, I ask him if he is willing, as some recognition of the suffering of the Jewish people in the Warsaw Ghetto, to stay with us for three months. I know that the Nazareth Kibbutz needs some help in establishing its farm, and he could be of considerable help in that regard. Hearing ended!"

Charles slumped back down onto his seat. He could not believe what he had heard.

A nominal sentence of three months, which legally was unenforceable!

Charles indicated his willingness to help the Kibbutz but requested that he be allowed to have lunch with his defence before making the journey north.

When David got back to England, he went immediately to the farm. When he found Maria, she was in the bakery. He saw the blood drain from her face as he called out to her from the door. Her fear was clear. As soon as they got outside, David took her hand and told her that he had good news.

"Good news?" Maria stuttered.

Once in the farmhouse kitchen, David told her that Charles had been found not guilty and the case dismissed. Maria almost fell into a chair. "Tell me, David, tell me when he'll be home."

David told her about the judge's request for help on the Kibbutz and explained that although he was not obliged by law to agree to it, he had.

"So, Maria, I think you can expect him home by the middle of August at the latest."

"David, I haven't even asked you how he is. Is he well? Did they treat him well? Oh, David, what a wonderful day this is!"

David refused the coffee Maria offered and said he should get home to Sara. Maria managed to press him to come for dinner the following Wednesday with Sara, and she hoped Matthew and Jenny would be there too.

"We'll have a little celebration," said Maria. "And thank you, David, thank you for everything."

She threw shyness aside and planted a kiss on his cheek.

The first thing Maria did as David left was to pick up the telephone and let Matthew know the verdict. Then she rang the monastery and conveyed the same good news to Gregory. Both men said they would come over to see her and hear about the judge's summing up and find out more about where Charles would be until August. The next telephone call was to Klaus to let him know the outcome of the trial, and he promised to come over to see them both once Charles was settled again.

The next weekend, the local newspaper carried on an inside page the news of Charles's acquittal.

Maria never knew how she managed to get through the months of June and July.

August came around. The weather was warm and sunny. The house was full of flowers from the garden. Every day, Maria waited for Charles, even when she was busy on the farm, she was half expecting to hear his voice. When she went to bed, she imagined every night, how she would greet him and fell asleep thinking how it would be.

It was a Monday. She had taken her after-lunch cup of tea with her to the bench at Bob's garden. She must have nodded off in the warmth of the afternoon sun. Something startled her into wakefulness. And there he was. The tall, slim, now grey-haired, good-looking man who was her husband, striding up the path. She ran to him, neither said a word, each clasped the other tight. No, not imagined. Firm bodies, held against one another. Their eyes met, almost as though they had to check that the other was really the one they thought they were. Then they kissed. Maria felt faint and clung to Charles as though she expected him to vanish. The moment for which she had so long waited had come, and its joy was overwhelming. Both, when they looked at one another again, saw the tears in the eyes of the other.

"My darling, you are home," Maria managed to whisper. "I have longed for you so much."

Arms entwined, they went into the farmhouse, forgetting the teacup on Bob's bench, forgetting Charles's bag on the path. In the hall, the front door now closed, they kissed again. Charles had still not spoken a word. Maria took his hand and drew him into the kitchen. They automatically took their usual chairs on opposite sides of the table, their hands reaching across it and clasping.

"I have imagined this moment over and over, ever since the acquittal. My dearest wife, here, waiting for me and longing, as I have, to hold one another. Oh, Maria, I can hardly contain the joy of it. You look just the same, beautiful as the day we married. No, more beautiful."

Charles glanced around the kitchen. "Everything is as it always is."

Then, mischievously and with a twinkle in his eye, he said, "Shall we make a pot of tea? How I long for a decent cup of tea."

Maria laughed and as she put the kettle on, retorted, "Charles, you are becoming more and more like an Englishman."

After Charles had had some tea, hand in hand they went around the farm. First, Maria showed him the new staff centre, which he thought was a very good idea. On their way to the bakery and Tea Shop, they saw Michael Collins, who hurried over to greet Charles. They shook hands.

"Thank you, Michael, for everything you have done. I don't really know what to say. I can see that all is running smoothly, and I am delighted with the new centre for the staff."

"Well, Charles, most of the credit should go to your wife. She has kept us all together through what was definitely a difficult time. We have all missed you. Welcome home!"

It was the same at the bakery and the Tea Shop, staff genuinely pleased to see Charles back again. Charles, never for one moment letting go of Maria's hand, made a little detour to seek out the young boys who worked in the fields and the orchard. To them also, Charles expressed his thanks and appreciation of their work whilst he had been away. Then, the pair of them made their way back to the farmhouse, gathering up the cup and saucer on Bob's bench and Charles's bag from the path and returning once again into the privacy of their home. The perfume of the roses in the sitting room, the sun streaming through the windows, wrapped them in a sense of well-being and relaxation. They sat together on the settee.

"What do you fancy to eat this evening?" was Maria's lazily spoken question.

"You," was the quick reply. "And have we got a decent bottle of wine to precede you?"

And then, in a very practical tone of voice he said, "Oh, Maria, I've just remembered that I intended to ring David Neuberger and let him know I'm safely home. I must go and do that now. He was absolutely wonderful in Jerusalem. I owe him a great deal."

He tried to disentangle himself from his wife. "Please, Maria, I'll be only a minute." He planted a kiss on her forehead, and she released her grip on his hand.

When he came back in, Maria asked him if he had also rung Matthew. He smiled and told her that Matthew had picked him up at Norwich station that morning and driven him home.

"But I didn't see him," said Maria.

"No, Matthew is a gentleman. He dropped me just down the lane so that we could be reunited without anyone else around."

Then Charles turned his attention to the bottle of white wine he had brought in.

"It's a Sauvignon Blanc because I think your delicate flesh requires a wine that will not drown its beauty." He laughed as he threw himself back beside her on the settee.

"Now, Mr Hartman," Maria endeavoured to say as she wriggled out from under the flood of kisses planted on her, "I have some beautiful fresh trout. It's from Cox's Farm Fresh. Would you like that, with some vegetables or salad?"

"Yes, provided I can have you for dessert. Here, now, a glass of wine." Charles handed Maria her glass.

"Let's drink to our never again being separated. A life filled with love and English Tea."

"Charles, you have become quite wicked. What did you get up to on that Kibbutz?" A little later, Maria went to the kitchen to begin preparing their meal. Charles went upstairs to have a bath and change his clothes. They finished the wine with their meal and Maria went to the larder for the fresh fruit and cream.

Charles came behind her as she did so and put his arms around her waist and kissed the nape of her neck.

"You promised me I could have you for dessert."

The next morning, after breakfast and after having helped Maria to clear away the previous night's dishes, Charles sat down to write to Gregory. He wanted to congratulate him on his forthcoming year in Rome and let him know that he himself was well and very happy to be home again. He told him about the Kibbutz, which had impressed him with its ideals and its wonderful community spirit. Maria added a paragraph telling her son how happy she was that his father was home.

Then Charles telephoned Matthew. When he put the phone down, he told Maria that Matthew had some news for them. They both wondered what it could be. Another baby? No, thought Charles. He's won the pools? But he doesn't do the pools. They decided they would have to wait until they saw him the next day.

On that Wednesday evening, Matthew came alone. When they were sitting waiting for dinner to be ready, Matthew told Charles and Maria that he had decided to retire.

"I'm getting on, and it's time to hang up my stethoscope," he said with a grin.

Apparently, he and Jenny had decided that the workload for both of them was too much. The children were getting into the beginning of their school years and would require less care at home. If Matthew retired, he could be there for the children when needed, Jenny's parents would like often to have care of them, and Jenny could go back to paediatrics full time.

"We're combining it with a move," Matthew said. "We're going to buy a house in Bressingham, mainly so that we can have a bigger garden but also so that Jenny's parents can see more of the children. Jenny has got an appointment at Norwich Hospital, quite a jump up in her career and is happy to do the drive there each day. It will be quite a change, especially for me."

Matthew looked at Charles and Maria, trying to gauge their reaction. Maria realised how concentrated she had been on her own affairs over the past year, taking Matthew and Jenny very much for granted. They had always been there for her and now perhaps it was time for her, and Charles, to put them first. Charles too was looking at Matthew with fresh eyes.

"Matthew, you have always been our very best friend and you have, I know, been Maria's steadfast support during my absence. Bressingham isn't far away, and maybe without the demands of the surgery on you, we may be able to see more of one another. You deserve a wonderful retirement, and maybe I'll be thinking about it also before too long. But I can't begin to imagine a life without you."

"You don't have to, Charles. You and Maria, from soon after we first met, have always been family for me. But the decision we have made is really only about my needing to retire. I've had enough, and after all, I am past the usual retirement age."

"Is there anything we can do to help you with this, Matthew?" asked Charles.

"Yes, Charles, there is." Maria, looking at the mischievous twinkle in Matthew's eye, knew something odd was about to be uttered.

"You could buy a little car." They all laughed. "No, seriously, it would help us to see one another if you could just jump into a car and be with me in ten minutes or so."

"Yes, Charles, let's do it. And Matthew, let us know if there is anything we can do to help you with the move, I mean other than buying new vehicles. I can always look after Emily and Sebastian if Jenny's parents can't be available."

"Well, Matthew, maybe I'll join you in this retirement plan. It's time we had some fun. We could take up new interests and get involved in all sorts of things." Charles wasn't joking.

"That sounds a good idea, Charles," said Matthew, chuckling at the thought of it.

The next day, Charles rang a local car agent and arranged a visit to look at some models of small cars. In a few days' time, Maria and Charles had a blue Austin 1100 sitting on the drive, the first car they had ever owned. Now, driving lessons had to be organised! It seemed incredible to both Charles and Maria that just a short time ago Charles had been in Jerusalem, neither of them knowing whether or not he would ever be free again. Now life seemed to be re-configuring itself in new patterns. But it was life, together, with their loved ones and lots of new opportunities presenting themselves.

By the end of August, Jenny and Matthew had found a house they liked in Bressingham. Charles went with Matthew to look at it. A medium-sized detached house, standing back from the road, with a curved drive, it looked pleasing. A bay window either side of the front door, and three smaller windows on the first floor gave the exterior balance. The bay windows belonged to the dining room and sitting room, the kitchen stretched along the back with a door to the garden. Upstairs were four bedrooms, the smallest of which Jenny earmarked for her office. The bathroom was large but needed some modernising. Matthew liked the garden because it gave ample scope for the children's play. But one of the best things about it was that it was more or less opposite Jenny's parents' home. Matthew took retirement at the end of August, and Jenny began her new job on September 1, the same day as little Emily began nursery school, aged almost three.

Everything seemed to happen at once for Matthew and Jenny, but Charles was on hand to help with the move, and Jenny's mother looked after the children's needs. With all this talk and activity going on about retirement, Maria began to think about her own working life. She realised that Charles might also soon decide to do less, although he was nowadays not doing a great deal on the farm. It might be a good idea if she also reorganised her schedule so that she had more free time for Charles. She decided to give it some thought.

As Christmas approached, Jenny and Matthew asked Charles and Maria if they would join them on Christmas Day together with Jenny's parents. Klaus was included in the invitation, since he was arriving on 23rd to spend the festival with Charles and Maria. So, Matthew and Maria went to Mass at the monastery together on Christmas Eve, leaving Charles and Klaus at home with a nice bottle of wine on the coffee table in the sitting room. The pair of them had been given the job of making sure the meal was ready for Maria when she got back. Since she had planned cold meats, it was not too onerous a task.

The next morning, Charles, Maria and Klaus drove over to Bressingham for a family Christmas with two excited little children, their parents and grandparents. The new house had quickly become home and everyone felt comfortable and relaxed, although it was quite a large gathering. Charles made an early New Year's resolution to help Matthew sort out the garden when he saw that he had not yet made a start on it.

Early in spring 1966, Charles asked Maria if she could arrange to be away from the farm for a few days. He told her that he wanted to take her away to fulfil a desire she had expressed many years ago and which he had at that time not been able to meet. He would not give her any other details, for he wanted it to be a surprise. Maria checked with the staff in the bakery and spoke with Michael Collins, and they were all sure that they could cope without her for a few days. So it was that soon after Easter they set out for Heathrow Airport.

Once there of course, Maria quickly learned that they were on their way to Berlin. They knew they were going into a still-divided city and one still to quite a large extent recovering from the ravages of war. They stayed at the Angleterre Hotel on Friedrichstrasse. Maria couldn't help remarking that it was rather different from where they had stayed the last time they were in Berlin, although it was in the same street. After an early dinner, arm-in-arm they walked down Friedrichstrasse, along Unter den Linden until they came to the magnificent Brandenburg Gate. "This, I think, is what you wanted to see and look there is the Reichstag."

The pair stood quietly surveying the scene, memories of the past a part of their present appreciation of the site.

The next morning, Charles suggested they walk again down Unter den Linden as far as Lustgarten where they could sit for a rest and enjoy the gardens, and then maybe choose a museum to visit.

In the afternoon, they returned to the hotel for a rest, and a change of clothes. That evening, they went to hear The Berlin Philharmonic play Beethoven's 9th Symphony conducted by Herbert von Karajan. As they moved along the row into their seats, Maria leading the way, a tall gentleman stood, very obviously in greeting. It was Klaus! Maria sat beside him, Charles on her right. Charles had arranged this, and he told her that they would be having dinner in the hotel with Klaus afterward and would not be going back to England the next day but to Frankfurt to stay with Klaus for a couple of days.

The concert was magnificent. Maria could not help thinking how very much Gregory and Matthew would have enjoyed this. It was a most moving and powerful performance.

Afterward, the three of them walked back to the hotel and went straight into the restaurant. Klaus told them that he had retired from his job at the end of the year and was still in the process of thinking how best to make use of his time.

"Well," said Maria straightaway, "you can come over to England and spend longer time with us. That would be nice. You two" – she looked from Charles to Klaus – "could make up for some of the lost time."

Back in their room, preparing their case for the onward journey, Charles asked Maria if she had enjoyed her trip to Berlin.

"Charles, it has been wonderful. Thank you, darling, for organising it. Berlin is a truly magnificent city."

"Yes," said Charles, "and although it is probably debateable, I think it has the best orchestra in the world. And the rebuilding of the city is not yet finished. It is hard, even now, to remember that it was in utter ruins only twenty years ago."

Klaus stayed in the hotel overnight, and the three had breakfast together the next morning, then they took a taxi to the airport for a flight to Frankfurt. Maria was thinking of Klaus beginning his retirement. She was thinking that it was sad that he was starting this wonderful new phase of his life, having no one with whom to share it.

The flight to Frankfurt was short, and a car was waiting to take them to Klaus's home. It was a large house facing the river and just a little way from one of Frankfurt's elegant museums, still in the process of being rebuilt. Klaus's home seemed almost like a small hotel. It was elegant and almost luxurious. He had a housekeeper who greeted them as they arrived and took Charles and Maria up to their room. It was a large room, overlooking the River Main, not far from a bridge, with its own bathroom. They unpacked, tidied themselves and went downstairs to find Klaus.

"I thought we would have some tea and then take a little walk before dinner. Tomorrow the real sightseeing can begin. If that's all right with you," said Klaus.

"This is a beautiful house, Klaus. Your housekeeper looks after things for you?"

"Yes, she is resident, and she cooks my meals and takes care of everything really."

After breakfast the next morning, they set out for the Old City. Klaus wanted them to see the picturesque old Town Hall. Picturesque was indeed a good word to describe the pretty wooden-framed building. Klaus explained that much of what they saw had been totally destroyed in the war but had been rebuilt as near as possible to its former state. From there, they made their way to the cathedral.

"Yes," said Klaus, looking at Maria, "it's Catholic. Gothic, as you can see. Would you like to go in?" Whilst Maria sat quietly the two men wandered around looking at the chapels and statues.

Next, Klaus decided they should go to the Goethestrasse, where, he thought, Maria would surely love to look at the luxury shops and where they could find a nice restaurant to have a lunchtime snack. Both Charles and Maria were amazed at the prices of products, and Charles's gentlemanly offer to buy Maria a dress was gently refused by her on the grounds not of cost but of its unsuitability in Scole, Norfolk. Both Charles and Klaus saw that Maria was right. After a light lunch, they took a taxi back home.

"Tomorrow, if you like, we could have a look at Goethe's house and go to one of the museums just near here." Charles and Maria agreed and were very glad to spend the rest of the day at home with Klaus. He showed them around the house, at Maria's request, and they loved the spaciousness of it and its central paved area with a glass roof. There were some exotic-looking plants standing in pots there and some chairs for lounging.

"I think it's too hot to sit here," said Klaus. "Let's go into the sitting room."

Both Charles and Maria were amazed at the way Klaus lived. Compared with their simple farmhouse, it was a palace. But for Maria, at the heart of it was one lonely man.

"Klaus, when are you going to find a wife to share all this beauty with?" she asked.

"Oh, one of these days," replied Klaus, laughing. "Actually, Maria, I'd much rather live in your farmhouse than here. It's a home, this is just a residence."

The next day, they went to see Goethe's birthplace, and Charles bought a beautifully bound copy of Goethe's poems. Then they went to the Museum of Art, where they had some lunch. The evening, like the day before, was spent at home, chatting and relaxing together.

Their last dinner was enjoyed with champagne, and the three of them sat in the library afterwards, with coffee and chocolate truffles.

"Thanks, Klaus, for this wonderful visit. We've had a marvellous time here."

"Well, I hope this will be only the first of many visits. I don't want to think about your return to England tomorrow, but the car will come to take you to the airport. You should be ready to leave at eleven."

So, their first visit to Frankfurt came to an end, and Charles and Maria boarded their flight back to London. From London, they took a mainline train to Norwich where Matthew was waiting to drive them home.

A few days after their return, Charles brought up with Maria something he had been turning over in his mind ever since Matthew had retired. He wanted to retire too, and Maria, so that they could have time to enjoy life with one another and with Matthew and his family, and Klaus as well. So, one morning, having discussed it at length with Maria, Charles wandered up to the staff house to find Michael Collins. He was working at his desk.

"Can you spare me a moment, Michael?" asked Charles.

"Of course, please take a seat."

"Michael, both Maria and I want to retire from our responsibilities on the farm, and I would like you to take over the entire control of the business. In many respects, you are doing that already, and I have absolute confidence in your ability to continue to run and develop things in the future." Charles gave Michael a moment to absorb what he had said, then asked him, "How do you feel about that?"

"I hardly know what to say. The farm is my life, and I would love to think it would be my work too, well into the future. Do you mean that I would have sole control over decisions?"

Michael was trying to understand the extent of this new role and feeling not only shocked by Charles's proposal but somewhat apprehensive at the amount of responsibility he would have. Quite sensibly, he wanted to be clear what Charles was offering him.

"Yes, that is exactly what I mean, Michael. I would hope that for anything major, you might want to talk it over with me, as I would remain the owner and finance-provider. One of your first decisions would probably involve the bakery side of things. If Maria were no longer involved, you'd have to think about how it could continue to run. It is a very financially successful part of the farm."

"That's easy, Charles. Pauline is very reliable and capable of running that side of things, and I'd have to check with Maria, but I think the new girls she has been training are able to continue the standard of baking to which we have become used. We would need to adjust Pauline's salary to reflect her new responsibilities."

"Yes, of course. And talking of finance, we would adjust your salary accordingly."

"But Maria gave me a substantial increase when you were away, Charles. I don't need another."

"Well, Michael, I can't have you running the farm on an under-manager's salary. Your income must reflect your new position. All I shall want to know each month is how the finances are. I will show you how to keep the accounts. All I shall want to do is cast my eye over them."

"Well, Charles, I don't need time to think about it. I feel honoured and deeply grateful for the offer you have made me. I can say yes, Charles, I would like to do it."

Charles and Michael discussed an appropriate salary for both him and Pauline, and Charles said that he would like to invite both Michael and Pauline to dinner as soon as they could be free. He left Michael, saying that he would now go and tell Pauline about the change in leadership, but that he would leave it to him to discuss with her how it would affect her personally.

Charles, in his now not often frequented lawyer mode, had a contract drawn up for Michael in order to protect his future should anything happen to Charles that would render him incapable of controlling the financial affairs of the farm. The next decisions, about what Maria and Charles would like to do with their time, were not so easy.

The first thing Maria did was to sign up for a yoga class once a week. Wednesday dinner with Matthew and Jenny would continue so long as Jenny's mother could look after the children. Maria and Charles signed up together for a rambling club, and Matthew and Charles joined a Music Society.

Sometimes, as they had their car, Maria and Charles would drive to Norwich for the day, and in the summer months, they would, with Matthew, take Emily and Sebastian to the coast.

In the autumn, Maria decided that they should buy one of those new televisions, and although Maria thought of television as something new, it really wasn't, it was just that the Hartmans were rather slow at adopting new things for the home. At the same time, Charles suggested they invest in a good gramophone and begin a collection of classical records, so that he could prepare for his music classes. Both purchases were made. Maria marvelled at how modern the farmhouse was becoming!

The following week, Charles and Maria welcomed to dinner, Michael Collins and Pauline with her husband Mark. They talked about how the farm had been in the days of Jimmie and Ethel Cox and what they each thought of the present government. The evening passed pleasantly, and when their guests left, both Charles and Maria felt that the farm would be in good hands and could probably continue successfully well into the future.

And so, time slipped by, and the Hartmans and Halls adapted to their new way of life. The farm did indeed continue to run well, keeping very much to its Fresh Local Produce policy, and Dr Jenny Hall enjoyed her work in the children's department at Norwich Hospital. Perhaps the only family that found themselves rather more busy than usual were the Sullivans who spent more time now looking after their grandchildren. They did not complain and neither did the children. And when Charles and Matthew sorted out the garden, adding a sandpit and a swing to it, the children were thrilled.

In October that year, Gregory left for Rome. Neither Charles nor Maria felt greatly affected by it, for they both saw that Gregory was settled in the direction his life would take. Gregory would be studying at the English College, and he told his parents that he might be there for well over a year. When he returned, he said, he hoped that sometime near his twenty-fifth birthday he would be ordained to the priesthood.

Early in 1967, Charles experienced once again, the abdominal pain he had had earlier and which Matthew had sorted out. Although Matthew was now retired, Charles spoke casually to him about it. Matthew thought it was a weakness that was likely to recur throughout his life, especially on occasions when he might be more than usually stressed.

"But I have only just retired, what have I got to be stressed about?" Charles commented. Matthew knew Charles well. He looked intently at his friend.

"Maybe it's an interior anxiety about something that has not yet happened. You have a weakness here, Charles, and it seems to make itself felt whenever you feel deeply threatened or unhappy. If it persists, you should see your new doctor at the surgery for his diagnosis and prescription. I can't prescribe for you now."

Of course, Charles being Charles, he never did consult his new doctor.

As spring began, Charles suggested to Maria that they take another break away somewhere.

"What about Cyprus?" he suggested. He actually felt unwell and thought a break away with Maria might help him.

"I've never been there," said Maria. "Would it be warm?"

"Yes, I think so. It would be a relaxing holiday, not so much sightseeing. I think most of our time would be spent swimming and sunbathing on a beach. We could probably find a nice hotel with good facilities. Shall I make some enquiries?"

"You know, it would be nice if Jenny and Matthew could come with us. But I don't suppose it could be done. The children are still a bit young, and Jenny would have to get time off work."

Charles did the research, contacted a travel agent, and soon after Easter, the pair were off to Limassol. It was the first time they had had a holiday like it, and Charles in particular, benefited from the warmth and the beautiful hotel situated right on the beach. They swam most days, and Maria noticed that Charles ate well and did not complain of any pain. Sometimes they took the bus down to the harbour and wandered around the shops there. They both returned home with a light tan, vowing to go again with Matthew, Jenny and the children.

Before they knew it, it was 1968, and early in the New Year, Gregory returned from Rome. Maria had begun to think that he would never come back. His ordination to the priesthood was fixed for Friday, November 1, All Saints Day and Gregory's twenty-fifth birthday. Charles and Maria, together with Matthew and Jenny, were all invited to the ceremony, which would take place at the Monastery Church. Gregory asked too that Rabbi Neuberger and his family be invited. Klaus travelled over the day before the ceremony. Gregory's old room had become 'Klaus's room' by this time.

Whilst Gregory had been in Rome the monastery had been raised to become an abbey. Maria assumed it just meant a change in name, for she could discern no outward changes, except for the building of a community hall on the side of the church.

The bishop would come for the ordination, and afterwards, there would be a gathering for the whole Benedictine community and the congregation in the new hall.

November 1 arrived. Getting ready for the Mass that morning, Charles could not help but feel miserable and anxious. He still thought that what Gregory had chosen was a waste of his life. He had always hoped that his son would change his mind, but now his future seemed certain. He had, to some extent, become used to the fact that he saw very little of Gregory. Now, with Gregory affirming a life Charles could not understand, he felt it was almost like a death to which he had to accustom himself. He felt empty and already bereft. Charles had never fully realised the extent to which he relied on Maria and Gregory for his sense of security and well-being. He felt that this was a final step in the loss of his son, and his emotional reaction robbed him of any ability to be rational about Gregory's vocation. Klaus tried hard to cheer him up, but wherever Charles was, Klaus was unable to reach him.

When they arrived at the church, it was obvious that it would be a large congregation, for it was a Holy Day, the bishop would be celebrating Mass, and there would be an ordination. It was quite an occasion!

Charles and Maria found Matthew and Jenny waiting for them in the porch, so they were able to find a pew where they could all sit together. Later, as Charles looked around, he caught sight of Raphael and his parents sitting towards the back.

The Mass proceeded as usual, as far as the day's Bible readings.

Then began the presentation and questioning of the candidate, Gregory Charles Jan Hartman, for the Rite of Holy Orders.

Maria was overcome with a mixture of love and pride.

Charles sat glum and cold beside her, trying to bear what his beloved son was voluntarily undergoing.

He managed to maintain control until it came to the prostration. To see his son lying face down on the sanctuary floor, arms stretched out as though he were on the cross, was too much for him. He felt angry and helpless. He got up quickly and left.

Outside, he gasped in the sharp cold air of November, blowing his nose fiercely into his handkerchief and striding up and down the forecourt. *I have lost my only son*, he was thinking. *He is as good as dead to me. Why, oh why did you choose this, Gregory? My son, my son.* Charles began to feel nauseous. He tried to breathe deeply and slowly. *Was it my fault*, Charles thought, *that you chose this way of life?* He remembered the day Gregory had discovered the swastika badge in the loft and had fled to this very monastery. Was all this now, what he, Charles, had driven him to? Was Gregory thinking that by living this life he could atone for his father's crimes? Charles could hardly bear to think these thoughts.

Then he was suddenly aware of a hand placed on his shoulder. It was David Neuberger.

"It must be tough to take," he said.

Charles merely nodded.

"Come back inside, Charles, and sit with Sara and me. It's cold out here."

Charles went back in with David, who slipped forward to Maria's pew and whispered that Charles was with him. Charles sat for a time with his eyes closed. Then it came to Holy Communion and a lot of people began moving out of their pews towards the sanctuary. Charles whispered a thank you to David and rejoined Jenny and Klaus, waiting for the return of Matthew and Maria from communion.

Quite quickly, then, the Mass moved to a joyful conclusion. The congregation waited for the formal procession out, then, in a very disorderly muddle, they made their way to the hall.

Each person was greeted by the newly ordained Father Gregory, who when it came to his mother, embraced her and whispered something into her ear that no one else heard. Charles followed. His son clasped his father's hands in his and could only say 'Papa'. Gregory understood the ordeal it all was for his father.

Later, as Father Gregory circulated around the people, he met up with David Neuberger. David asked him a little about the church's new document on its relationship with the Jewish people. He asked Gregory to get in touch with him as he thought they might be able to do some work together relating to it.

"Of course, I will. Where's Raff?" Gregory asked him.

"Just look for the prettiest girl, and that's where he'll be." David laughed.

Charles watched Gregory, moving easily among the people, smiling and seeming as though he had something special to say to each one. The time in Rome seemed to have changed him, he thought. He had to admit that his new role appeared to suit him.

Father Andrew came up to Charles. "This cannot have been an easy experience for you, Mr Hartman," he said.

"No, Father, I must be honest and say that I do not understand any of it."

"Well, all I can tell you is that from the time that your son first stayed with us for a few weeks, a long time ago now, until this very day, he has been an outstanding applicant for the religious life. I don't think that any of us can fully understand the vocation of another, whether it be to a ministry such as ours, or to any other profession. You were a lawyer, I believe, Mr Hartman?" The conversation was interrupted by the abbot, Father Vincent, asking for people's attention.

"A number of people are asking for a speech from our new young priest. Father Gregory, will you say some words to us?"

Gregory, his parents knew, was not really comfortable with addressing large groups of people. They were quite surprised therefore, to see him stand, smiling and at ease, facing the large assembly.

"Happy Feast Day and thank you all for coming. A very special thank you to our bishop also." He paused. "My father came to this country in 1943, escaping the reach of the Nazis in Poland, of which he was one, as no doubt many of you, if you are local, will know from the somewhat lurid accounts in our newspapers. He came through all the dangers of a Nazi-occupied Europe, with my mother and me, although I must tell you that I had a very comfortable journey, unlike my parents, because I was not yet born. That was more than twenty-five years ago. I happen to know that with us today is at least one highly qualified paediatrician who would, I am sure, confirm what I am about to say. The character of a man, or woman, is formed by the upbringing they receive in the first seven or so years of their life. If there is any good in me at all, it is because I have the most wonderful parents in the world. I remember, on my fifth birthday, being in considerable trouble. There may be some of you here, having bought potatoes from Cox's Farm at that time, who found them bruised and split when you got them home. The fault was mine. No, actually, there is a friend of mine, here today, who was complicit with me in causing the ruination of sacks of potatoes by making a slide out of them." Gregory looked towards Raff with a smile. "My father, in spite of it being my birthday, sent me to bed in disgrace, but my mother, as so often mothers do, soon came to my room and persuaded me to say sorry. I tell you this little story not because I remember to this day the displeasure of my father but because I have always remembered the love with which I was embraced when I stood crying before him, trying to say sorry. There were many other occasions of correction; I was rather a naughty child, but always I knew that I was loved. Twenty-four times twenty-four ad infinitum, my father told me was the amount I was loved! Thank you, Mama and Papa, for caring for me in a way that has brought me to this wonderful day. I must also pay tribute today to my godfather, who many of you will know as Dr Matthew Hall. He has always been there for me, above and beyond the call of duty, not only a wonderful godfather but the best of friends. Thank you, Uncle Matt. And my Uncle Klaus I thank too for so many happy times with him and especially for a never-to-be-forgotten Safari experience.

"Lastly, I want to thank Rabbi David Neuberger who has been a wonderful friend to my family in ways for which I shall eternally be grateful.

"So, as I set out on my life as priest and monk, from such a secure foundation, I turn to my new religious family and thank them for receiving me, also with love, into the worldwide Benedictine community. The love I have received throughout my life has been a reflection of God's love, and I will spend the rest of my life in striving to bring that love to all I shall have the honour to serve. Thank you!"

There were a few seconds of silence, and then a gentle and growing sound of clapping echoed around the hall. Charles took Maria's hand, whispering to her how proud he was of their son. Maria could not speak, so full was she of emotion that was a mixture of joy and tears.

Many of the community of monks began to leave, but most of the congregation hung around a little, and Father Gregory began to circulate, having a word here and there. As he moved towards a different group, he felt a tap on his shoulder.

"You don't remember me, do you?" said a female voice. Gregory turned. It took only a moment, then he said, "Lucy, it's Lucy! How wonderful to see you. But I didn't think you were Catholic?"

"No, I'm not. I came because I wanted to be at your ordination. Do you know, Father Gregory," Lucy said, with a mock air of accusation, "you broke my heart when you became a monk. But please don't be too upset. I should like to introduce my husband to you."

Then, Gregory was delighted to be able to spend a little time with the Neubergers, especially to talk with Raphael and to hear about what he was doing. He promised David that he would ring him about planning some shared work on Jewish-Christian relations. After, knowing he must join the bishop and his community for lunch soon, he made his way to his family. Charles and Maria, Klaus, Matthew and Jenny were standing nearby. Gregory embraced his mother first, then each member of his family in turn. Then he turned again to his father.

"Papa, you have lost your son, as many fathers have done before you, be they fathers whose children died in this last war or fathers whose children live but are in some way lost to them. Your sacrifice will go with me and enable me, through whatever good I am able to do in my ministry. You will, together with Mama, always be with me. I love you both twenty-four times twenty-four ad infinitum. Forgive me, I must go." And he was gone.

The family, together with the Neubergers, went then to the farmhouse, to have lunch. Pauline had offered to prepare the self-service meal, taking care to follow Maria's instructions about keeping meat and milk separate out of courtesy to the family of the rabbi.

The sitting room and kitchen were still in considerable disorder, with empty plates scattered around, when the clock struck four. A car drew up on the drive, which hardly anyone noticed, so energetic was the conversation. When the doorbell rang, it was Matthew who jumped up quickly and went out to open the door.

"I've a big surprise for everyone," he announced as he opened the sitting room door. He stepped aside. In walked Gregory.

"He's fed up with it already," joked Raphael, his eyes beaming with merriment.

"Gregory, whatever are you doing here?" asked Maria.

"Can't I spend time with my family on my birthday?" Gregory went straight to Maria and planted a big kiss on her cheek. "I came for a decent cup of tea." Gregory laughed.

"You sound just like your father." Maria got up and disappeared into the kitchen.

Sara and Jenny began to clear away some of the dishes, Klaus too got up to help, and Pauline came in with clean tea plates. She asked everyone to sit down and together with Matthew, returned to the kitchen. Maria had been sent back into the sitting room by Pauline, who soon came back in carrying a tray with a pot of tea. Behind her came Matthew bearing a birthday cake with many candles flickering on it. Gregory's face was to be seen to be believed. 'Happy Birthday' was sung by everyone, and Gregory was pushed forward to blow out the candles.

"What I want to know," he said, "is who is the rascal who got this organised and how did you know I would come? It was only about an hour ago that I was told, actually ordered, to get the community car out and drive over to spend the rest of the afternoon with you."

"I must admit to it" – Matthew laughed – "it was actually that charming man Father Andrew who rang me a day or two ago to say he wanted you to come for some family time. Then I thought a birthday cake would be fun, and it all sort of snowballed from there. It was actually Pauline who did most of the work."

Maria gave Matthew a big hug. She whispered to Jenny, "You could not have made a better choice of husband."

"I know," replied Jenny.

Then Maria went over to Pauline and gave her a hug, thanking her for all she had done.

Gregory saw that his father's eyes were full of tears. He went over and sat on the floor at his feet. For a moment, Gregory felt a stab of anxiety for his father.

"Thank you for what you said this morning," Charles said quietly to his son. "It was a very beautiful occasion, although I did find some of it hard to take. But you know, Gregory, I was very disappointed about one thing."

"What was that, Papa?"

"I was quite sure you would preach on The Prodigal Son. All these years I have been waiting for an expert explanation of this story. I bet the rabbi here knows more about it than I do."

The following Sunday, Father Gregory was saying the morning Mass. Jenny stayed at home with the children, preparing lunch for everyone, and Matthew went with Charles and Maria to be at Gregory's first public Mass. When it came to Holy Communion, Maria whispered to Charles that he too should come forward so that he could receive a blessing from his son. As they left the church, Gregory was greeting all the parishioners as they made their way home for Sunday lunch.

"Papa," said Gregory, "I am so sorry that today's Gospel was not the Prodigal Son, but I promise to let you know when it comes up. Mama, Uncle Matt, have a lovely Sunday."

Charles returned with Maria and Matthew to Bressingham, where a nice smell of Sunday roast was coming from the kitchen. The children ran to greet them, with shouts of 'Daddy, Auntie Maria, Uncle Charles'. And now, Charles began to feel a little more at peace.

But for Gregory, he felt the hollowness of being without his family at, and after, Sunday lunch. It was the contrast in remembered family togetherness on a quiet afternoon, with the solitariness of a monk's Sunday afternoon, when Mass was over and the accompaniment of a single reader over lunch was the only experience of 'family' Gregory would have. It was a reaction that he would experience every Sunday of his religious life.

Chapter Thirteen
The Struggle Ends

A few weeks later, one morning as she was preparing breakfast, Maria saw that Charles was outside, sitting on Bob's bench. He had no coat on, and it was the middle of November. Maria hurried out, a growing feeling of unease rising within her.

"Charles, darling, what are you doing…?"

She stopped, seeing his eyes glazed and unresponsive, although he was breathing. As she looked at him, a cold dread crept over her.

He managed a whisper, "I am in such pain, Maria."

"Can you manage to walk? Hold on to me." Maria managed to get the bent-over figure, step by step, back into the warmth of the house. Each step was accompanied by a gasp of pain, until Maria got Charles back indoors and to the settee. He was very cold. She grabbed a coat from the hall and put it over him, tucking it tenderly around his shivering body.

Maria rang for an ambulance and went back to Charles. She sat close to him, trying to warm his body with her own. "Help is coming, darling, just hold on. Please, hold on." Maria held him as close as she could, as though her own life force would flow into him.

Charles seemed to have slipped into a semiconscious state. Maria wasn't sure what to do but thought she must try to prevent him from falling into unconsciousness. She took his hands, cold and blue, wrapping her own around them. "Darling, darling Charles. Please stay awake. We are waiting for an ambulance to come, and I will go with you to the hospital. Please stay awake." The fear she felt, sounded in her voice.

"Love you, Maria." Charles's head slipped onto Maria's shoulder. The voice was faint and slow.

"Come on, Charles, come on," Maria insisted with an urgency that made Charles open his eyes again. Maria was rubbing his hands. "Look, here comes the ambulance. You're going to be all right."

Maria quickly let the men in. Charles had slipped down from his sitting position and was now lying, his knees drawn up. His eyes were closed. One of the men asked Maria his name.

"Charles, Charles, open your eyes please. Open your eyes, Charles. Where is your pain?"

Charles's eyes flickered open. He put a hand on his stomach. The usual thing thought Maria. She explained to the ambulance man that this was something that happened to him from time to time and that he had been treated by his doctor. But, she said, she had never seen him as bad as this.

The ambulance man checked his pulse and heart, and then one of them brought in a stretcher from the van. Maria collected a coat, picked up the house keys and her handbag and followed the men into the ambulance, holding Charles's hand.

Once at the hospital, the morning became a haze of doctors and nurses, consultants and more nurses, registration and another consultant, until Maria was told that Charles would be admitted for observation. They then administered some pain relief and Maria accompanied Charles to the ward for general medical conditions not requiring surgery. Settled in bed, curtains drawn around, he looked a little better. His eyes seemed to have some life in them, and Maria began to be more hopeful. A nurse came in and put a 'nil by mouth' notice up over the bed, hung some charts on the rail at the bottom of the bed and then took a look at Charles.

"How is the pain now?" she asked. "You certainly look better than when you first came in. We'll soon get you to rights, don't worry." She leaned over Charles, taking his pulse.

"Better, a little better. Love you, Maria." Then Charles closed his eyes.

Maria smoothed his forehead and told him, in a whisper, that she loved him too and that she would go down to the cafeteria and get herself some breakfast but would be back. Charles seemed to have fallen asleep. Maria didn't consider whether or not he had heard her. She kissed his forehead and said again that she loved him.

Maria noted that it was Adamson ward. She knocked at the Ward Sister's door on her way out and told her that she would be back in a little while and then went down to the ground floor. She found a telephone and rang Matthew. She could hear the children's voices in the background as she told Matthew what had happened. The normality of the scene that she imagined at Matthew's home contrasted sharply with the tension and uncertainty she was experiencing. At the back of her mind, she was thinking how thankful she was that Matthew was always there for her.

"Do you want me to come, Maria?" was his response when he heard the situation.

"No, Matthew, but thank you for offering. I hope to see the consultant and get some idea of what is to happen to Charles, then I plan to go home and return for the afternoon visiting hours. If you felt you could come with me this afternoon that would be marvellous, but I know it is not so easy for you to get away."

"I will see if Grandma can have the children, and then I'll ring you at home around lunchtime. It's probably a good thing in a way, Maria. Maybe we can get this problem sorted out once and for all. Try not to worry. I'll speak with you again around lunchtime."

Maria sat for ten minutes in the light and airy cafeteria, with a coffee and croissant in lieu of breakfast. She thought about the last few weeks and how Charles had seemed better after the ordination. She herself felt easier now that he was in the hospital and something was being done to help him. She realised how frightened she had been. She had thought he would die. She glanced around at the few other people, also taking coffee there. At this time of the morning, they must also be in a similar position, she thought. For a moment she empathised with what she imagined might be the crises going on for the people at the other tables.

She returned to the ward and saw that Charles was still sleeping. She stood for a moment looking at him. The ward sister walked over to tell her that the consultant had not yet visited, but if she was coming back for afternoon visiting, she might have news for her then. Maria kissed Charles very gently on his forehead, not wanting to wake him, then left.

She took a taxi home. She cleared up the kitchen and tidied the bedroom. She found out clean pyjamas for Charles and got a bag of toiletries together for him. She decided to go up to the Tea Shop to have a coffee with the staff. She told them what had happened to Charles.

Later, back at the farmhouse, Maria heated some soup for lunch and was just finishing when the telephone rang. It was the hospital.

"Is that Mrs Hartman? This is Sister Joan Fletcher at Adamson Ward. Mrs Hartman" – there was a hesitation in the voice – "I am so sorry; I have to tell you that your husband died about fifteen minutes ago. In fact, he didn't wake up again after you left him."

There was a crashing noise on the line, and Sister Fletcher lost contact with Maria.

Maria lay on the floor. When she came to, she registered the telephone still swinging just a little. What had happened? How long had she been on the floor?

She wandered, dazed, into the sitting room and fell onto the settee where not so long ago she had sat with Charles. She couldn't think what had happened. She did not know how long she had sat there when she was startled by the sound of the doorbell. Matthew let himself in with his emergency key. He had grown very anxious when he had not been able to get a response from Maria's telephone, and after having called his mother-in-law, he had jumped into his car and driven over to the farmhouse.

He noticed the telephone hanging off the hook as he passed the kitchen and found Maria sitting on the settee in the sitting room.

"He is dead, Matthew. He is dead." Maria spoke in a monotone, without emotion.

Matthew had never been more shocked. He sat down next to her. He put his arm around Maria, cupping her head onto his shoulder. He had no idea what to say. They sat there together for some minutes, neither speaking.

"Did the hospital ring you, Maria?" Matthew spoke softly.

"Yes."

"Can you manage to tell me the name of the ward? I will ring and see what the position is. Would you like to go with me to see Charles if that is possible?"

"Adamson ward." The rest of Matthew's question went unanswered.

Matthew rang the hospital and once through to Adamson Ward, spoke with Sister Fletcher. He returned to Maria. "Maria, if you want, and you feel you can cope, Sister Fletcher says we can see Charles in about an hour. I think it would help us both but especially you, to see him now." Maria just nodded.

"I will make us some tea. We don't need to leave just yet. Maria, would you like me to let Gregory know?"

Once again, Maria just nodded.

Matthew made a pot of tea, turned off the soup still heating on the stove, then called the monastery. He asked to speak to Father Andrew.

"Father Andrew here. Who is this?"

"It's Doctor Matthew Hall, Father Andrew. Father Gregory's mother has just been told that her husband has died this morning in the hospital."

Matthew took a breath, still unable to believe that what he was saying was real.

"He was taken ill early this morning and Mrs Hartman went by ambulance with him to the hospital. She had not been long at home when they rang to say that he had died. I thought I should make sure that Father Gregory is told as soon as possible."

"Dr Hall, this is a terrible shock, and I am so sorry to hear it. Gregory is at home just now. I expect he will want to go immediately to the hospital. I will let him know straightaway."

"Mrs Hartman and I will be going back to the hospital soon. The ward sister said we could see Charles at about two o'clock."

"I will let Gregory know at once, and I am sure he will want to join you at the hospital. I am so sorry, Dr Hall. Am I right to assume that you are with Mrs Hartman? She is not alone?"

Matthew replied in the affirmative. The call ended. He took the tea into the sitting room. They had hardly drunk a cup, when a car drew up in front of the house. Matthew went to the door.

It was Gregory. He just said 'Matt' and went straight into the sitting room.

"Mama, Mama! How can this be true?" He sat beside his mother, holding her hands and gazing, distraught, into her eyes. Tears were running down his face.

Maria seemed to pull herself together at the sight and sound of Gregory.

"He is gone, Gregory. His last words were that he loved me, and I think he heard me tell him that I love him too." Maria had the feeling that she should never have left him. She should have stayed and held his hand.

"He was asleep. But why, Gregory, why did he die now?"

Tears began running down Maria's cheeks. Gregory sat himself beside his mother, took her in his arms, and their tears mingled.

"No, no, it can't be right," she murmured, "he will surely be all right when we get back there?"

A determination was in Maria's eyes, and her voice too was strong. It was as though she thought she could change everything according to her will. He would surely come back to her, as he had done before.

Matthew came back into the room.

"I think we should get ready to leave now."

Maria went with Matthew in his car, she sat still and quiet beside him, the silence in the car heavy and full of dread. Gregory followed behind.

Once at the hospital, they took the lift to Adamson ward and found Sister Fletcher.

"I am so sorry," she said. "His passing was absolutely peaceful. The last thing he can have known, Mrs Hartman, was your goodbye."

Matthew spoke quietly, "It was I who spoke on the telephone with you Sister, and this is Father Gregory Hartman, the son of Charles."

Sister Fletcher acknowledged Matthew and Gregory.

"I will take you to see Mr Hartman. Then his consultant will see you. When you are ready, will you come back to my office on the ward?"

Maria glanced over at the bed where she had last seen Charles. The curtains were pulled around it.

Sister Fletcher led them to the lift, down to the ground floor, along a corridor and stopped at a door, which she opened a little and then closed again.

"Mr Hartman is here. Go in when you feel ready."

Matthew asked Maria if she would like to go in with Gregory on her own. He was afraid of trespassing on this intensely personal moment.

Maria spoke firmly, "No, Matthew. You are Charles's family. And I need both of you with me." She glanced at each of the men, noticing their pallor and sensing their fear. She registered subconsciously that she was the one who had to be strong for them.

She pushed open the door and led the way to the still figure lying in the centre of the room. Charles looked peaceful. He looked like himself at his best. Except, Maria knew at once, that he was not there in that room. Somehow, that understanding calmed her. She touched his forehead, smoothing his hair and very gently and with great reverence, kissed his cool cheek. She knew now that he was dead and would not be coming back to her. The acceptance of it bestowed on her a sense of the holiness of death. It was not to be feared, she thought. All that was to be feared was her life without him.

"He knows that I love him. It was the last thing I told him."

Gregory, standing on the other side of his father, tears flowing down his face, now also leaned over and kissed Charles on the forehead.

"Papa, my Papa. You are with God, I know. But I love you dearly and will miss you every day of my life."

Maria saw the depth of Gregory's distress, and she moved around to her son and stood close to him, her arm around his waist. Both just stood there, looking down at Charles.

Matthew moved forward, placed his hands on Charles's still, folded ones. Matthew bowed his head and closed his eyes. He stayed there for a moment, then gently and quietly walked out of the room.

The meeting with the consultant was just a blur to Maria. She noted that he did not know the cause of Charles's death and that an autopsy would be necessary. She sat back, remote from the conversation, leaving everything to Matthew and Gregory.

The three of them returned to the farmhouse. Matthew went straight up to the staff house where he found Michael. He told him that Charles had died and that he would go and let Pauline know. Out of courtesy, he stayed a few moments with each of the staff and then went back to join Maria and Gregory again.

"I think none of us has eaten properly since breakfast. Oh, you have, Gregory? Anyway, I will put some food on the kitchen table. Will one of you see to a hot drink for us?"

Maria went into the kitchen. Both Matthew and Gregory were amazed by the composure she showed.

As they sat around the table, Maria voiced the worry she had about Charles.

"Is it really necessary that there should be an autopsy? I don't like the thought of it, and I don't see why Charles should have to undergo such an indignity. No, I don't want it."

It was Matthew who attempted an answer. "Maria, I understand completely how you feel. But I think it is something that the hospital and the law requires. At the moment, no one knows the cause of Charles's death. As simple a thing as the death certificate needs a cause to be written down."

"I know the cause; that should be enough." Time seemed to be suspended.

Matthew and Gregory looked at one another. Neither of them knew quite how to deal with this, and Matthew could see that in any case, at the moment Gregory was not sufficiently able to handle it. The anguish on Gregory's face told Matthew that Maria's statement was best left unanswered for now.

Gregory stood. "Mama, I must go back to the community for a short while, but I will be back. Matthew, do you have the time to stay here until I return?"

Maria and Matthew saw him out and returned to the sitting room. Over the next few days, Gregory stayed with his mother, returning to the monastery early each morning for an hour or two and then coming back to be with Maria. Together they did all that was necessary to prepare for Charles's funeral and to attend to his estate. Gregory wrote to Klaus who let them know immediately that he would come over for his brother's funeral. The service was to be held at the abbey out of consideration for both Maria and Gregory and with the abbot's full approval. Maria remained outwardly brave. Only at night, clutching Charles's pillow did she give way to her grief.

Klaus arrived the day before, he was picked up at Norwich by Matthew, and it was with Jenny and Matthew that he stayed. The day before the funeral, Maria was issued with the death certificate for Charles. Under 'cause of death' the entry said:

Perforated peptic ulcer.

The day of the funeral dawned, bright but very cold. By this time, Gregory was already back with his community, so it was Matthew, Jenny, and Klaus, who accompanied Maria in the funeral car. The heavy scent of the flowers on the coffin had made Maria feel faint, but she felt emotionally controlled.

As they made the procession into the church, Matthew was aware that there was a very large congregation present. He noticed Michael and Pauline and some of the young boys from the farm there. Matthew knew that Michael had decided to close the business for the day. He noticed, too, some people from the Music Group that he and Charles had attended. Many may just have been local people who had long been customers of Cox's Farm Fresh.

The service was not, of course, a Requiem Mass, for Charles was not a Catholic, but a service of prayer and thanksgiving for his life had been beautifully crafted by his family. Matthew had asked David Neuberger to share a reading with him, and Father Andrew read a passage of St Paul. Klaus read, in German, a short poem by Goethe, the translation of which was given in the service sheet. He read from the book Charles had bought in Frankfurt. Maria spoke with great dignity about her brave and beloved husband. Then it was Gregory's turn to speak and to make the final blessings in readiness for the committal of Charles's body.

Gregory stood in the centre of the sanctuary. He wore a black suit and his clerical collar. He carried no notes.

"St Luke tells us a story which we call The Prodigal Son. I expect most of you here today will know the outline of it. I would like to suggest, respectfully, that this story has been misnamed. Yes, it is about a son who thinks only of himself and goes off and lives so recklessly that eventually he has no home, no food, and it would seem, no friends left.

"But I think the story concerns the nature of God, or to put it in the terms of the story, the love the father has for his son, rather than the selfishness of the boy. In a way, the 'wastefulness', the prodigality, belongs to the father."

For a moment, Gregory looked down, as if considering his words even more carefully but perhaps taking a second or two for reflection. Then he re-engaged with the congregation.

"My father, Charles Hartman, as most of you know, was a Nazi officer in Warsaw, overseeing the creation of the Jewish Ghetto. He abhorred the plans for the Final Solution, and as soon as he could, he escaped with my mother and fled to England, to Cox's Farm where he remained until his death."

Gregory took another short pause. What he wanted to say was painful to him, and he did not want to lose control of his voice. He breathed in deeply.

"What he was never able to escape, though, was the guilt he felt for the part he played, however unwillingly, in the death of hundreds of Jews. I want to tell you that Charles Hartman was a deeply moral person, brave, generous and a loving husband, father, brother and friend. But he was never able to escape the pain of his memories.

"When he measured himself on the scales of justice, he considered they fell heavily on the side of 'bad'. What he never took account of, was the eternal forgiving love of God. Not a God who waited at home for his erring son to return, tail between his legs so to speak, but a God who comes out to find him, wherever he is, in whatever condition he is.

"I think, weighed down by his own measure of his guilt, my father didn't see our Heavenly Father offering His loving forgiveness to him. And his overwhelming sense of guilt was something he could no longer live with."

Gregory paused again, his eyes so full of tears that he could not see the congregation ranged in front of him, but his voice remained steady and strong.

"The measure of a man, or woman, is not according to their faults but according to the good they do. There is a rabbinic saying, I believe, that tells us that one good man can save the entire world. Christianity is based on that belief too. My father's goodness, for he was certainly a good man, did not save the world, neither did it save him. My father is saved by the eternal, infinitely forgiving love of God, as depicted in the Parable of The Prodigal Son. God loves us twenty-four times twenty-four ad infinitum, as my father once told me was the measure of his own love for me. I know that that love is poured out to my father and that the forgiveness for which he so longed is granted to him. I know that he rests in peace."

Gregory stood still and quiet for a moment, the tears flowing down his face. He knew that his voice could no longer be relied upon. There was not a sound to be heard in the church.

Then Father Andrew came to Gregory's side. He placed a steadying arm on Gregory and then proceeded, with the assistance of one of the altar boys, to vest him so that he might carry out the final sanctification and committal of his father's body.

And so, Charles was laid to rest in the little cemetery outside Diss. He was a man who had travelled physically from Germany, to Poland, to England. But spiritually and emotionally, he had travelled much further. As a young man growing up in the province of Posen, his personality had been formed by an environment hostile to 'the other'. It had made him rather authoritarian and selfish. His redemption in this respect came through his love of his wife Maria, and the love she gave to him.

Maria is probably the heroine of this story, for within the gentle steadfast love of his wife, Charles became a considerate, kind and loving employer, friend, brother, husband and father. She it was who enabled him to grow into the best he could possibly be. His tragedy consisted in the fact that as his young son had told him many years earlier, he was not able to forgive himself for the part he had played in the systematic murder of Europe's Jews. Not even when pronounced not guilty by a Jewish court, nor when a friend who was Jewish talked him through his painful memories, could Charles feel within himself the peace that comes with the sense that one has been truly forgiven.

Perhaps Charles had not been seeking forgiveness at all.

Perhaps he had simply longed to have acted differently.

His tragedy was that he failed to do, in 1943, the one act of love that could have saved him. He walked past a dying child.

Over the next few months, Maria tried to cope one day at a time. She offered Michael and Pauline help in the bakery again and was pleased to resume her work there on the days when they were busiest. She continued to walk with the ramblers' group she and Charles had joined, and usually on a Wednesday, she drove out to Bressingham to spend the evening with Jenny and Matthew and their children. On Sundays, Maria attended Mass, sometimes with Matthew, sometimes alone, at the Benedictine Abbey at Quidenham. From time to time, she went over to Frankfurt to spend some time with Klaus.

When she thought over her life, she could only feel an immense gratitude for the blessing of Charles's love. She came to understand that the anguish she felt, now that he was gone, was a part of her love for him and like her love would be a constant thread running through the rest of her life.

In 1975, Father Vincent, Abbot of the Benedictine Monastery at Quidenham Abbey, died.

In due course, the community and the Benedictine Order in England elected unanimously Father Gregory Charles Jan Hartman as Abbot. He was, in living memory, the youngest abbot ever to be elected.